When the place you run to...
is the one place you can't escape.

STRANGERS

#1 Bestselling Author

Michaelbrent COLLINGS

website: http://www.michaelbrentcollings.com
email: info@michaelbrentcollings.com

For more information on Michaelbrent's books, including specials and sales; and for info about signings, appearances, and media,

check out his webpage,

"Like" his Facebook fanpage
or
Follow him on Twitter.

PRAISE FOR THE NOVELS OF MICHAELBRENT COLLINGS

DARKBOUND

"Really good, highly recommended, make sure you have time to read a lot at one sitting since you may have a hard time putting it down." – *The Horror Fiction Review*

"In *Darkbound* you will find the intensity of *Misery* and a journey reminiscent of the train ride in *The Talisman*…. A proficient and pedagogical author, Collings' works should be studied to see what makes his writing resonate with such vividness of detail…. You will not be disappointed in this dark tale." – *Hellnotes*

"*Darkbound* travels along at a screaming pace with action the whole way through, and twists to keep you guessing throughout.... With an ending that I didn't see coming from a mile away, and easily one of the best I've had the enjoyment of reading in a long time...." – *Horror Drive-In*

THE HAUNTED

"*The Haunted* is a terrific read with some great scares and a shock of an ending!" – Rick Hautala, international bestselling author; Bram Stoker Award® for Lifetime Achievement winner

"[G]ritty, compelling and will leave you on the edge of your seat.... *The Haunted* is a tremendous read for fans of ghoulishly good terror." – horrornews.net

"*The Haunted* is just about perfect.... This is a haunted house story that will scare even the most jaded horror hounds. I loved it!" – Joe McKinney, Bram Stoker Award®-winning author of *Flesh Eaters* and *Inheritance*

APPARITION

"*Apparition* is not just a 'recommended' novel, it is easily one of the most entertaining and satisfying horror novels this reviewer has read within the past few years. I cannot imagine that any prospective reader looking for a new read in the horror genre won't be similarly blown away by the novel." – *Hellnotes*

"[*Apparition* is] a gripping, pulse hammering journey that refuses to relent until the very final act. The conclusion that unfolds may cause you to sleep with the lights on for a spell.... Yet be forewarned perhaps it is best reserved for day time reading." – horrornews.net

"*Apparition* is a hard core supernatural horror novel that is going to scare the hell out of you.... This book has everything that you would want in a horror novel.... it is a roller coaster ride right up to a shocking ending." – horroraddicts.net

"[*Apparition* is] Riveting. Captivating. Mesmerizing.... [A]n effective, emotional, nerve-twisting read, another amazingly well-written one from a top-notch writer." – *The Horror Fiction Review*

THE LOON

"It's always so nice to find one where hardcore asylum-crazy is done RIGHT.... *THE LOON* is, hands down, an excellent book." – *The Horror Fiction Review*

"Highly recommended for horror and thriller lovers. It's fast-moving, as it has to be, and bloody and violent, but not disgustingly gory.... Collings knows how to write thrillers, and I'm looking forward to reading more from him." – *Hellnotes*

MR. GRAY (AKA THE MERIDIANS)

"... an outstanding read.... This story is layered with mystery, questions from every corner and no answers fully coming forth until the final conclusion.... What a ride.... This is one you will not be able to put down and one you will remember for a long time to come. Very highly recommended." – *Midwest Book Review*

HOOKED: A TRUE FAERIE TALE

"*Hooked* is a story with depth.... Emotional, sad, horrific, and thought provoking, this one was difficult to put down and now, one of my favourite tales." – *Only Five Star Book Reviews*

"[A]n interesting and compelling read.... Collings has a way with words that pulls you into every moment of the story, absorbing every scene with all of your senses." – *Clean Romance Reviews*

"Collings has found a way to craft an entirely new modern vampire mythology – and one strikingly different from everything I've seen before.... Recommended for adult and teen fans of horror and paranormal romance...." – *Hellnotes*

RISING FEARS

"The writing is superb. The characters are believable and sympathetic... the theme of a parent who's lost a child figures strongly; it's powerful stuff, and written from the perspective of experience that no one should ever have to suffer." – *The Horror Fiction Review*

DEDICATION

To...

All the people who read my books… thank you,

and to Laura, FTAAE.

Contents

Chapter Page

PROLOGUE 1
1 15
2 19
3 27
4 30
5 32
6 34
7 36
8 44
9 47
10 50
11 54
12 59
13 62
14 64
15 68
16 72
17 75
18 78
19 81
20 84
21 86
22 88
23 91
24 95
25 97
26 101
27 104
28 107
29 111
30 114
31 117
32 120

33 124
34 128
35 131
36 135
37 138
38 140
39 142
40 145
41 148
42 153
43 156
44 161
45 165
46 168
47 171
48 173
49 181
50 188
51 192
52 195
53 199
54 204
55 207
56 213
57 216
58 218
59 221
60 226
61 231
62 237
63 240
63 243
64 247
65 250
66 252
67 253
68 256
69 258
70 262

71 266
72 270
73 273
74 275
75 277
76 282
77 285
78 286
79 289
80 290
81 292
82 293
83 296
84 300
85 303
86 307
87 310
88 312
89 316
90 319
91 321
92 323
93 324
94 326
95 330
96 332
97 334
98 336
99 339
100 341
101 344
102 346
103 350
EPILOGUE 354
AUTHOR'S NOTE 357

PROLOGUE

Bob Jankowitz traveled through beauty on his way to murder and thought for perhaps the thousandth time that today might be a good day to quit.

Christmas lights twinkled on the eaves of many of the houses, which was a rare display of holiday spirit from the well-to-do. Jankowitz had discovered over the years that the more well-off a person was, the less likely that person was to indulge in such tacky items as Christmas lights, or tinsel, or holiday spirit. So it was a surprise to see so many of the large houses that lined this street glittering with reds and blues and greens, oranges and yellows and whites. A few of them had manger scenes, and a flourishing forest of ten-foot-tall neon candy canes had even sprouted on one of the lawns – though they could barely be seen behind the tall privacy wall that circled that particular property.

Still, even behind tall walls and foreboding stands of towering trees that stood like evergreen guards, there was *spirit* here. A sense that the people of this neighborhood hadn't completely withdrawn from humanity, in spite of their wealth.

A black cargo van passed him, driving slowly as though admiring the lights. It had bumper stickers on the *front* bumper, which Jankowitz thought was odd. "Honk if you Love Jesus" said one on the right side. And on the left, "Honk if you Love Satan."

Typical, thought Jankowitz. He wasn't particularly religious, but he hated how nasty people had seemed to become in the last ten years. Like the only things of value anymore were cynicism and the ability to belittle others. More and more it seemed that people were becoming enamored of the kind of argument the driver of the van apparently preferred: support what you want, but in doing so you'll also be co-opted into supporting the things you most despise.

Jankowitz craned his neck to see what kind of person would drive a van with such a nasty message, but the black vehicle had passed before he could spot the driver. And just as well. He was going to need all his patience, all his peace tonight.

He let himself enjoy the Christmas lights again, and for a moment the holiday displays flashing all around, glinting off the winter snow that packed the sides of the street, gave Jankowitz a rare flash of hope.

Then the Christmas lights faded.

They were replaced by a different kind of illumination. The warm holiday colors waned, overcome by bright white flashes as reporters clicked cameras, hoping for lucky shots, and by the random red and blue of police cruiser lights spinning around one another like children at play.

Jankowitz put his own roof light on his car, adding one more spinning blue light to the mix. He always thought of the old Kmart advertisements when he did that, the nasally voice he had heard when wandering up and down the halls of the store with his parents as a kid, announcing "Blue Light Special, aisle seven," and waiting for the moment he could leave, hoping that he would maybe get a cherry Icee out of the trip.

"Today's Blue Light Special, shoppers, will be on aisle seven," he said under his breath. "And you ain't gonna believe this one."

It was a guess – the dispatcher hadn't given him many details. But he'd been doing this long enough to smell an unusual night ahead. And the fact that there were so many vultures – sorry, *reporters,* he corrected himself – crowding around the police barricades certainly bore out his instincts.

He edged his sedan forward through the throng. A few of the buzzards – no, *newspaperpeople* – didn't notice his car until the last second, and he had a delicious moment where he both hoped and feared he might get to... *nudge*... one or two of them.

Jankowitz had nothing against human beings as a rule. But murderers, rapists, pedophiles, and reporters were all something that he viewed as items that had been missed by whatever Darwinian filters operated in humanity's gene pool. They all existed because of misery and pain, fed on tribulation and fear.

Sadly, the assholes – sorry, *journalists* – got out of the way at the last second. Jankowitz eased up to the police barricades, which were moved aside by a pair of the uniformed officers stationed there to keep curiosity-seekers and bottom-feeders out of the way of the crime scene, and then pushed up to the house.

No question *which* house it was. It looked like a human anthill, with more cops going in and out of it than any crime scene than Jankowitz had ever witnessed.

He groaned inwardly. This many cops was never good news. It meant inevitable miscommunications about who was in charge, about who was to do what, about... about *everything*.

He parked the car at the end of the driveway, engaged the parking brake, and sat for a long moment before getting out. Part of his hesitation was so he could enjoy one last moment of the warmth inside his car. It was blisteringly cold outside, and he had no desire to be tramping around in sub-freezing temperatures.

Mostly, though, it was to give himself a chance to think of the Christmas lights. Because in spite of nearly twenty years on the force, Jankowitz was still a person with hope. He hoped that people were mostly good, he hoped that humanity was worth saving. But with every case he investigated, he felt that hope curl and blacken a bit at the edges. He felt it withdraw into itself, lessen.

Die.

So he thought of the Christmas lights and clung to the memory of holiday cheer like a prisoner of war might cling to remembrances of hearth and home.

Then he got out of the car.

The sounds hit him fast and hard. Not that they were loud, but his car had been quiet, and calm, and almost peaceful. Out here, by the house, everything was contained chaos, barely controlled panic. Jankowitz could see it in the faces of the men and women going in and out of the house, in their postures and the way they were holding themselves.

He felt his pulse start to race.

The house before him was different from the others on this affluent block. Not in size or quality of architecture. But there *were* differences. For one, it was set back farther from the street, as though the owners didn't want to share in the companionship that the rest of the neighborhood enjoyed.

And it was dark.

Not only was there no evidence of any holiday display of any kind, but there was no light in the house at all, other than the dancing firefly glimmers of handheld flashlights. The structure hunched dark and silent, like a lifeless husk on a dead battlefield.

Jankowitz walked up the well-shoveled walk. His breath plumed, now yellow, now white, now blue, depending on what kind of light caught it in the night. The shifting colors brought no joy or merriment. The Christmas displays down the block had been colorful in a vibrant, gleeful way. The shifting colors here were muted, tense, terrified. The colors of mayhem ill-contained.

Jankowitz intended to head right into the house, but he veered away from the front door when he noticed a number of forensics officers crowded around a shattered window on the front wall, about fifteen feet away from the front door. A few of them were dusting for prints, but the others seemed to be just standing and staring, mouths half-open and all but scratching their heads in confusion.

Jankowitz knew every one of the officers, of course. Good men and women for the most part. But he focused on one of them, a short, chubby woman named Chantae. A lot of the CSI techs called her "Mama Bear," both because of her shape and because she fought for the CSI team come budget appropriations time each year. Jankowitz liked her, and the feeling was fairly mutual.

She was one of the standers-and-starers. Which was not like her.

"Getting anything?" he said to her.

"Nothing."

"You think you *will* find anything?"

Mama Bear looked at him. She looked drawn and weary, and the flashlights that the techs held cast knife-sharp shadows against her round face. She looked cadaverous in that moment, and Jankowitz could tell instantly that she had been in the house. And that things were much worse there than he had suspected.

"I think we probably have a better chance finding evidence of Santa Claus than we do of our guy."

Jankowitz nodded. He felt the lack of surprise at her statement, and that depressed him. Had he gotten so jaded that he *expected* the bad guys to win?

He made himself look away from Mama Bear's haunted eyes. The window. It was shattered, bits of glass clinging to the pane like the teeth of a saw. "Forced entry," he said.

He had been speaking to himself, and it hadn't been a question. But Mama Bear answered him. "Actually, we're not sure about that."

"Why not?"

She pointed with her flashlight at some of the snow piled beside the house. It glittered. More than snow should. Glass. "With forced entry there'd be more glass *inside*," she said.

"So... what?" said Jankowitz. "Someone trying to get out?"

"Not sure about that, either," said Mama Bear. "There'd be more glass *outside* if that were the case."

"It fell inside?"

"No, not much."

Jankowitz felt himself grow irritated. "Then where, if it didn't fall inside or outside? Did it disappear?"

"It mostly fell on the sill. Straight down."

She swung her light up at the window sill, which was slightly above her eye level, and Jankowitz now noticed that there *was* a large mound of glass on the lower sill. Nor did it look like someone had piled it there. It was in haphazard heaps, some of the shards hanging half off the sill.

"So someone broke the window, but the glass fell straight down?" he said. "How is *that* possible?"

Mama Bear shrugged.

Then something drew Jankowitz's attention away from the glass. Around the window itself there were a series of holes. Perfect circles, about the circumference of one of his fingers, evenly spaced about every six inches. They looked like dark eyes, staring at him in the night. He shivered, and only part of it was due to the cold air.

"What are those?" he said, pointing at the holes.

"We don't know yet," said Mama Bear.

"What *do* you know, Mama?"

"That it's cold out."

Jankowitz looked at Mama Bear again. Under any other circumstances, he would have guessed those words to be a joke. But her voice was bereft of humor. She sounded… *gray*. Like the house, like whatever she had seen inside it, had leached the life out of her.

He stepped back –

(*No, don't kid yourself, Bobby. You're not stepping* back, *you're stepping* away. *Away from Mama Bear. 'Cause she has truly, deeply creeped you out.*)

– and looked around the front of the house. He couldn't see all of it. It was too big, with a couple balconies and other architectural doo-dads getting in the way of his line of sight. But he *could* see six – no, seven – windows. Four were broken. And though it was too dark to tell for certain, he was pretty sure that all of them had those little holes around them.

Jankowitz looked away from house. He dropped his gaze to his shoes, as though to escape the dark vision of the crime scene. He knew he hadn't seen anything – not yet, not *really* – but he felt oddly tired. Oddly worried. Like he needed a break.

Between his feet, something peeked out of the snow. He shuffled the frosty powder aside with his left toe, then motioned for Mama Bear.

"Know what that is?" he said as she came over.

She shook her head. "Some kind of orange fabric," she said. "Looks heavy-duty."

"Have someone tag it and bag it and let me know what it is, okay?"

"Sure."

Mama Bear gestured for another forensics officer to bring her a camera and evidence bag. Jankowitz moved away. He didn't want to stay with Mama Bear any longer. He'd never seen her so listless, and it was thoroughly messing with his mind.

He tramped through the snow, back to the walkway that led to stairs up to the front door. He was about to walk up the short flight to the porch when Ed Royston came out the front door.

Ed was a grizzled veteran, the kind of guy who could always be counted on to act professionally and to keep it together. He never went in front of the press because he was too gruff and matter-of-fact, tending to refer to "corpses" and "stiffs" rather than "victims" and "deceased." Not a P.C. guy, which Jankowitz liked about him. He was rock-solid.

Which was why it was a shock when Ed, after inhaling deeply, lurched down the steps and then barely made it off the walkway before puking his guts out all over the snow.

Jankowitz just stared. He knew what to do when a rookie did that, but when someone who was tougher than a titanium rat trap did it, what then? Were you supposed to go to them? Ignore it?

"Geez, Ed," he finally managed. "You okay?"

Ed looked over at him, bile still dripping from his lower lip. He was white as the snow around him, the only color on his face coming from his eyes, which were bloodshot and fevered. "I... I never seen...."

Ed turned his face down and hitched again.

Jankowitz stepped toward the man. Patted him awkwardly on the shoulder, then headed up to the house. "Try not to puke on any evidence, Ed," he said. It was a lame quip, he knew, but to leave a seasoned cop without *some* kind of ribbing would be the worst kind of rebuke. It would be to acknowledge that what he did was not just embarrassing, but *dishonorable.*

He left Ed behind, still dry heaving with one hand planted against the side of the house for support.

A few steps up to the porch.

Then through the door.

He felt like he had stepped into another world. It was hot, for one thing. Too hot. He loosened his tie and collar, unbuttoned his coat, and felt sweat burst out on his forehead.

And the smell. It wasn't oppressive, but it was definitely unpleasant. A musky, slick scent. It smelled like a wild animal's den, or perhaps a tiger's cage in an under-funded zoo.

Dark forms moved all around, uniforms and plainclothes officers, all wearing latex gloves and holding flashlights that cast weird shadows in the cavernous darkness of the almost-mansion.

Jankowitz felt his brow knit in confusion. So there was heating? Then....

"Where's the light?"

As with Mama Bear outside, he was speaking mostly to himself. And as with Mama Bear outside, someone answered. Jankowitz didn't even see who it was, just one more black shape moving past him in the foyer. "Not working," it said.

Jankowitz rolled his eyes. "Obviously," he said. He reached into his jacket pocket. He had been caught in a crime scene under a house early in his detective days, looking for a corpse in the near-dark. Since then he always carried a light. Good thing in this case.

He pulled out a small Maglite, twisting the bottom to activate the powerful bulb. As soon as it came on, he swung it up, and as he did he realized another tidbit that his subconscious had picked up on: all the cops in the area had their lights pointed *down*. Like they were looking at their feet.

And the moment his own light swung up, he understood why.

The foyer looked like it had been poorly painted. Not in the whites or creams favored by this kind of place, but in a red-rust-brown mixture. Blood. It had been splashed all around the walls and was now congealing into a scab-like layer of gore.

Jankowitz stared at it, shocked. "Where'd all this come from?" he said. This time he *was* hoping for an answer. But this time none came.

He moved into the house. He didn't want to. But it was his job.

He noticed as he went that there was a pile of wood in the foyer. Looked like it had once been a nice table. He passed it. Other rooms had similar piles of wood.

What the hell did these people do to their furniture?

He saw knocked-out windows from the inside, their jagged teeth gnashing in pain in the night. More blood on the walls around them.

The smell grew stronger. It was the blood, obviously. But there was more to it. Something beneath the metallic scent of blood, something darker.

He moved deeper into the house, his instincts pulling him toward what he sensed was the hub, the center. The place where he might find answers.

Movement. He glanced to one side and saw what looked like a child's room. Several cops and forensics officers swarmed around something. Then they parted and Jankowitz glimpsed feet and legs jumbled together. No bodies. Just dismembered feet and legs piled together like poorly stacked firewood.

He pushed on. Deeper into the house.

He started to hear something. It sounded like... talking? No. It was too rhythmic, too cadenced. It was almost a chant, a low litany that could only be heard in this church of the damned.

Another room. A chair. A body, dead but not falling over. Not falling over because it was tied to the chair by loops of barbed wire that held it fast and tight, its head thrown back in a forever scream.

Jankowitz moved down a long hall. He passed an office where he glimpsed a form swinging from the ceiling. Flashes popped as pictures were taken, and images seared themselves into his mind: a woman, her skin trailing from her body in long curls, hanging from a meat hook that had been jammed through the roof of her mouth.

The smell got worse. It was... it was....

He didn't know yet.

Jankowitz followed the chanting, like sonic bread crumbs in a forest. Only he wasn't finding his way home, no, he was following the crumbs *to* the witch's house.

The kitchen.

He stepped in. Slipped. He looked down and the flashlight reflected off a red river. Unlike the walls in the foyer, the blood on the floor had not begun to congeal. Jankowitz couldn't tell if it was because it was still too new, or if there was simply too much of it.

He looked to the source of the chanting, and saw a pile of wood that he supposed was a table and chairs at one point. And beside it....

Jankowitz walked toward the wood. There was another cop there, a lone detective in this otherwise empty kitchen. Jankowitz tried to remember the man's name but couldn't. He gave up and just moved forward, stepping carefully and trying to ignore the wet sucking noises his shoes made in the river of blood below him.

The other cop was huddled over something. Something that was making the noise. Something that was the source of the smell, that familiar smell.

Jankowitz saw it.

"Holy shit," he said.

It was a man. Or it had been, once. He was lying in a fetal position on the floor, covered in blood. His eyes moved rapidly back and forth, back and forth, but Jankowitz could tell that the man didn't see him or the other cop or anything else in the room. There was nothing in the man's gaze. No comprehension, no reality. Only terror. Madness.

The man wore the ragged remains of what had once been a nice suit, but it had been cut to pieces, and the skin that showed was bruised and battered. He had been cut, burnt, abraded. It looked like every possible kind of physical trauma had been visited upon him.

"He was everywhere," said the man. "He was everywhere and I told. Everywhere and I told. Everywhere and I told." He repeated the words over and over, his eyes flashing sightlessly in the darkness, trapped in some hell that Jankowitz could not even guess at.

"How long's he been like this?" said Jankowitz.

The other cop's voice was low, almost reverent. "Since he was found."

"Everywhere and I told ...."

"Jesus," said Jankowitz. He was not a religious man. But he crossed himself all the same. His mother had done that, and in this moment it seemed the only appropriate thing to do.

The man on the floor seemed to see the movement. He remained curled up in the blood, his eyes continued to dart back and forth. But his voice began to raise. "He was *everywhere* and I told. *Everywhere* and I told. *EVERYWHERE AND I TOLD*."

Jankowitz realized what the smell was. Not just blood and sweat and shit and tears and trauma.

It was madness.

The man's voice continued to rise, louder and louder and louder until it cracked like the windows of the once-lovely house. Jankowitz wanted to leave, wanted to join Ed outside and maybe throw up himself.

But he didn't.

He stayed.

He watched.

And felt insanity wash over him. Felt hope's last life curl and die within him.

Knew with the sound of the man's screaming that humanity was a lost cause, and the only relief to be found was death.

1

Jerry Hughes drove down a dream, but knew as always that the dream would end badly.

He was awake, of course. But even awake, he knew that this street – *his* street – represented the pinnacle of success, the peak of hope. He was driving down the American Dream.

It was a long street, but not so long that it felt like a thoroughfare. No, it was just long enough to give a sense of grandeur and permanence. Long enough to give those who drove its length a chance to rubberneck, to appreciate, to gape and gasp a bit and – perhaps most important – to grow more than a little jealous that *they* did not live on such a street of dreams.

Each house was different. Not that the street seemed at all thrown together. No, each house was different but somehow they all seemed to fit together, presenting different facets of one overarching message that bespoke wealth, progress, and hard-earned superiority.

Of course, to know that you had to look hard, because these houses, these individual bits of dream on the larger dream that was the street, were mostly hidden from view. High privacy walls shielded all but the tops of most of the houses from the prying eyes of the unwashed masses. And behind many of the privacy walls tall evergreens stood as well. The trees added life to the picture of perfection that was each home and, not coincidentally, also added another ten or twenty feet of obscurity, of privacy, of secrecy.

Part of the American Dream, Jerry mused, is complete separation from one's neighbors. Once upon a time we lived in communities, hoping to build a better life by banding together with those around us to create things that were more than we could have done apart. Now we hoped only to do enough to provide ourselves with that most fleeting of goals: the illusion that we were masters – or, even better, sole inhabitants – of our own tiny domains, like feudal keeps surrounded by rivals not so much hostile as simply ambivalent to our existence.

Jerry sighed. He wondered, as he often did, what would happen if he rang the doorbell of any of the houses bearing a plate of cookies. Just a neighborly thing to do, a thing that he remembered his own mother doing often when he was a boy.

As always, he immediately knew the answer: there was no way in hell he'd even get to the door. The walls and trees and gates were designed to keep such things from happening.

Welcome to the American Dream.

He only knew one of his neighbors. Other than that, he didn't even know the *names* of the people on the street. Didn't know what they did as occupations. Hell, he didn't even know what most of them looked like.

Perfect isolation.

The illusion that we are alone in the world.

And, he thought, it's not like I'm any better. I don't even know what it's like outside the car. Hot? Cold? Is it spring?

That was going too far and he knew it. He knew exactly what time of year it was, what the *date* was.

What today meant.

No, try not to think of that.

He looked at the car's dashboard. Jerry drove a Mercedes: an acceptable vehicle on this American Dream Street. It was a late model, one he had purchased just a year or so ago. He had bought it, he remembered, not because he *needed* a new car, but because he *could*. And really, when it came right down to it, at some point the *ability* to have something became synonymous with a requirement to acquire it.

Still, he didn't like this new car. It had too many buttons. Too many controls. The dashboard looked like something he would expect to see inside a high-tech research department.

But it did tell him the temperature. Which was nice, he supposed. He also supposed he could have just rolled down the window and stuck his arm out, but....

Seventy-three degrees. Perfect temperature. Not too hot, not too cold.

Nice night for a swim?

Jerry shivered. For a moment he saw a bright green circle in his mind, a red mass to one side like a malignant tumor.

He pushed the thought away. He'd been doing so all day. He'd keep *on* doing so. Until this day, the worst day of the year, was over.

He slowed. He was almost home. He looked at the clock, wondering how late it was, how much hell he was going to catch.

The clock said "8:16 PM" in orange letters that were almost too bright. Next to the time was today's date.

Nice night for a swim?

Jerry felt his face draw tight, his cheeks tautening over his skull. He'd lost weight in the last year. Lost weight, lost sleep... lost hope.

And now, worst of all, he was home.

2

The American Dream Home – *his* American Dream Home – sat at nearly the end of the long cul-de-sac that he had just traveled. Like the other houses it was large, prestigious. Like the others it bespoke prosperity without being ostentatious. Like the others it was protected from the intrusions of the outside world by a high wall. The wall was beige. Wrought-iron barbs jutted spear-like out of the top of the front wall, adding another six feet to its already impressive height and, Jerry supposed, dissuading any would-be climbers.

At the front of the property the wrought-iron barbs seemed to crawl down the wall and link hands to form a large gate that was the single way in or out of the property. The gate sat on a track and, at the touch of a remote control, a chain would pull the gate to the side, allowing the house's inhabitants and invited guests to enter freely.

Jerry's own remote control was clipped to the visor of his Mercedes. He thumbed it as he drove up, slowing down as he did so. After living here for a few years he knew exactly how fast the gate opened, how slow he had to go to *just* squeak by without losing a side mirror to either the still-opening gate or the silently crouching wall. His wife hated that he did that, hated that he didn't just wait until the gate was completely open, but Jerry liked to get home as fast as he could.

Or at least, he *used* to like getting home as fast as he could. Now he supposed he mostly did it out of habit more than desire.

Still, he slowed down a bit. Because if there was any day he didn't want to be home, it was today.

He glanced at the dashboard again. At the date.

One year.

His eyes darted forward again.

"Shit!"

The word burst out of his mouth, more surprise than rage or fear. His foot, already resting on the brake pedal, now jammed down hard.

The gate wasn't open. Not the slightest bit.

Jerry frowned. He must not have activated the remote correctly. He flipped his visor down and thumbed the button again.

The gate didn't move.

Jerry's first thought was that the remote's batteries had died. But even as he thought that his finger punched the button again, and this time he was aware of a faint grinding noise. It sounded like a garbage disposal into which some enterprising toddler had jammed a handful of spoons. He hit the remote again and got the same result.

He sat still for a moment. An insane thought occurred: maybe he should just go back to the hospital. Sleep in one of the on-call rooms, curl up in a ball and sleep the night away, pretend none of this existed, that today was just a dream.

But he knew that wouldn't end well. He was going to be in hot water as it was for working so late.

Jerry got out of the car. The night air was just as the car had advised: just about perfect. A bit more humid than in the car, where the filters and conditioners stripped much of the moisture away. But nice.

Nice night for a –

Jerry shoved the thought away. He left the motor on, the engine idling and the lights aimed at the gate. He walked up, wondering what he was going to do. Unless it was something fairly obvious, he doubted he'd be able to fix it.

Still, what was the alternative? Just sit in the car all night?

As he walked up to the gate a dark shape came bounding forward over the well-manicured lawn. It moved like a piece of shadow that had sheared itself off the night and now made a beeline for Jerry, barking excitedly. A moment later Socrates' muzzle was poking through the gate and the dog was licking at Jerry's hands and wrists, yipping with delight to see one of the masters of the castle come home.

"Hey there, boy," said Jerry. He smiled at the pooch. Socrates was a mutt they had picked up at a shelter about six years ago. Looked like he had some Alsatian, maybe a bit of Elkhound. He was a big dog, but well-groomed and affable. He had one of those mouths that always seemed to be curled up in a puppy's grin, a long pink tongue lolling over his teeth and adding just the right touch of silly affection to his demeanor.

Socrates barked in reply, licked Jerry's hand, then barked again.

"Yeah, good to see you, too," said Jerry. He patted the pooch's head one more time, then turned his attention back to the gate. He had brought the remote from the car, and now he pressed the button again.

The grinding sound was worse up close. Like someone had replaced the bones in Jerry's skull with slate and was raking their nails across his temporal bones. He winced but hit the remote once more. Socrates didn't like the sound either, yipping and barking as the whir/crackle/grind rent the otherwise still night air.

"Sorry, Soc," said Jerry.

The sound was coming from just beyond the gate, just to the right of the privacy wall the surrounded his home. The bars of the gate were close-set, about five inches apart, so Jerry couldn't stick his head through to see what was there. He tried moving to the left, hoping he would be able to spot what was causing the problem.

Just call the house.

Sure. That'll be a great way to come home.

No way to come home that'll be great. Not today.

Jerry took another step, pressing his head against the bars of the gate as if by doing so he might silence the internal argument sounding in his mind.

Socrates started barking again, as though weighing in on the debate.

"Easy, Soc."

Socrates didn't pay him any heed. Also typical. Jerry often reflected that there might have been a time where a man was the master of his domain, but that time was not now, and that place was not here.

"What?" he said. The sound was almost a breath, just a surprised exhalation that became the barest ghost of a word.

He thought he had seen something wedged in the chain mechanism that drew the gate out of the driveway.

Jerry moved back to the left. Socrates kept barking. "Soc, shut up," he said. Again, the dog kept barking. Jerry couldn't tell if the dog was excited by the general adventure of the moment, happy to see his master, or simply being a dog.

He reached through the gate, questing fingers feeling for what he had glimpsed from his oblique angle. He touched something. Wood, rounded edges. A splinter bit his finger.

Somehow a rake had fallen into the chain winch.

Jerry's brows pulled together. The gardeners weren't due today, were they? Then he shook his head. Didn't matter. No matter how the rake had gotten there, he had to get it out.

Socrates' barking took on a more urgent tone. At first Jerry thought the mutt was cheering him on as he reached for the rake, urging his master to get it get it get it *get it you can do it master get it!* Then his bones and his skin almost jumped in separate directions as –

"Can't you shut that damn thing up?"

Jerry's head smacked against one of the bars of the gate with a clang. He pulled his arm from between the other bars, his hand going to his forehead as he swiveled to see who had startled him. Even though he already knew. Indeed, he should have known from the moment Socrates went nuts, because very few people rubbed the good-natured dog the way that the man standing behind Jerry did.

Ted lived next door. Jerry didn't know his last name. He was pretty sure he *had* known it once, but he didn't anymore. The man was just "Ted." And that was quite enough.

Ted was about five-eight. Maybe a hundred eighty pounds. Perennially hurried, perpetually sweaty. Beady eyes that seemed to float just a tad too close together in the pasty mass of his face. Comb-over that was only slightly less revolting than having a toupee made of dead ferrets would have been. He was a judge, Jerry thought. But he couldn't be sure. They were *neighbors;* that didn't mean they knew each other.

Jerry stared at the middle-aged man, rubbing his head until the sharp pain where he had whacked himself subsided, then turned back to the gate. He reached back through and tried to push the rake out of the chain where it had fallen.

"Hey," Ted said. His voice rose a notch, both in volume and tone. He was the epitome of the "I live alone because I can't stand people" type. "Did you hear me?"

Jerry sighed. Kept reaching for the rake. "I heard you, Ted. But I'm trying to ignore you."

He tried to close his fingers around the rake handle, but couldn't quite gain purchase on it. It was just barely out of reach.

"Well, doesn't that just –"

"Ted! I'm concentrating."

Ted went silent, though whether respecting Jerry's wishes or simply taken aback, Jerry couldn't say.

Jerry felt the rake. Handle worn smooth through use. He tried to grab it. Couldn't get a grip. Switched to pushing instead.

The rake fell away from the winch chain. It clattered to the concrete driveway with a skeletal rattle.

Socrates kept barking.

Jerry turned back to Ted. The man was scowling like he had just found out his favorite fantasy football team had been eliminated, right after a bad colonoscopy.

Jerry pasted a too-wide grin on his face, wishing Socrates would shut up. "Now," he said. "What were we talking about?"

Ted fumed for another moment. Jerry could almost hear the squat man's teeth grinding. Then Ted exploded, stepping forward and waving a short sausage of a finger in Jerry's face.

"I should call animal control and have that mutt hauled away!" he nearly screamed. "And your kids were listening to their stereo loud enough to hear it over the *wall* again!"

Jerry had no doubt that Ted was telling the truth about the kids: Sheri and Drew listened to their music at levels that could only be described as seismic. But he still felt his blood pressure going up like a bottle rocket. Because even though the kids might be in the wrong on this one, they were *his* kids, and he was damned if he was going to let some Napoleonic twit with an attitude bitch them out, even *in absentia*.

Jerry felt his grin grow wider, creeping up until the corners of his mouth felt like they were resting just below his earlobes. "Tell you what," he said. "You cut back your tree – you know, the one that keeps dropping branches on my wife's garden – and then I'll talk to my dog. Maybe even my kids. Until then, Ted, please kindly shove it up your ass."

Jerry turned away from the shorter man's glowering face. He was suddenly struck by the fact that Ted looked like a badly-coifed version of the Stay-Puft Marshmallow Man from *Ghostbusters* and had to quell a rising fit of laughter. Instead he hit the remote, praying that the gate would open. He did not want to have to go back to the gate right now. Not with Ted-Puft glowering at him like he was trying to incinerate Jerry with his mind.

The gate opened.

Jerry got into his car. Back into the sterile non-temperature of the Mercedes. He put the car into drive, then pulled into his property. Socrates followed the car, barking in a way that sounded oddly like he was saying "Nyah-nyah, nyah-nyah!"

Ted stayed where he was the whole time. Arms crossed. Glaring at Jerry's car in a way that probably would be lethal to small woodland creatures at ten paces.

Jerry kept watching Ted in the rearview mirror as he drove up the driveway. Longer than he should, in fact. Longer than was safe.

3

For the second time in minutes, Jerry almost slammed into something. He turned his eyes forward just in time to see the woman in front of the car and mashed his feet down automatically, practically standing up in his seat as he put all his weight on the brake

The car shuddered to a halt, and he was treated to a glimpse of a rage-soaked face that seemed to be lit half by his headlights and half by internal combustion. Then the face was gone as the woman flitted around to his side of the car. She pounded on the hood as she walked, tiny fists hitting it with dull thuds that resounded even in the sound-proofed interior of the Mercedes.

Then the face was at his window. Jerry stared at the woman. He knew her, but... *didn't.* He had seen her almost daily for – how long? Years? – but now she suddenly seemed unfamiliar. Her eyes, normally soft and compliant, shone down hard and angry. Her mouth was drawn firmly across her face like a thin slash that someone had cut with a razor.

What the hell is going on today?

Jerry rolled the window down. The woman said nothing, simply continued to stare. "Hey, Rosa," he said.

Rosa didn't say a thing for another moment, a quick second that was long enough for Jerry's heart to do a fast lub-dub and for Jerry's mind to wonder if he should roll the window back up and maybe call 9-1-1 on his cell.

Then she started screaming.

Jerry didn't understand it. Not a word. She was shrieking full speed in Spanish, her hands flapping like the wings of a hummingbird in a karate class.

"Easy, Ro –" he began. That just resulted in even louder shrieks. He noticed she was still wearing the apron she always wore when working at the house, but none of the cleaning supplies she usually carried in its pockets were present.

After another second Rosa slapped the car. Still screaming in Spanish, she shook her finger in his face, then stomped away down the driveway. Jerry leaned out to track her progress. Rosa marched down the drive, then seemed to reconsider halfway down and moved onto the grass, lifting her feet extra high with each step and then ramming them down as though to smash as much grass as possible on her way out.

Then she was out the still-open gate – Ted was gone by now – and turned past the privacy wall and disappeared from view.

Jerry watched the empty driveway exit, as though if he stared at it long enough normalcy might return to the day.

Fat chance.

Socrates barked once. No longer gloating, the bark was sharp and almost angry. Like he was warning something. *Stay away,* the bark said. Which was ridiculous, because Jerry could see nothing in the night other than him.

The universe has gone nuts.

On that thought, he clicked the remote and the gate slid shut. He meant to make himself feel better, as though closing out the evils that threatened him in the outside world. But the closing of the gate did no such thing. Instead he felt suddenly as though he knew how an insect must feel, swallowed up in a Venus flytrap. Like he was seeing his last view of the outside world.

Like the house was swallowing him.

4

The man gets out of the black van. Because it is his *turn* to get out of the van.

Of course, there is no one in the van but him, so it is *always* his turn. But still, care must be taken. Attention must be paid. There are rules to any game.

He does not break rules.

He stands outside the still-open door and watches Jerry and Ted fight. He has never understood why people fight like that. Or rather, why people *squabble.* He understands fighting – certainly, fighting is struggle and struggle is understanding and understanding is necessary to life – but merely *squabbling*?

He sighs.

"Why would they do that?" he says in a whisper. And then he answers himself, as he so often does: "Because they have not yet been brought to enlightenment. They are still hiding."

"From whom?" he wonders, though he knows the answer. And, knowing, he says, "From themselves."

The squabble – the quarrel, the *tiff* – finally ends. Jerry goes to his car and leaves. Socrates follows. Barking happily. Socrates is a good dog. The man likes dogs. Dogs have no secrets. They are open books. They have only love or hate. Purity.

Ted watches Jerry drive away. Then he smirks as though he has seen something funny and begins the long walk to his own driveway, to his own property. Next door, but a whole world apart.

Perhaps the man will visit Ted someday.

No, probably not. Ted seems thoroughly… *unredeemable*.

But he knows that the fun is going to begin. Because Rosa has been cast out from among them. And Rosa needs to be dealt with.

This family is going to be fun. More fun, more riveting, more *teachable* than any of the others. Not even the last family, the ones who died in so much pain while Christmas lights drew colorful pictures outside their home, will hold a candle to this one. He knows it. He can *feel* it.

He's getting better and better at this. Each family that he teaches, teaches him in turn. This will be his best visit ever.

"Whose turn is it?" he says.

"For what?" he answers.

"To teach a lesson."

He giggles. The sound pleases him.

"Why, mine, of course."

5

Jerry clicked another button on the remote, and this time the garage door rolled up.

He glanced at the rearview mirror. He didn't know why he did it. Habit? Perhaps he was hoping to catch Ted standing at the driveway gate, glaring at the house. It'd serve the crabby turd right, to stand there alone all night, hoping to intimidate the family or something.

Ted was not there.

But something else was.

At first Jerry thought it might be Rosa, come back from whatever bout of insanity had gripped her. But no, whoever it was simply stood there. No movement toward the callbox that would allow him or her to call the house. And even from this distance Jerry could see that the shadow was considerably larger than the diminutive Latina.

He stopped the car before going into the now-open garage. Turned in his seat so he could look out the rear window rather than staring at the mirror.

The person was still there.

The face and figure were cloaked in shadow, just a dark patch in the night. But it moved, and icy coils crawled up Jerry's back and gut. He couldn't be sure why at first, but then he realized: it looked like whoever it was was *sniffing* the air. Smelling it like an old lady enjoying a rosebush, or a child sniffing a pot of fudge… or a hyena inhaling over a fresh-killed corpse.

Jerry watched the shadow for a long time. Then the person stepped back. The night seemed to take him. Hold him. Swallow him.

Gone.

Jerry watched another second. Waited to see if the stranger would come back.

The person – whoever it was – didn't.

Jerry pulled into his garage. As fast as he could.

6

The man waits at the gate. Watches as Rosa stomps away. But by the time she gets in her vehicle, a small blue economy car, he is already waiting for her there.

It is impossible for anyone else. But not for him. He is much, much faster than anyone he has ever met. It is one of his gifts. One of the things he has given himself.

He watches her, fumbling in her pocket for her keys, her mouth moving as she mumbles to herself, probably saying nasty things about the people in the house.

She wipes her eyes with the back of her hand. Crying. Perhaps that is why it is so easy for her not to notice him. Perhaps it is just another one of his gifts. He has so many.

Finally, she fishes the keys out with shaking hands. They jingle, a light *tinkity tink* that he rather likes. It sounds bright and happy.

She gets in the car and drops the keys on the seat and that sound, too, is deceptively jolly in the night. She leans over in the darkness to fish around for them – he already turned off the dome light – and when she finally straightens up with them he sees her eyes widen in the rearview mirror and knows she has seen him.

She gasps. Inhales, clearly ready to scream.

Before she can scream, he snaps his hand forward. He is fast. Very fast. Her inhalation cuts off as his hand clamps over her mouth. The sound she makes – a muted "*Hrrrk,*" the sound of a scream being stuffed backed down her throat – is funny and he giggles.

He reaches for her. Smiling. Then says "No!" in a stern voice. He rolls his eyes, but knows he is right. He glares at the woman. "You're lucky," he says. "Lucky it's my turn." He nods. "Yes, because when it's *my* turn things can get ugly."

Rosa whimpers.

"Still," he says. "You *were* stealing. Not so nice." He nods agreement. He makes a good point, as he so often does. "No. Not nice at all."

Rosa whimpers again, but this whimper disappears and turns into a gagging scream.

"Shhh," says the man. "It's better this way." He leaves his hand on her mouth, puts another over her throat, and push-pulls in a practiced motion. Something pops and shatters and Rosa's larynx rips to pieces in her throat. Her whimper turns to a breathy gasp. She is still alive, but will not scream again. Not ever.

The man smiles to himself.

The night's play has really, truly begun.

7

Jerry pulled into the garage. The tires squeaked on the epoxy-coated floor that was maintained at a high gleam by both Rosa –

(*What the hell was* that *all about?*)

– and by a pair of men who came twice a year to clean, polish, and buff the garage floor. The sound usually made Jerry smile. It was a good sound, a clean sound. The kind of sound that said, "You're home, and things here are A-okay and under control."

But that was the case less and less of late, and not at all tonight. Tonight the sound was just a tortured shriek of rubber on a floor that simply wished to be left alone.

Socrates was still running around the yard, barking at the grass and the sky as he chased his tail in circles. That was a bright spot. Hopefully the mutt would keep it up all night, long enough for Ted to go nuts and maybe consider putting his house on the market.

As if I'd be so lucky.

Jerry hit the garage door remote and the light switched on in the garage as he got out of the car. The light cast bright flares of illumination onto the many mostly-bare surfaces. There were bikes for each member of the family on one wall, a few cleaning supplies.

And his tool board.

Jerry didn't remember leaving it open. But since it was, he stood for a moment to admire it. It was a large pegboard wall on which hung every kind of hand and power tool available to mankind, along with a few he was pretty sure hadn't been invented yet but were only available via time portal technology exclusively licensed by Home Depot and eBay. He had never used the great majority of the tools and had no idea if some of them even *worked.* But that was all right, because they were his.

If he needed something he liked to have it available to him. That was the whole point of a tool collection: having the right tool for the right job at the right time. Whether you actually used it was irrelevant. *Availability* was the point, not utility.

Jerry realized he was stalling: something he did more and more these days, putting off going into the house for precious minutes or seconds. But the house – and the people in it – weren't going to change or go anywhere no matter how long he stood here.

He might as well go in.

He grabbed the wide door to the right of the tool display. It was on rollers that were cleverly hidden in the floor and ceiling of the garage, and when it slid home it hid the tools completely. Just another blank wall. White and clean, no clutter or confusion, which was pretty much Jerry's own personal definition of happiness.

He hung his keys on the hook near the door that led from the garage to the house. He squared his shoulders and took a breath, half of him feeling like a soldier preparing to go into battle and the other half of him feeling idiotic for feeling that way.

He went in.

The door opened soundlessly. He poked a head in, blanching as though expecting to be gunned down by sniper fire.

The house was silent. Mostly dark. The kids were probably upstairs.

What about Ann?

She could be anywhere. The house was over five thousand square feet. Vaulted ceilings, lots of hallways and interlocking doors and jack-and-jill bathrooms. It was a labyrinthine layout – one that you could easily get lost in, if you had half a mind to do so. Jerry himself was continually getting turned around, forgetting nooks and crannies the place possessed. Fun sometimes, a real pain at others.

Jerry sighed. He'd either see her or he wouldn't. He beelined for his office, and as soon as he was in he put down the attaché case he'd brought in from the car. He put it next to the closed laptop on his desk and briefly thought about taking out the papers inside and going over them, then discarded that idea. A minute or two of malingering outside was one thing, but if Ann came in and saw him working in the office she'd really lose it.

When did things go so bad? he wondered. When did everything fall apart?

He knew. He knew exactly. But he didn't want to think about it. It was too *hard* to think about.

He pulled his cell phone out of his pocket and plugged it into a charger. Then all movement ceased; every muscle in his body went rigid as a sound slid into the office. It wasn't loud, but it was strident. The kind of sound someone made when they were being particularly careful to be very care*less* with their steps. Stepping around in such a way that anyone within fifty feet would have no alternative but to hear them.

Jerry cursed under his breath.

He turned off the light in his office and walked the short few steps across the hall and into the kitchen.

Ann was there.

As always, Jerry felt his heart leap into his throat when he saw his wife. Even now, even after almost two decades of marriage, Ann was still one of the most stunning women he had ever seen. She was older now, of course. No longer the brightly smiling woman he had taken to his heart and to his home and to his bed when they were both barely out of their teens. But where she had once had youth, now she had so much life, so much experience.

She was still a knockout, too. Judicious eating and borderline obsessive use of a Stair-Master had kept Ann Hughes at a level of fitness that most high school cheerleaders would envy. Dark hair tumbled in thick waves well past her shoulders, and her eyes, though deep brown, could light up enough to power a city when she was happy.

Now, however, those eyes seemed to pull light out of the room, a pair of small thunderclouds that spat lightning at anyone who dared to approach.

Behind her, Jerry noticed that the door to the basement was open. He wondered why. Then realized he was searching for excuses to avoid talking to Ann… and that in so doing he was only going to make things worse.

He forced himself to look at his wife. Tried to plaster a smile onto his face, much as he had with Ted. Only he couldn't muster up even the insincere, go-screw-yourself smile he had aimed at his neighbor. All he managed was a strange squiggle-mouthed expression that probably made him look more gassy than anything.

"Sorry about having to work late today," he said.

Then even his weak attempt at a smile disappeared as Ann said, "What else is new?" She turned her back on him and when she turned back around she was holding a glass of wine. Another thing that hadn't happened before life started to splinter: Ann never used to drink at all. Now it seemed like she never missed a day without at least a glass of wine, and often much more than that.

His wife's words stung him. Probably all the worse because of their truth. He pushed down the flare of anger that rose up within him. "If he hadn't needed an emergency surgery, I wouldn't have gone in," he said finally, keeping his words neutral and his tone even. Ann said nothing. Just stared at a point in space about a foot in front of her.

Jerry decided to change the subject. "Did you know there was a rake stuck in the chain that pulls the gate back from the driveway?" Still nothing. Ann looked like she was trapped in her own private world of thought. "Honey?"

Jerry took a deep breath. He knew what she wanted, though he really didn't want to oblige her. Didn't want to deal with it. Not today. Not *today.*

But she wasn't going to move, he saw. Not until he asked. "Okay," he said, and was surprised how tired his voice sounded. "What happened with Rosa?"

"Bitch was *stealing from us*!" shouted Ann, her words coming so hard and fast in response that Jerry literally stepped back. His hands went up in front of his face, not as though to calm her but more as though he was worried she might try to hit him. He had never seen her respond like this to anything. Not even....

"Whoa," he said. "What do –?"

Ann grabbed a large, antique silver ladle off the counter and waved it around like a sword in her right hand while her wine sloshed out of the glass she still clutched in her left. "And not little things, either. It wasn't just a fork, or the ten bucks we leave for the kids' lunches. This was big, *big* things!" She approached Jerry, jabbing at him with the bowl end of the ladle like someone enrolled in a bizarre remedial fencing class. "Did she think we wouldn't *notice*? Did she think she could just stick this down her bra and *hide* it?" Ann slammed the ladle against the counter. The implement clanged, a strangely empty sound in the large kitchen. "I shoulda jammed this thing down her throat and let her keep it *that* way! See how she likes it then!"

The ladle punched out at him again, and Ann inhaled like she was going to head into another rant. Jerry felt like hiding under something. Then the air seemed to trickle out of Ann. The ladle slowly lowered.

"Today, of all days," she said. She was looking at something. Jerry didn't have to follow her gaze to know what it was. A picture. Her and the kids. *All* of the kids. "Why today?" Her voice was almost a whisper.

Jerry felt something tugging at him. Something close to the way he had felt for her before everything started to come down around them. He stepped toward Ann and slowly reached out. Wrapped his fingers around the haft of the ladle, then pulled it from her now-loose grip. He put it down on the counter, then took his wife in his arms. He held her carefully, as though she were a cracked porcelain doll, an antique that might come apart with the barest breath of a breeze.

He could feel her. Still looking at the picture.

"Let it go," he whispered, and wasn't sure if he was talking to her or to himself. It probably didn't matter, he supposed; probably neither of them would be able to do such a thing. "Let it go for tonight."

He pulled back and looked at Ann. She was still staring over his shoulder and wouldn't meet his gaze no matter how he tried to catch her eyes with his own. "Let's enjoy ourselves," he said. "No one bothering us, no phone calls, no nothing but the family. Okay?" She didn't answer until he gave her a small shake and added, "Okay?" one more time. Then her chin went up and down about a half centimeter. Her gaze was far away, long ago.

Not too *long, though. One year. Just a single year.*

"Why don't we order some take-out?" he said. "We can have a nice, low-key dinner. Sound good? Just the family."

Ann nodded again. Her movements were slow. Delayed, like she was processing everything at one-quarter speed. Which perhaps she was.

They all were. Life was moving too slow for her, just like it was for him. Passing by, minute after agonizing minute, moving toward… what?

Jerry looked over his shoulder. Finally let himself look at the picture.

Three children.

Three *happy* children.

Three.

He swallowed, feeling a hard lump forming at the back of his throat. "I'll make the call for the food," he said. Ann didn't answer, and he wondered if she was even with him right now. Or was she *there*? One year ago, finding him? Finding their son?

"I'll make the call," he said again. Because in spite of the fact that he held his wife in his arms, in spite of the fact that he held her close and could feel every curve of her body, he still felt as though he were alone in a room full of nothing but memories and ghosts.

8

It took a while, but he gradually got her to move away from the counter, from the ladle that she had been swinging about. Though truth be told, it was almost nice to see some emotion in Ann's eyes, some life. She had been so passionate, so fiery when they met. Sometimes that was a royal pain in Jerry's ass, but Ann had never been boring.

But since the night it all fell apart, Ann had settled into a state of doldrums that bordered on the comatose at times. The whole family had. They moved like people, but acted more like zombies, or maybe those weird automatons you might see at Disneyworld. Jerry wouldn't have been surprised to hear twin clicks when his eyes closed each night, wouldn't have been surprised to hear near-silent whirrs as he powered down for another nightmare-streaked sleep.

He called in an order for Chinese food from their usual place – though the voice that answered was not one he recognized – and when he came to the table Ann was running a finger along the edges of the wineglass, lazy circles along the rim that he knew he would have found subtly erotic not too long ago. Now… nothing. Especially since she was still looking at the picture.

The three kids. All three of them smiling like life was fine and forever. Like the universe owed them a debt of happiness.

Wrong.

Jerry and Ann sat in silence. He didn't try to talk; could tell that his wife wouldn't respond even if he did. And before he knew it the doorbell rang, startling him. He looked at Ann. She didn't seem to have noticed the sound.

"Must be the food," he said. "You want to get the kids, or take care of the food?" His wife said nothing, just continued tracing those circles around the rim of the glass. He moved it away from her. Her eyes moved away from the picture she'd been staring at, but didn't quite manage to focus on him. "I'll get the kids," he finally said.

She nodded. Again, the movement was slow. He wondered if she was like this for everyone. Or was it just for him?

He stood and headed for the front stairs. The house had two sets, one that led up from the foyer, and another that ended in the back of the kitchen. As he stepped toward the hall, Ann spoke.

"Jerry?"

He turned. Hope bloomed. He didn't know what he was hoping for, exactly. Maybe that she'd run to him, that she'd hold him, that she'd tell him it was all going to be okay; that they'd get through this and survive.

None of those. "How'd he get up?" she said.

Jerry blinked. "Huh?"

"How'd he get through the gate without ringing?" Her brow furrowed in irritation. "Did you leave it open?"

Jerry tried to think. He remembered griping out Ted, remembered Socrates barking like crazy. Remembered the rake in the mechanism and Rosa screaming at him. And, of course, he remembered his reluctance to come home, the melancholy he'd felt all day on this worst of anniversaries.

But had he closed the gate?

He shrugged. "I guess I must not have."

Ann sighed, as though she had to put up with horrors like this on a regular basis, and only her supremely charitable soul kept her from lashing out and doing something terrible. Jerry had to fight to keep his eyes from rolling. To remind himself that they were all hurting, and getting into a fight right now wouldn't help anything.

"You gonna get the food?" he asked.

She nodded and moved toward her purse, which was on the counter near the opposite end of the kitchen.

Jerry nodded and ran up the steps. Or rather, he started to run. But with every tread his feet slowed a bit. Because he knew that Ann wasn't going to be the only one who was difficult to handle today. Not the only ghost in this huge tomb masquerading as a home.

No, there were still the kids to deal with.

9

Because he was moving slowly, he was only halfway up the front stairs when Ann emerged from the kitchen. The roof was vaulted high above them both, with some naked beams showing, adding a rustic look that was both incongruous and strangely compatible with the rest of the modern house.

Jerry watched as his wife moved to the front door, holding three twenties in front of her. She moved with a shuffling, almost stumbling gait. If he hadn't known better he would have guessed she was drugged. And now that he thought of it, maybe she was – melancholy, grief, denial, anger… they could all affect the mind as potently as any man-made pharmaceutical.

She passed the baby grand piano that sat at the edge of the living room, and Jerry saw his wife touch its keys. She used to play. Not anymore. Music was gone from the house. Music along with so many other things.

He saw it for a moment in his mind. The thing that had killed the music. The green. The jewel-green with streaks of red reaching through it and a dark form at its edge.

Then Ann opened the door, and Jerry was grateful for the interruption to the memory.

He couldn't see the delivery man. The angle was wrong and the porch light must have burnt out, because though Ann flicked the switch no light flooded in when she opened the door. So all he saw was a dark form and the shape of a baseball cap with the Chinese restaurant's logo on it. Still, the figure seemed unfamiliar to him, and he thought they knew all the delivery people.

A sobering thought itself.

When did we start eating exclusively takeout food?

"Hey," said the delivery man. He held out two white plastic bags, knotted tightly at the tops. "That'll be forty-nine fifty-two."

His voice was strange. Nothing wrong with the tone, but it was oddly emotionless. Or no, that wasn't right, Jerry realized. It was more... *contained.* Like he was trying desperately to hold himself back, like he was on the verge of flying to pieces. As though if he let himself show the slightest trace of emotion, even vocally, he might completely lose all control and God only knew what would happen then.

That's ridiculous, Jer-Jer. Get a grip.

Red on green. Tendrils in the light. Beauty and death.

Ann took the bags, handed him three twenties. Then she frowned. "I thought I knew all the delivery guys at Chang's."

The man shrugged, the dark shadows of his shoulders going up and down once. "It was my turn to come out," he said. "My turn," he added. He giggled, then turned away before she could say anything else.

Ann watched him go, clearly confused, then swung the door shut behind him and went back to the kitchen. Jerry watched her go and felt like calling out to her. He suddenly wanted company. Something about what he had just seen had... disquieted him.

Admit it, Jer-Jer. That weirded you out.

He shook his head. Started to climb and as he climbed he even managed to convince himself that he was shaking his head because Ann would have been angry to discover he was watching her and not to deny how terribly frightened he suddenly was.

10

Jerry turned down the hall. Three enormous rooms up here, all interconnected with jack-and-jill bathrooms. He had loved that fact when he had first seen the house. It seemed fanciful, whimsical. Like a labyrinth in a fairy tale, and when they moved here the plan was that every single room would hold a treasure, would be the end of the maze, the gold at the end of the rainbow.

Now, though, the magic seemed to have leached out of the house. The bright colors of his life had dimmed to faded pastels, here as everywhere else.

Jerry went to the first door. Knocked on it.

Drew answered. "Yeah?"

"It's me," said Jerry.

There was a pause, long enough that Jerry started to get irritated. He believed in giving the kids their space and a sense of privacy, but it was rude to just leave him out here like this.

He was at the point of saying something when Drew's voice came again: "Come on in."

Jerry opened the door. Stepped in.

His son's room was huge. That was what always hit him when he came in. So much bigger than anything Jerry had ever had as a kid, but he was glad of that. Glad that his son could enjoy nice things, could enjoy life.

The walls were papered haphazardly with pin-ups (none too risqué, thank goodness) and posters of rock groups that all looked like they were in serious needs of a good stylist and someone to wash their clothes on at least a semi-annual basis. But his son didn't take after them. Drew was fifteen and had that fresh, well-scrubbed look that Jerry knew would stand him in better stead than trying to be on the cutting edge of fashion. Fashions changed, trends moved too fast to keep up with, but cleanliness and good grooming never went out of style.

Jerry loved his boy.

(Your remaining *boy.)*

He felt tears threaten to rise up behind his eyes at that thought, and as much to avoid them as to salute Drew he walked to where the kid sat. Drew was at his desk, feet propped up on it while he read a school book and enjoyed a nice breeze coming in through his open window behind the desk.

"Hey, kid."

"Hey, Dad," said Drew. He didn't look up from his book. He studied hard and got almost straight As, though things had dipped a bit in the last year. Hardly a surprise. "What's new?"

"Not much," said Jerry. "Just a long day of 'stickin' it to the man.' You?" He was joking.

Drew answered. He *wasn't* joking. "Despair as corporate America becomes more and more faceless." He sighed. "I really wonder what I'm going to do after high school, since it's less and less likely that a college education is going to help me out in the job market."

Jerry kept his face impassive. That was a conversation for another time. Though he was concerned his son might be right: college was turning more and more into an extremely expensive babysitting experience, after which most graduates emerged *without* their virginity (those few that still had it going in), *with* an extremely high tolerance for low-quality alcohol... but with no marketable skills whatsoever. Jerry thought education should teach a person something that would benefit them in real life and not just serve to put real life off for another four years. But he didn't want to tell his son that; at least not now.

Drew saved him from dealing with the issue, though at the cost of dealing with something else Jerry didn't want to face tonight: "How's Mom?" said the kid.

Jerry shrugged. "How are *you*?" he finally said.

Drew was quiet for a long time. He stared at nothing, reminding Jerry of Ann. Would the whole family look like that soon, capable of vision but unable to see anything of value in their lives?

"I miss him," Drew finally said. He hesitated, and Jerry saw his cheeks color as if the kid was embarrassed. "But I can't remember what he looked like. I see his pictures, but it's like looking at pictures of someone I've never met." He looked up, his eyes boring into Jerry. "It's only been a year, Dad. Shouldn't I remember him better?"

Jerry didn't know what to say. That was one of the things no one told you about becoming a parent: that it was the thing that would make you feel stupider than anything else. So many questions, so many *important* questions, and the only constant in all the answers was that you knew as a parent that your answer was likely the absolute worst one possible.

So Jerry didn't answer. Not today. It was too raw, too real. Too hard. He just looked at his son, his beautiful, only remaining son, and said, "Dinner's downstairs. We're going to watch some TV while we eat. Just the family."

Drew nodded. He looked like he understood why Jerry couldn't answer. Looked like he understood… and hated Jerry for his weakness.

That was okay with Jerry. Because he knew he deserved the hatred. That was the one answer he *could* confidently give his children.

Go ahead and hate me. Hate your old man. Because any hate you have for me is earned.

He forced a smile onto his face.

"See you downstairs in five."

11

Jerry felt like he had been through a five-minute round with a heavyweight MMA fighter. He wondered if things would ever get back to normal, if talking to his children would ever just be something he *did,* ever be something that simply *happened* again.

Probably not. Not since what had happened. Not since a year ago.

Don't lie to yourself, Jer-Jer. It wasn't a year ago. It was before that. It was since the girl. Since you –

He knocked on the next door. "Round two," he said under his breath.

"Hold on," came Sheri's voice. "I'm not dressed!"

Another wait, though this one was much shorter than the one he had endured outside Drew's room.

"Okay, it's safe!" she said.

Jerry opened the door and walked into another large room.

A computer sat on a small desk near the door. Off. Not surprising. Jerry had bought the thing for her several years ago and near as he could tell Sheri hardly ever used it.

His eyes went to her. She was sitting in bed, her blankets pulled up to cover her up to her neck. She was clearly getting ready to go to sleep. And even getting ready for bed, even as merely a floating head against a backdrop of bedding, Jerry could see – as always – that his seventeen-year-old daughter was what the kids called a "hottie." He went through the usual ritual of convincing himself he didn't have to worry about her. She rarely went out, she never partied. She was almost always in her room, and when she *did* go out it was with her girlfriends, usually shopping, and always back at a decent hour.

Another thing no one told you about being a parent – specifically about being a dad – was how many different homicidal urges sprang to life around the time your daughter started wearing a training bra.

He sat down at the foot of Sheri's bed as she scooted her feet up under the covers to make room for him. "Hey, Princess. Hitting the hay early?"

She nodded. "I'm tired. Studied my behind off today."

"Test tomorrow?" Another nod from his daughter. "Well, don't work too hard. You know what the doctor said."

Sheri rolled her eyes. "Yeah, yeah: I gotta take it easy."

Jerry smiled. "Just trying to watch out for you."

"And I keep telling him – and you – that I'm not made of spun sugar."

Jerry nodded but didn't address the statement. Sheri's condition was something she had to live with, whether she liked it or not, and he didn't want to have the usual circular argument with her about it. So he sidestepped. He rubbed her feet through the blanket and said, "Anyway... the family's doing dinner and a show."

Sheri yawned widely. "Not really interested, Daddy."

"I know you're tired, Princess. But you know what day it is. And I think we should do this for your mom."

"I think she'll be okay."

Sheri wasn't going to budge, he could tell. Jerry stopped rubbing her feet. He kept his voice even but firmed it up around the edges. "This isn't really a request," he said. "We should be together."

Sheri glared at him. Jerry let her glare for a while, hoping she would get tired of it. She didn't, so he got up and walked to her door.

"If we should be together today, then why'd *you* disappear?"

Jerry stiffened. He felt his face twist, felt the pain of well-earned guilt writhe across his features. He didn't turn around. Just resumed walking.

"I'll expect you in five minutes."

He left. He thought he heard her say something. Maybe not.

Or maybe she said, "I hate you."

And that would have been more than he deserved.

He was barely two steps down the hall when he heard Sheri cry out. All thoughts of what was happening to the family fled in an instant. Her voice was startled – no, *panicked* – and he turned and bolted back through her door.

She had been facing her window, but when Jerry barreled into her room Sheri whipped around to face him, yanking the blanket that she had half-wrapped around her so that it completely covered her from neck to ankle. Her face reddened.

"Geez, don't you *knock*?"

"I... I heard you yell."

The flush in her cheeks died. The flare in her eyes faltered as well, and she glanced back at the window. Jerry stepped farther into the room. "What is it?"

"I don't know." Her voice was small, and Jerry was suddenly reminded of the little girl who had run around the yard in nothing but a pair of shorts and a sunbonnet. She needed him again, just like that four-year-old had needed him.

Jerry looked out the window. "Did you see something?"

"Maybe."

"What?"

Sheri was silent. She bit her lower lip. "I thought for a second that someone was watching."

A taloned finger seemed to trace its way up Jerry's spine in time with her words. "You sure?"

Sheri shook her head. "No. It was just a second."

Jerry had a thought. "Could it have been Ted?"

"Our neighbor?" Sheri thought about it. "I don't know. I don't know for sure if I saw anyone at all, Dad."

Jerry reached out and touched his daughter, almost hugged her. But didn't. Not quite. Not because he didn't think she wanted a hug, but because a part of him thought – a part of him *knew* – that she deserved better than that. "Well, maybe we should call the police. Just to be safe."

"No," she said. She seemed to gather strength from his willingness to make such a call. Or maybe it was just the fact that the shadow she had seen apparently wasn't visible anymore.

The pale lies we tell ourselves in order to sleep better at night, Jerry thought. And for a moment he thought how much Sheri looked like another young woman he had known in the not-too-distant past.

He looked away from her. Don't go there, he thought.

"Do you want me to make the call?" he asked.

Sheri shook her head. "No. Just... I'll be down in five minutes, okay?"

Jerry nodded and left without looking at his daughter again.

12

It took about ten seconds for Jerry to know this wasn't going to pan out the way he had hoped.

What did *you hope, Jer-Jer? That Chinese takeout and a TV show would solve the world's ills? That'd be a helluva cable subscription.*

Still, he had hoped for at least some interaction. But so far the only interaction had occurred when Ann handed out the food. Even that passed in almost total silence. No "Please" or "Thank you," only an occasional "No, that one's not mine," or "Can you pass the sauce?"

Then silence. Broken only by the low sounds of people eating and the noise of whatever cop show Ann had turned on. She liked police procedurals, and though no one else particularly enjoyed them it seemed they didn't even want to argue over *that* – just wanted to show their faces for the bare minimum required, eat, and get back to their rooms.

Then Jerry realized that Sheri wasn't eating. She was staring out the large bay window that allowed a panoramic view of the backyard from the media room. The media room itself was large enough to allow for plenty of space for each member of the family, but Sheri was hugging herself as though crowded on all sides. And staring.

Jerry followed her gaze.

He saw what she was staring at.

The pool.

Jewel-green, with red tendrils –

"Can you hit the blinds?" said Sheri.

"Huh?" Drew said. He had to have heard, but he apparently was pretending fascination with Ann's show. Jerry didn't know if that was just sibling rivalry or some passive-aggressive bullshit, but either way he could see that it was going to send Sheri over the edge, and fast.

"The blinds, Drew," said Sheri. Her voice sounded strangled.

"Why?" said Drew innocently. Then he seemed to know he had gone too far, because he reached for a nearby remote and clicked a button. A thick panel of blackout curtains reeled out from the wall, covering the view of the pool. And not just that, but the lights in the backyard, the neighbors' lights, the lawn furniture, even the low moon all disappeared. The media room now seemed to exist in a universe that consisted solely of itself and nothing else. You could look up and see the second floor balustrade, but if you kept your eyes level it seemed to be a lone room hanging in an otherwise unfinished universe.

Drew wasn't done. He hit the rest of the buttons on the curtains remote. Jerry felt a low rumble/whir and knew that similar curtains had been lowered or pulled closed in every room in the house. Total isolation.

He wondered if Drew was being sarcastic and geared up to have a minor bitching-out with his son, but when he looked over he saw Drew's hand on Sheri's knee. "All gone," said the boy.

Sheri nodded. She didn't say anything, but there was a bright, shining "Thank you" in her eyes. A nice moment.

But it was just a moment. And then it was over. All eyes returned to the show.

They were sitting together. They were eating together. But they might as well have been transients in a truck-stop, Jerry thought. Passing time in the same space, but not sharing anything more than oxygen.

We're strangers, he thought. He thought he should do something about it. Should fix it. But he had no idea how to go about such a thing.

And a minute later he sighed and he, too began watching the show.

13

The man watches as they divide up the food. Like a good family should. No fighting that he can see, no spats that he can hear.

He smiles and takes the hat off. He hates hats, and normally he refuses to wear them. He never matches when he wears a hat. But the restaurant the family prefers has their delivery people wear hats, so he acquired one and wore it. Because they still don't know what's happening. What's begun.

It didn't begin with the call, either, when Jerry spoke to him as he sat in the van and answered his call and Jerry thought he was speaking to the host at Chang's Chinese. No, all this began much earlier. And the family never knew. Never suspected.

Which, of course, is part of the fun.

He tosses the hat on the ground. He'll pick it up later. Or maybe he won't. He hasn't decided yet. He'll talk it out with himself when he has a moment.

But for now, he's watching them eat.

Then Drew moves, and the curtains drop inside the room his family is sitting in.

"That was rude," he says. And as usual, he answers himself. "Cut them some slack."

"No, rude is rude is rude is rude." It is a saying that the man's father always loved, and he is right in this, as he was right in everything.

As if to highlight the veracity of his father's statement, the curtains all over the house begin to drop. He sighs. They wish for their privacy, their isolation. And their wish is about to come true.

"Shall I?" he asks himself. And the answer is obvious: "Yes."

He's already standing near the junction box. He opens it, and only a moment later is in position. Most people wouldn't be able to do what he has to do, wouldn't be able to get all the pieces in place. But he's always had a head for organization. He's always been very good about using his time well. It's part of his gift.

"Ready," he says. He counts to one hundred. Then pulls one of the wires. He giggles as it comes loose.

"Time to play."

14

Jerry had barely decided to just do what everyone else was doing and simply surrender to the numbing influence of the television show when he realized that the kids were no longer even watching anymore. They were both on their cell phones, texting.

He had no idea who they were sending messages to, but that wasn't the point. It was just one more reminder of how shattered the family was. Here they were for a dinner and a show that was the closest thing to an official meal they'd had in ages, and the kids would rather send text messages that most often boiled down to a play-by-play description of how bored each party was than attend to their own family.

"Kids," he said. His voice had that official "Dad" lilt to it, the patent-pending sound that hinted at groundings and time in the cellar if the voice was not heeded.

Both kids looked up... and both went right back to their phones after only a second.

Jerry didn't know whether to pursue the issue or not. It wasn't like you could *force* people to enjoy themselves, right? And at least they were here, so that was something.

He took a bite of his food. Even that tasted off: mealy and chalky, like someone had put a layer of uncooked flour over everything.

Perfect night.

He looked at the wall. There were family pictures in every room, and this one was no exception. Four people in the room. Five on the walls.

I miss you, bud.

Then Jerry almost leapt off his seat as a loud *pop* bounced through the room. The TV dissolved into a blizzard of static. A second later even that disappeared and a blue box with the words "Cable Signal Lost" appeared over a field of black.

The family groaned as one.

"Again?" Drew half-shouted.

"What is this, like the tenth time?" Sheri said.

"Eighth," said Ann. But she said it in a tone that made it clear eight was just as bad as ten would have been. Maybe worse.

Jerry felt like putting his head in his hands. What else could go wrong today?

Happy anniversary.

He took another bite of the mealy-tasting Chinese food, then set his tray down and opened up the television cabinet. Under the cable box was a phone number, and Jerry grabbed a cordless phone off a nearby charger base and called the number.

"Don't worry," he said to everyone and no one at once. "We'll take care of this."

It *was* a cable company. So it took over twenty minutes of being routed from electronic voice to electronic voice, before Jerry heard himself explaining the situation with a voice that was entirely too whiny, then listening to the operator calmly telling him they'd fix it right away.

"*When*?" said Jerry. "*When* is it going to be fixed?"

The operator's voice was weird, he thought. It was almost machinelike, lacking in emotion. But at the same time it… *bounced* was probably the best word for it. Just at the end of some sentences, and during some words. As though the guy was really excited, but was trying to keep it under wraps. Like he was planning a surprise party and didn't want the world to know about it.

"I'm really sorry, sir," said the operator. "I'll put a stat ticket on this and we'll have someone out there first thing in the morning."

"Tomorrow?" Jerry heard his voice grow shrill. Somehow that was almost the worst of it. That he had been pushed so far that losing cable reception was the last straw, that it created this kind of desperation in him. But try as he might, he couldn't rein in the jags in his voice. "We need the TV now. Tonight." His fingers tightened on the phone, so hard he could hear the plastic creaking. "We want this fixed, or we're cancelling service."

"I don't blame you at all, sir," said the operator. "And I'm so glad it was my turn to talk to you." Jerry blinked, thinking that was a weird thing to say. Then the operator continued, "I promise we'll get on this first thing. And I'm going to credit you for this month, since there's been an ongoing problem with this."

Jerry said thank you, because that's what you say at the end of a service call, even when what you really want to say is that you hope the person you're talking to dies a horrible death and rots in a special circle of hell.

The operator's strangely monotonous voice brightened a bit. "Thank *you,* sir. I really look forward to helping you. I'm glad it was my turn to talk."

Then he hung up. Jerry stared at the phone in his hands, and was going to comment on what a weird freak the cable company had employed, but before he could Sheri said, "Well?"

He looked around and realized the rest of the family was staring at him. They all looked like they were holding their breath. He felt like he had just walked out of the O.R. and had to deliver the bad news of how a tricky operation had gone on everyone's favorite uncle.

"Nothing they can do about it tonight," he said. "They'll be out tomorrow."

Ann, Drew, and Sheri all deflated. Their shoulders slumped. All hope was gone. Uncle Fred was a goner. Jerry almost laughed, not because it was funny but because it was so damn sad the only thing he could think to *do* was laugh.

Either that or start screaming. And he was afraid if he did that he might not be able to stop.

15

Without the television on no one seemed to have the energy to even *pretend* to be engaged in the "family dinner." Ann was the first to leave. If it had been one of the kids, maybe Jerry could have made a stink, but he could hardly reprimand her, could he?

Still, the minute she was gone he saw Drew and Sheri eyeing one another as though trying to gauge when the most appropriate moment to make their escape would be. Less than thirty seconds later they were out of the room as well, both of them tramping up the stairs with heavy footsteps. He could hear them yawning and thought they were probably doing it for his benefit – *Here, let's show Dad it's 'cause we're so tired, and not because the family's such a mess* – though he supposed they might actually be ready to hit the hay. Both had seemed pretty fatigued as they left, and he felt bone-weary himself.

Death anniversaries will do that to you every time. It's the new workout craze.

Jerry sat alone in the media room for another minute or two, trying to eat some more of his food. It still tasted awful. Bitter and mealy. Chang's would be getting a call tomorrow. Actually....

His hand went to the cordless he had replaced on its charger cradle after calling the weirdo at the cable company. Maybe he should call Chang's now. Give them a piece of his mind and let them know they wouldn't be getting any repeat business.

He actually started to dial the number before stopping and replacing the phone.

He wasn't that mad over the food. The family had been ordering Chang's for five or six years and this was the first time they had ever done anything wrong. He was hardly going to make a fuss over one error.

No, he was just avoiding what he knew had to come next.

But as with everything else tonight, avoiding it was just going to make it worse. Avoiding things *always* made them worse.

And you know all about that, don't you?

He pushed that thought out of his mind, then went in search of Ann.

He considered looking around the house, maybe starting upstairs in their room. But he knew she wouldn't be there. In truth, there was only one place she *could* be.

He walked through the living room. There was a door that led to the backyard, and he opened it and walked out.

It was like entering another world. A brighter place, a place where hope still existed and time still ran at full speed. He hadn't realized how dark the house was, but now that he thought of it most of the lights were off inside. That coupled with the blackout curtains still being drawn converted the house into something approaching a dungeon, in feel if not reality.

Jerry went to the pool. It glowed in the night, an uneven green oval with a bright light at one end.

Ann stood on the opposite side of the pool, looking at the deck about five feet from where she was. Jerry watched her. She didn't look up or even acknowledge his existence.

"Kids are in bed," he said. Still nothing. "Ann?"

"I try, but I just can't understand."

Jerry sighed. He had known this was coming, but he didn't want to do this again. Not again. Not this same conversation, this conversation that always turned into the same argument. "Honey... he fell. He slipped."

"I can't believe that." Ann finally looked at Jerry, and he almost blanched before her gaze. The passion he had been hoping for only a short time ago was there, but now he wished it was gone. Or at least directed somewhere else.

"The police said –"

"The police said it looked like it was 'probably' an accidental death," she said. The words spat out of her mouth like bullets from a machine gun. "And then they didn't do *shit*."

Jerry did cringe this time. He hated when she spoke words like that. It was just another mark of how far they had come from where they once were. There had been a time when Ann would have just about died rather than speak a four-letter word. Now, though....

"Something happened to my boy," she continued, "and they didn't care enough to give it more than a half-hour to find out what." She looked back at the deck. The same spot. Jerry didn't. He didn't want to look.

Ann returned her gaze to his eyes. "They just gave up," she said. And he knew she was really saying, "*You* just gave up."

"He fell," said Jerry. His voice came out as a monotone. He didn't have the strength to keep fighting this battle anymore. "He was alone."

"I should have been there," whispered Ann. Then she pointed at Jerry and almost screamed, "*You* should have been there."

Then she stomped past him in a whiff of perfume, and he wondered if life would have been better if *he* had been the one to die a year ago.

He turned to follow her. Because this could be fixed. It *had* to be fixed. The family couldn't continue like this. It was imploding, falling into itself. And soon there would be nothing left.

But he stopped halfway through his turn. Because he thought he saw something. Or at least some part of his brain insisted that something was out there, even if nothing had actually been *seen*.

He scanned the huge backyard. Lawn furniture, patio. Gazebo far away near the northeast corner of the privacy wall that ringed the property. A stand of trees near the opposite corner, which wound along the wall until they came nearly to where the pool sat in shining simplicity near the house.

Nothing out of place. Everything was as it should be, and as it had been every day and every night he could remember.

So why did he feel… *watched*?

He looked around. Wondered if he should call the cops. Then his gaze fell to the deck. To where it had happened.

He shivered and all but ran back into the house.

16

Jerry caught up to Ann as she opened the door to their bedroom. It was on the second floor, at the far end of the hallway, so he was panting a bit – not to mention yawning every four seconds, so apparently it was past his bedtime. But he had also formulated a plan. They had to get out of this rut. *He* had to get them out of it. He loved Ann, and he hoped she still loved him.

But they were losing each other.

So he had to move. Had to act.

She opened the door to the room. Darkness beyond.

He caught her in his arms. Held her tight, and unlike when he had held her in the kitchen, he concentrated on really being there for her. Not for her pain, not for her anxiety, but for *her*.

He pulled back a moment. Smiled. "At least we never have to live through today again," he said.

Ann felt limp in his arms. She was letting him hold her, but wasn't reciprocating. Jerry felt his own arms fall to his sides.

He stepped away from her. Flicked on the light and entered the room. He sat on their bed. Dejection seemed to have hung leaden weights around his neck and shoulders, and he slumped under their mass.

The bedroom was the biggest room in the house. Four-poster bed, gas fireplace. Attached sitting room with settee.

Walk-in closet. And yet Jerry felt crushed by it, like the walls were closing in on him.

Ann disappeared into the closet. He watched his wife go, silent, uncomfortable. He wondered if it would be better for him to sleep downstairs tonight.

A moment later Ann reappeared.

Jerry felt his mouth drop open so far he wouldn't have been surprised to learn he had dislocated his jaw.

Ann had changed out of her clothes. And changed into something a great deal more revealing. A corset, purple lace panties and matching bra, and he saw now that what he had thought were pantyhose were really stockings, held up by a garter belt.

She couldn't have changed into that in just the short time she'd been in the closet, he realized. So that meant....

Hope bloomed as he understood that Ann wanted things to work, too. That she hadn't given up. Things were hard now, but they could get better.

She walked over to him. She smiled, and he remembered the smile she had given him on their wedding night. She'd been wearing something similar, and that smile had been so hesitant, so loving and worried and excited and scared. "Do you like it?" she said. He'd never seen anything so beautiful.

Ann kissed Jerry. Hard. He felt himself grow aroused. Put his arms around her.

And then he felt tears wet his cheeks. He thought they were hers at first, then realized that he was feeling his own tears, that he was weeping.

Ann must have felt the tears as well. Her embrace, so heated a moment ago, grew suddenly awkward.

She pulled away.

Tried to touch his cheek.

He shook his head. Moved to his side of the bed.

I'm not giving up, he thought. Not giving up. But I can't. Not tonight.

He yawned.

Not tonight.

A small part of him noticed that he was far too tired. Even given the fact that it was one year after his son's death, even given the toll of the other problems he'd been facing – or avoiding – he didn't think he should be this tired.

He almost rolled over to talk to Ann. Then he thought he heard a low snore. Realized she must have slept as well. And that was wrong, too, wasn't it?

Then that thought floated away, born on a wave of exhaustion that pulled him into soft sleep. But it was a sleep tinged with darkness. A sleep in which he knew nothing, but even knowing nothing he knew that nothing was right.

17

The man watches.

The house is dark.

But he waits.

He is patient.

It doesn't work unless he is patient.

"What time is it?" he wonders. He looks at his watch and answers himself. "After midnight."

The house doesn't move. Nothing moves.

But a moment later he does.

It's his time.

It's his *turn*.

Getting in is easy. It's what he's prepared for. What they *begged* him to do. So he's walking through the back door a few moments later, after pausing to look at the pool.

"So much sadness here," he says. And then he says, "Yes, but we'll fix that." And he's right. He's always right. It's part of why he talks to himself. Because no one else gives him the same amount of wisdom, of knowledge, of hope.

Inside. The living room. The couch, the television – he's never seen a house with so many televisions, one in every single room – the beautiful, silent baby grand piano. It is a lovely instrument, but in the darkness it hunches like a huge dark cockroach, and the man doesn't like cockroaches.

"I'm going upstairs," he tells himself. And so he does. Upstairs is where the fun is *really* going to start.

The stairs creak a bit as he walks up. He tries to step silently, but he can't seem to walk with his usual stealth tonight. Perhaps it's the excitement. Besides, he knows no one will be awake. He saw them all eat the food before the blackout curtains shut. They'll be deep asleep. Just a pinch of the right drug on their Kung Pao chicken – more than a pinch, actually – and they'll sleep for a long time.

So will the delivery man he had to kill a few weeks ago to take the uniform and hat, preparing for tonight, but that couldn't be helped.

"Sheri, or Drew first?" he wonders aloud. And he answers, "The girl." Again, and as always, the answer is the right one. She's so lovely, so beautiful. Even though her beauty is like the beauty of a home that is riddled with termites and dry rot. Gorgeous, but spoiled within. He knows this because he knows her secrets. He knows all their secrets.

Still, even though her soul is black, her skin is so soft.

He goes into her room. She is asleep. Sweat prickles her brow. She moans as though gripped by nightmares. She probably is.

Sheri moans again. One of his hands wipes the sweat from her forehead. One of his hands goes to her chest and lifts her blanket up higher to preserve her modesty.

Then to Drew's room. This room makes him uncomfortable. The rock-and-rollers on the walls seem to stare at him with accusing eyes, and the man wants to tear them down. His hand actually reaches for a poster, but he stops himself, gripping his own hand by the wrist. "Later," he breathes. "Later."

Drew moans as well. The man kisses the boy on the cheek. "You'll feel better soon."

Then into Ann and Jerry's room.

Ann is still as death. Silent as a corpse. She already is dead in so many ways. The man smiles. He likes dead people. Being dead is the closest thing to perfect that most people will ever be. No lies, no secrets. They are what they are and nothing more.

Then Ann breathes deeply, and the beautiful moment is ruined.

And ruined more when Jerry screams out in his sleep. A nightmare. He screams a name. Not the name of any of his children, not the name of his wife. But the man knows the name. He smiles.

The secrets are surfacing.

The fun has begun.

He puts a hand on Jerry's arm, rolling back the man's loose long sleeve, exposing the crook of his elbow.

"Remember," he says, "this will sting a bit. But it's for the best."

18

Jerry lurched upright in his bed, and bit back something that could only be a scream.

He'd been dreaming. Nightmaring.

What was the dream?

It was fleeing, even as the scream fell away from his lips. Nothing but images, confused images that withdrew from his consciousness like objects sinking below the troubled surface of a storm-darkened sea. He thought he heard Socrates barking. He thought he saw someone leaning over him, someone that split apart and became two versions of him, then became the girl….

The girl….

Jerry didn't want to think about her.

He wiped his hand across his forehead. It came away wet. Not just damp, not just a bit sweaty; it felt like he had gone for a swim.

Swimming… another memory he preferred not to think about.

He twisted to the side, then swung his legs off the bed and stood. The room lurched away from him and for a single confused second he thought he was on a boat. But no. This was his room.

Wasn't it?

He looked around. The effort of turning his head increased the room's back-and-forthing, and suddenly Jerry felt sick to his stomach. He went to the master bathroom as fast as he could – not terribly fast, considering that his feet didn't want to work and the floor had the consistency of a water bed – and barely made it to the toilet before he began retching.

Nothing came up, just a thin slick of clear bile that burned the back of his throat. He dry heaved for what seemed like a solid year but was probably only thirty seconds, then grabbed some toilet paper and wiped at his lips before dropping it into the toilet and flushing.

He lay his head on the toilet seat until he felt like he could move without vomiting again, then stood. The room started to tilt once more so he stood still and waited until things solidified around him, then slowly shuffled back to the bedroom.

Once there, he saw a small light blinking on and off. He thought at first that it was just another aspect of whatever illness had assaulted his system, but then realized that the light was real. He squinted.

"Ann!" he said. He regretted the outburst: as soon as he said it, he had to stop moving again as the need to vomit became almost unbearable.

Ann jerked upright like she had been electrocuted. Her eyes were so wide Jerry could see the whites all around her irises, and her breath came in quick, sharp gasps that sounded almost painful. She must have been having a nightmare as well.

She whipped her head back and forth, looking around frantically in the dark bedroom. "What?" she said. "What is it?"

Jerry pointed at what he had seen with one hand while he used the other to grip his forehead. "I think we overslept."

Ann looked at the clock. It was digital, with bright blue numerals that provided the only illumination in the otherwise dark room. And they were blinking on and off repeatedly: "12:00."

"I think we lost power," he added.

"What…?" said Ann. She got out of bed, then her knees buckled and she only saved herself from falling by grabbing one of the posters on the bed.

"You, too?" said Jerry. He grimaced. "Must've been something in the takeout." He swallowed thickly. "I thought it tasted bad."

"What about the kids?"

"What?"

Ann started for the door, wobbly but determined. "They could be sick, too."

19

Jerry noted that Ann must have changed before she laid down. She was dressed in sweats pants and a long t-shirt. He was still dressed in the clothes he had come home in the night before.

Ann slipped into a pair of tennis shoes on her way out the door. Jerry followed suit, putting on his own shoes. He wondered why as he did so – did tending to a pair of kids' food poisoning require footwear? – but something deep inside him demanded it and he followed the mandate of his subconscious.

In the hall, Jerry moved to Sheri's room as Ann peeled away to Drew's. He pounded on his daughter's door, Ann hammering on their son's.

No answers to either.

He looked at Ann. She was pale, her face almost aglow even in the dark hall. He wondered if he looked as ill as she did.

By unspoken agreement, both of them opened their respective doors.

Sheri's room was dark and Jerry saw her as just a lump under the covers. He staggered over to her. Shook her. She moaned. He shook her again, worried that she might not awaken. He knew that was an irrational fear, knew that they probably just had food poisoning. But knowing it didn't stop the terror that had gripped him. What if she was really sick? What if she was dying?

Like Brian.

"Honey," he said. "Sheri, wake up."

Sheri moved. His heart stopped chiseling chinks in his ribcage as she sat up and looked around the darkness. She blinked blurry sleep away.

"What's going on?" she asked.

"The power must have gone out during the night," he said.

She frowned. As in Jerry's room, Sheri had a digital clock that was blinking, sending on-off-on-off shadows through the cavernous space of Sheri's room. The intermittent flashes made her look strange; alien. She was suddenly robbed of her beauty and made to look like a thing that should have died, like a thing that never should have been born. Jerry shuddered internally. He didn't believe in omens, but the feeling that gripped him now felt almost prophetic, like he was looking at a vision of his daughter's doom.

"What time is it?" she said.

"I...." He shook his head, trying to cast away the disturbing thoughts that had forced their way into his mind. He realized he had no answer for her. "I don't know."

Sheri fumbled for something on her bedside table. A moment later a small square of greenish light appeared and Jerry realized she was looking at a watch. The light was enough to show her face clearly as she frowned.

"What is it?" he said.

She shook her head. Jerry took the watch and looked at it. "Ten o'clock?" he said. "That's impossible." It didn't *feel* like ten o'clock. It couldn't be that late.

Could it?

He moved to the window. A dark black patch in the greater darkness of her room. Moving like a blind man to get there, hands in front of him as though that might save him from falling. Luckily Sheri was a tidy girl – or at least, Rosa was a good housekeeper –

(*Rosa* used *to be, she's not with us anymore she was fired....*)

– so nothing tripped him up as he made his way to the thick blackout curtains that covered every window in the house, thanks to Drew's actions last night.

(*Was it last night? It felt so long ago.*)

He threw the blinds back.

Still in her bed behind him, Sheri gasped.

Jerry felt the world spin again. But this time it had nothing to do with whatever illness had gripped them all.

20

It was dark beyond Sheri's bedroom window.

But it wasn't the dark of a cloudy morning, or even a normal night sky. No, it was the dark of....

Nothing.

It was like the world ended at the glass of Sheri's window, like the universe had shrunk down to perfectly fit around the room, and beyond it was only the deepest black of utter void. Darkness uncreate.

Jerry put his hand against the glass, a part of him expecting to feel unnatural cold or strange heat emanating from the window. Neither. It felt normal. Whatever the darkness outside signaled, it was something that did not intrude into the room. But nor did it allow for vision beyond its confines.

"Dad?" Sheri said. The single word held a wealth of questions.

Jerry moved his hands to the window latch and slipped it open. Then he put his hands on the ridge of the sill and pulled.

The window didn't move.

He pulled harder. Then flipped the latch back the other way, just in case it had already been open and he had inadvertently locked it.

No difference. The window stayed shut. The darkness beyond it stayed absolute.

He looked at Sheri. She was huddled in the corner of the bed, her pale face still looking like a cadaver in the blinking light of the clock.

"Get dressed," he said.

Sheri nodded. Normally he would have been thrilled to have her agree with something he said and not put up a fight, but now it just made his stomach feel like it was coated with lead. Something was wrong. Beyond wrong.

Maybe not, he thought. Just take it easy. Check out what's going on with Drew. Maybe it's just something easily explained.

Then he heard Ann call out, "Jerry!" and her voice was terrified and he knew whatever was happening wasn't over.

It was just beginning.

21

Jerry moved as fast as he could into the hall, then to Drew's room. The door was open. Drew was sitting on his bed, pulling jeans on over the boxer briefs he slept in, the light of a small lamp clamped to his headboard spreading a meager glow through the room.

Ann was standing at the window in Drew's room. The curtains had been thrown back and she was looking out. Looking out at the same nothing that Jerry had seen through Sheri's window.

She spun around as soon as Jerry came in. Pointed at the darkness behind her. "What's happening?" she said.

"Does the window open?" he asked.

She shook her head, her frustrated expression clearly showing she'd already attempted that. Jerry tried as well, doing the same pull the window/flip the latch/pull the window/flip the latch routine he had done in Sheri's room. With the same results.

Ann watched. She didn't look irritated that he was trying the same thing she had already done, just worried – disturbed – when he failed to open the window.

A noise made him spin around. It was just Sheri, coming in through the jack-and-jill bathroom that connected her room to Drew's. She had dressed, pulling her hair back in a quick pony tail and wearing the same outfit she wore before bed the night before. That stood as a true testament to how worried she was, since Jerry didn't think it was permissible under United States law for teenage girls to wear the same outfits twice in a row. Boys might wear the same pair of jeans until the pants actually tried to flee of their own accord, but not girls.

Drew yanked his pants the rest of the way up. "Good hell, Sheri, can't you knock?"

Sheri didn't even acknowledge him. She just looked out the dark – no, the black, the *blank* – window. "What's going on?" she said. "What do we do?" Then she weaved on her feet and had to lean on Drew's dresser for support, one hand going to her mouth.

"Don't puke in my room," said Drew. Though the boy's face was pale and Jerry thought it looked likely his son was going to vomit at any moment himself.

Whatever bug got us, it got us hard, he thought.

Out loud, he said, "Let's just wait a second, and as soon as everyone's up to it we'll go downstairs and go outside. See what's going on with the windows. Okay?"

He looked around. No one nodded. But no one dissented either. He wondered if they were thinking about what he was: what if there *was* no outside?

It was ridiculous. But just because something was ridiculous didn't mean it wasn't capable of causing fear. Just because something was ridiculous didn't mean it couldn't absolutely terrify.

Sometimes ridiculous things could even kill.

No, he thought. There's an outside.

But it sounded like a lie, even in his own mind.

22

They filed down together. Jerry went first, holding onto the banister as he went down the long, spiraling staircase that led to the foyer. Sheri and Drew came next, almost holding onto one another. Ann came last. She was wild-eyed, looking around as though the darkness itself might come alive and take her somewhere beyond imagining.

Jerry flipped the foyer light on at the bottom of the stairs. The small chandelier was equipped with "soft glow" bulbs that were meant to emulate the dim illumination of candles, so it didn't banish the darkness completely, but at least it pushed the shadows back a bit.

He looked at the rest of the family. They were all holding each other now. Gripping each other's shoulders. He felt like the odd man out. Which he supposed he was.

Still, he put a smile on his face as he flicked the lock on the door. No question about this one. Unlike the kids' windows, he had opened this lock a hundred thousand times. He knew which way the lock was pointed when it was open.

"All righty," he said. "Let's just see what kind of practical joke's been played on us."

He felt better. Partly that was because the sickness seemed to be ebbing. He wasn't as nauseous, and the world didn't tilt radically every six steps. But partly it was because he really believed it in that moment. This had to be a joke, right? No one woke up in a house in the middle of *nothing*. It was too incredible, too *impossible*.

Then the smile froze on his face and became an unnatural rictus as he turned the knob, pulled…

… and the door didn't open.

The door was unlocked, he could see that clearly. He could feel the latch sliding back from the striker plate as he turned the knob.

But the door itself wouldn't budge.

Ann saw him struggling. "Here, let me try," she said.

Jerry moved away. Ann pulled a few times, then her hands fell to her sides. She looked at him through eyes wide with confusion and terror.

"Let's go to the garage," Jerry said. He tried to sound reassuring and confident, as much for himself as for her and the kids, but he heard cracks in the edges of his tone. Heard crevasses beginning to open in his self-control. Heard madness creeping into his reality.

He moved through the hall, past the kitchen and his office, then to the garage door. Something pushed past him halfway there. Drew. Panic was drawing jagged lines across the teen's face, and he clearly couldn't force himself to walk the way Jerry was doing.

Drew got to the garage door a few paces ahead of Jerry. He grabbed it. Turned the knob. Yanked the door. It rattled but didn't open. Drew kept at it, jerking on the knob with movements that were almost spastic before letting go and saying, "What the *hell*?"

"Drew, language!" said Ann. It sounded like she was speaking reflexively, just a knee-jerk response. Jerry didn't know if she even realized she had done it.

"It won't open!" Drew whined. He sounded almost like a toddler who had been told his favorite treat would be withheld.

Jerry tried this door as well. There was no way it was going to open, he knew. But he had to do it. He couldn't just let it sit there without touching it, without trying it. As though he was incapable of believing that he had found himself in this weird version of reality without verifying for himself.

Nothing. The door was shut tight. "What gives?" he muttered.

"Not the door, apparently," said Drew, and laughed a crackling, jagged laugh.

"*Da*-ad," said Sheri.

Jerry looked at his daughter. She was standing still, but he saw her hand move up, like she was going to touch her shoulder but then stopped herself. He felt ill again. Sheri, of all people, shouldn't be in here. What if she had an attack? She had to get out. *He* had to find a way out.

"Back door! Back door, everyone!" he shouted.

Through the hall. Into the living room. The back door that opened into the yard.

Jerry pulled it. The last door, the last door out.

It was shut tight and wouldn't open no matter how hard he pulled.

They were sealed in.

23

The second Jerry's hand dropped from the back door, the mood shifted. Only a moment before, the tension in the room was almost visible. Now it dissipated, replaced by an even more cloying emotion: terror.

He looked at the family, then beyond them. The entire wall of the living room was essentially glass, a series of windows that stretched nearly floor-to-ceiling.

All covered by blinds.

He knew he should uncover them. But he didn't want to. Because what if there was nothing outside them? What if they were alone?

Drew beat him to it. The teen grabbed a window control remote off a coffee table, then pressed a button.

The blinds pulled away from the windows.

One by one the windows were exposed. Six of them. Six dark eyes that gazed at Jerry with the blank stares of a line of corpses.

As with the upstairs windows, they showed nothing. No lights, no sun or moon. Just blank black darkness more fearsome than any vista imaginable.

The middle four windows were permanently shut, but the two on the ends could be cranked open to allow a cross-breeze to run through the house. Drew flipped open the crank and tried to turn it.

His face turned red and he grunted, "It's jammed." He exhaled then looked at the family. "Just like the doors." He ran to the other window, finding the same result. "They won't open!" Hysteria was bleeding into his voice, tingeing in with crimson tones that bespoke worse things to come.

Jerry went to the middle window. He cupped his hand against the glass and looked against it. He probably looked like he was trying to see into a dim parlor on a hot summer day. But he was trying to pierce the darkness that had captured them. Trying to breach the void in which they found themselves suddenly swimming.

"What's going on?" said Sheri. Her voice sounded small, childish. She had a hand on her chest, just under her collarbone.

Jerry had no answer. "I'm sure it's nothing," he said. Which was totally untrue, but what was he *supposed* to say? "Don't worry, baby, we're entombed in our house and floating in nothing but it'll probably get much worse soon so we might as well enjoy the moment"?

Ann snorted. "Is that your answer to everything? 'It's just nothing'?"

Jerry did his best to let the reference to the night before slide, though part of him marveled at her ability to bring that up at a time like this. He looked away from Ann, and his gaze fell on the cordless phone that sat on a small desk near the wall. He picked it up.

"I'll just call…."

His voice dropped away.

"What?" Ann said. "What is it?" He held the phone out. She took it, turned it on and off and on and off. "No dial tone," she said.

"No worries," said Drew. "I got my phone." His voice was still a bit crazed, but he was grinning madly, his terror clearly converting to wild hope for a swift resolution to this situation.

He dug in his pocket. Then his expression changed from excitement to confusion to concern. He pressed several buttons, and Jerry could see that the phone wasn't lighting up.

"It's probably just out of power. Just plug it in," said Sheri.

Drew didn't make a move for the stairs. He pulled the battery compartment of his phone open. And his face changed. He took a quick hitch of a breath that was almost a sob.

"What is it?" said Jerry.

Drew held up the phone. Even by the ambient light of the hall Jerry could see that Drew's phone had had its guts removed. There was no battery, no circuitry. Just an empty shell.

Sheri was already pulling her own phone from her pocket. Hers was a different model, a touchscreen without the buttons that Drew's phone boasted. But when she tried to turn it on she got the same lack of response, and cracking it open revealed a similar void where the phone's internal workings should have been.

Jerry ran to his office without a word.

"Jerry, where –" Ann began, but he didn't answer.

His own phone was on the charger, just where he had left it. He pulled it off. Was it lighter than he remembered it being? He didn't remember.

He began to turn it on, then stopped himself. What if it didn't work? He ran back to the living room, as though by being among others their combined hope might force the phone into function.

He pressed the button.

Nothing.

Pressed it again.

Nothing.

Nothing.

Nothing nothing nothingnothingnothing*nothing!*

And when he broke the phone open, working his nails between the seams that held the front and back halves together, it fell apart far too easily. The pieces fell to the carpet with a muffled lack of sound that was still somehow deafening.

Jerry's phone was empty, too. Hollow inside. A shell that held nothing but false hope which dissipated when exposed to plain view.

"What's happening?" Sheri asked.

No one answered.

24

Jerry pulled his eyes away from the empty plastic bits that had once been his primary mode of communication with others.

When did I stop talking to *people*? he wondered. When did I stop having friends that participated in my life, instead of contacts that just existed in my phone?

Then he pulled his eyes away from the phone. Looked at his family. They were staring at him like they expected answers. A solution. What could he give them? They were locked inside, the phones were out. That left....

"The laptop!" Drew practically shouted.

Jerry nodded, and again he headed to the office. But this time he flipped on lights as he went, as though every burning bulb contained the power to banish the evil that had invaded their home and made it something alien and hostile.

The family followed this time, moving so close he worried they might trip over one another. Afraid to be alone.

Jerry grabbed the laptop off his desk. At first he was relieved to see it there – what if it had been missing? – but then he was gripped by the certainty that it, like the phones, was empty inside. Hollow, just like Drew's phone, just like's Sheri's. Just like –

(Just like you, Jer-Jer. Just like you and the family have all become: looking like people, but empty inside.)

– just like his own had been.

He flipped the laptop open.

It hummed to life, its drive spinning up from sleep mode and the screen coming on in all its sterile, blue-white glory.

Ann exhaled almost explosively. Sheri grabbed her chest again, and Jerry wondered how much of this she was going to be able to handle.

He grinned at her. Things already looked brighter – literally, now that some of the house lights were on. But with the electronic chime that announced his computer was ready for use, he felt buoyed up and reassured. Technology had become, he realized, not merely a tool, but a proof of life. No start-up sounds? Why, you might as well be dead!

Still, Jerry smiled at the family and swung the computer around so they could see the working screen with its familiar icons. They'd be able to email someone, maybe directly message the police... *someone*.

"Twenty-first century technology to the rescue," he said.

Sheri gasped. Ann frowned, and confusion rendered Drew's face nearly unreadable.

Jerry looked at the computer.

"What the...?"

25

The screen was gone.

The *hardware* was still there, of course, but Jerry's homescreen had disappeared. Gone were his icons, his browser shortcuts, his desktop background picture – one of Leonardo Da Vinci's drawings of his famous dissections, showing the internal organs of cadavers he had cut apart himself – all had disappeared.

In their place was a webcam view, whether live or recorded Jerry couldn't tell. The cam showed a closeup of a woman, from the neck to the knees. The room behind her was obscured by shadow and blurred, as though the woman was all that mattered in this particular cyberworld. And Jerry knew enough about this kind of thing to know that, for her clients, she *was* all that mattered. For now at least, for the time it would take to feel like they had gotten their money's worth.

The woman swayed. She wore a pink miniskirt and a blue tube top that seemed to stay on in direct defiance of gravity and physics. It was tight enough that it was painfully obvious that she wore no bra beneath it.

She began a striptease. Pulled her miniskirt down, inch by inch, revealing a thong before she reached up to her top and –

The screen flickered. The picture disappeared, replaced by a black screen over which the words: "Cannot find server. Internet connection unavailable," appeared.

"What was *that*?" Ann said. Her face was curled with disgust, and Jerry shook his head. He knew his wife's attitude about porn on the web. And he agreed with her, especially since he had had to do an emergency surgery some years before on a young girl who had come in beaten and sliced nearly to pieces after she didn't turn in enough money after a night on the streets and her pimp took it upon himself to "teach her an economics lesson." Porn, he knew, all-too-often ended up like that for the girls involved; and even if it didn't, it fueled a massive demand that could only be satisfied by pressuring and even forcing women and girls to do things like they had just seen on the screen.

Nevertheless, he didn't say any of that, or respond to Ann. He might be disgusted, he might be upset. But he didn't want to have a discussion right now, he just wanted out.

He tried to get rid of the error screen, but failed. Tried to reset the computer. Nothing.

Finally he pulled out the power cord and yanked the battery out. The laptop turned off, deprived of its power sources.

He put the battery back in and hit the "On" button.

The laptop stayed dark.

He put the power cord back in. Still nothing.

Sheri started to wheeze. Jerry looked at her with concern. She was staring at the now-black laptop screen like she was worried it might come alive and attack her.

"Princess?" said Jerry. "Sheri, let's stay calm."

Ann and Drew pulled closer to Sheri, and Jerry could see them struggle through their own fear to reassure the teenage girl.

"It's okay, sweetie," said Ann.

Drew reached out and touched his sister's hair, almost petting it. "You don't want to end up in the hospital again," he said.

That seemed to get to Sheri. Her breathing slowed. She managed to pull her gaze away from the dead eye of the laptop. She looked at Jerry. "Actually, being in a hospital doesn't sound too bad right now."

Jerry had to agree with her.

Sheri looked around as though their home had become a beast, a strange leviathan that had swallowed them all in the night. Her gaze started to jerk around erratically, and Jerry was about to put his own hand on her shoulder, about to try calming her as well, when Ann pulled Sheri away from him.

The motion stung him. But only a moment, because in the next instant he realized that Ann wasn't really pulling Sheri away from *him,* but from the laptop. Turning their daughter away from the screen.

He turned and flipped the laptop closed. There was no help there.

The fear among them had increased. He could practically see it, crawling among them, breathing terror into their minds. And it was only growing. Only getting stronger. They were going to break soon. They were going to –

And at the moment when Jerry was most certain someone was going to go mad, at the moment when he *knew* they couldn't take this anymore, Drew screamed.

An instant later, so did Ann. And Jerry, spinning around, wanted to scream himself. Because they weren't looking at each other. Nothing had happened in the room.

No, they were looking… *away*.

They were looking outside the office.

They were looking outside, down the hall.

They looked like something was coming for them.

26

"Holy crap," Sheri shouted. "What the –" she broke off suddenly as Jerry rushed to join them.

"What is it?" he said. His voice was trapped between a shout and a whisper, like he didn't know whether to be stealthy or try to frighten away his fear with anger.

Sheri stood silent.

But she slowly…

… raised…

… her finger…

… and pointed down the hall.

At the far end of the still mostly-dark hall was an extra room, one that Ann used for crafts and sewing and the rest of the family used as a "miscellaneous storage" room. A place for things you might want to get to easily, but probably wouldn't need in the next few weeks.

The door to the room was open.

The room was dark.

And barely visible in the dark room: a figure. Shadowed. Motionless. A tall man-shape in a dark coat, a hat pulled low over his face.

He was watching them.

Jerry felt a plum-size knot in his throat, and wanted to swallow but was afraid if he did he'd start coughing and wouldn't be able to stop. Not a good time to start choking on his own fear.

"What do we do?" asked Ann.

"Call 9-1-1," said Drew, his voice strained, panic tightening his vocal cords like overstretched harp strings.

"On what?" Sheri spat. "Your Etch-A-Sketch?"

"Quiet!" Jerry half-barked.

He thought. He looked around, thinking. No one else to call, no *way* to call anyone else.

It was up to them. The family was all there was.

Shit, he thought.

But out loud he called, "Hey!"

There was no movement. The figure just stood there, watching. Watching. Jerry felt like the skin around his testicles was starting to crawl. He wanted to puke. The figure, he realized, had to be close to seven feet tall.

"Stay here," he said to the rest of the family.

"You're kidding," said Ann.

"I'll be fine," he said. Part of him was glad she was resisting the idea of letting him brace the intruder alone. But he knew it was his job. His responsibility. He was the father. He was supposed to keep the family *safe*. "I'm just –"

"*No*." Her voice came out loud, probably louder than she intended or expected, and everyone looked down the hall.

The intruder had not moved. He was still watching. And for some reason that was worse than if he had been rushing at them like an insane fiend from hell. An attack Jerry would know how to react to. He probably wouldn't last long in a fight against someone that big, but at least he would *know* what to do.

But being watched like this....

"No one goes anywhere alone," Ann insisted.

"But...," Jerry began.

But I'm supposed to do this. It's my job. My chance to make things right. *To* atone.

He didn't say any of that. He nodded. And as one, the family tiptoed down the hall. Someone turned on every light they passed, pushing back the darkness that had come into their home, forcing it to retreat, foot by aching foot.

"Hello?" Jerry said. "Hey! Hey!"

Still the darkness reigned in the room at the end of the hall. And still the figure watched. Silent.

They reached the doorway.

The hall was bright, and the light sent a cone of yellow illumination into the sewing room. But the figure was standing against the back wall. Motionless, still cloaked in shadows, hat still low.

Dark.

Deadly.

Frightening.

Jerry raised a trembling hand. "We don't want to hurt you," he said.

Behind him, Drew mumbled, "We don't want *you* to hurt *us*," under his breath.

Jerry did his best to ignore that, continuing, "I'm not going to come in, just...." He reached his shaking hand into the room. "... just want to turn on the light."

He flicked the switch.

27

The light came on.

The intruder was shown.

And Jerry… *laughed.*

A moment later, Drew did, too. Then Sheri. Ann last of all, like she was resisting the urge. But finally she started chuckling as well. Soon they were all hooting and howling in a near-hysterical release of pent-up nervous energy.

The intruder still stood there. All seven feet of him. Made of wood, wearing a coat that had been thrown on his thin frame, a hat put on his hook-head.

He was a hat rack.

The laughter went on for what could have been minutes, or could have been hours. It seemed to drain everything out of Jerry. Not just the fear, but the adrenaline burst of energy he had enjoyed for the trip down the hall. He didn't feel at all ill anymore – thank goodness – but he felt weak and drained. He suddenly remembered the funeral. The numbness, the sensation of having nothing left to give anyone.

He felt like that now.

The others quieted as well.

Ann straightened. He saw her looking at something. There was a window in this room, too. The blinds pulled back as they were now pulled back from all the windows.

Like the windows in the bedrooms, the windows in the living room, this one was black. They still floated in a nothingspace of sunless void. They were still cut off. Alone.

Jerry touched her elbow, then gestured for her to follow him. She nodded, and he led the family back into the living room.

The lights blazed here, the heart of the house. But though it was bright, he only had to look over his shoulder at the floor-to-ceiling windows to see that the brightness was an illusion. Their home was infected with some malignant force. Something he didn't understand and couldn't begin to deal with.

"What's happening, Mom?" said Drew.

Ann had no answer. She just looked down at her feet, then up at the ceiling as though searching both Heaven and Hell for answers and finding nothing in either plane.

Jerry turned away before anyone asked *him* that question. He tried to open the two end windows, just as Drew had. Neither yielded.

On the second window, Jerry felt his movements grow frantic and jittery. He knew he was losing whatever semblance of control he had managed to maintain to this point. And part of him knew that he couldn't afford to do that; couldn't afford to lose command of himself, when he had already lost command of everything else –

(*everything, Jer-Jer, even the ability to keep people alive*)

– in his world.

Rage gripped him. He spun and grabbed a wooden chair that sat near the windows, an antique piece that he and Ann had bought as one of their first-ever "nice" purchases when the money finally started to come in. When their lives had seemed perfect.

"What are you doing?" she said.

"Getting us out," said Jerry.

He turned to the window. Reared back with the chair held in both hands, ready to crash it through the dark glass. Part of him feared to take that step. What if there really *was* nothing outside? What if he swung, and instead of granting them escape, he merely allowed the void to enter, and take them?

Then he threw off that concern. This wasn't *The Twilight Zone*. There was an explanation for this. There was a world outside.

And he was getting his family out.

He swung the chair.

28

CRACK!

Jerry had his eyes closed, his body half-clenching in automatic preparation for the explosion of glass it was sure must be coming. So it took a half-second for him to realize what had happened.

He looked at the window.

It was still intact. Still whole.

Still dark.

He looked at his hands. He was still holding the chair. *Parts* of it. The two legs were gripped tightly in his fists, the varnished wood smooth against his sweaty palms. The rest of the chair had fallen to kindling and lay in pieces on the floor beside him.

"What happened?" he said dully. He felt stupid, like his IQ had just dropped by half or more.

"The chair just fell apart," said Sheri in a voice that Jerry would have expected to hear from someone who had just witnessed Christ turning water to wine. Only this miracle was a different kind of miracle. A dark miracle. "It just broke."

"Why would the chair break?" said Drew. He, too, sounded shocked. But where Sheri's voice was tinged with awe, his was tinted by terror.

Jerry dropped one of the chair legs. It fell to the top of the heap of wood beside him and he was visited by an image of bone falling on bone, of skeletal remains cast aside by a predator that had stripped them bare and sucked them dry.

He felt the end of the leg. Not the bottom, where it sat on the floor, but where it had parted company with the rest of the chair.

"It feels like… like it's been sawed through. Or is it 'sawn'? I can never remember." He had to quash a giggle. His mind still wasn't working.

"Sawed through?" said Drew, and the tint of terror became a fully-rendered painting of panic. "What do you mean *SAWED THROUGH*?"

"Who would do that?" said Ann, speaking almost on top of Drew.

Jerry couldn't think. He could only move. He dropped the remaining chair leg and grabbed another chair. Even older. Finer. More valuable, purchased well after the ornamentation of this life had become second nature.

It, too, fell apart in his hands.

The panic that had been drawn across Drew's features now communicated itself fully to Jerry. He whirled through the living room. He grabbed end tables, chairs. Anything small enough to pick up, but big enough to throw through a window.

A moment later, Drew joined him in his mad quest.

Everything collapsed. Nothing held.

Ashes, ashes, it all falls down.

There was only kindling, only bits of nothing that had once been furniture and appointments and decorations. Only wood and plastic and metal that was good for nothing but a reminder of how meaningless their lives had become, how when it was taken down to its basic pieces, it served them not at all.

Ann watched, clearly blown away. Sheri took deep breaths, her hands clutching her shirt with knuckles that glowed white, then letting it go, then clutching it again.

Jerry moved to the baby grand. He tried to move it. Couldn't.

"Drew!"

Drew came over. Even together, the instrument was too heavy.

"The couch!" shouted Drew.

They each went to an end of the couch. Jerry recognized in his mad dash that this was ridiculous – wasn't even the leg of a chair enough to smash the windows out? – but he was gripped by a panic so severe it bordered on hysteria. It wasn't just about getting out right now, it was about finding out how deeply their world had been cut apart, how completely their life had been destroyed.

Jerry bent over at his end of the couch. Gripped under the heavy piece of furniture. Lifted.

Jerry was braced for the weight of the piece. So he almost threw out his back when it came up far too easily. Then it fell out of his hands, and he stared with mouth agape at the six sections the couch had been cut into.

No one moved.

Jerry was panting, Drew gasping for breath in the aftermath of their activity. Ann watched them with eyes that looked haunted.

Sheri was taking breaths that were clearly conscious attempts to remain calm. She looked like a yogi in a battlefield.

Other than the breaths, though, all was silence. But not the silence of peace. It was a *heavy* silence, the kind of silence right before a bullet fires, the silence before a tidal wave rushes over land and sweeps away everything in its path.

Sheri finally spoke. "How could someone have done this? All this? In one night?"

Then she screamed. Jerry did, too, and he thought Drew and Ann joined their voices to the banshee chorus. But he couldn't be sure.

Because in that instant the lights – all the lights, everywhere in the house – had all gone out, and it was as though the perfect black outside the windows had made its way in and taken them into its harsh and loveless embrace.

29

Jerry heard something. Movement. He held up his hand, but couldn't see it. It was right in front of his eyes, he knew it, but he couldn't see it.

He had never been in this kind of darkness before. He felt blind, would have worried he *was* blind, if it weren't for the fact that the others were all moaning and groaning as well, crying in the black that had clutched them all in an instant.

The movement continued, then a clatter. Drew cursed, and Jerry realized his son was moving around. He couldn't figure out what his son was doing, but then he heard a familiar *tic-click tic-click* and realized his son had found one of the small lamps that had sat on the end tables – the end tables recently by the sofa, now in piles of wood next to pieces of what had once *been* a sofa – and was flicking it on and off, on and off, on and off in the hopes that it would chase away the terrifying black that had enveloped them all.

"The lights aren't working," Drew muttered. Then he said it again louder, and then he shrieked the words, "The lights *aren't working!"*

Jerry wanted to reach out to the boy, to comfort him. But he couldn't tell where his son was in this perfect darkness, and not only that but he feared there might well be no real comfort to be had.

Then, just as fast as they had gone, the lights came back. They couldn't have been off for more than a minute, but Jerry blinked and held a hand above his eyes like a man who had been trapped in a mine shaft for months – or years.

Ann was standing stock-still, her mouth moving like she was praying to herself. Drew was, as Jerry had thought, bent over the bits of the end table and held a lamp in his hands.

Sheri was hyperventilating. Her face was a uniform shade of white.

The sight galvanized Jerry. He couldn't lose her. Not his Princess. Not like he had lost Brian.

He didn't think. He just acted. He spun and lashed out with his fist. Punched the nearest window.

It broke. Glass shattered around his fist, falling to the sill, falling to the floor around his feet. Some of it made its way into his flesh, sticking out from between his knuckles like the red-stained claws of some strange beast. Blood flowed.

Jerry barely registered the pain that surged on electric currents through his hand and arm. He stared at the window. Not the glass, but the window, the hole that was left behind.

The glass was gone. But behind it was still dark. Nonetheless, with the glass gone he could see that it wasn't void beyond, it wasn't a formless nothing waiting for some dark god to come and speak the words that would call forth creation. No, it was....

"What is that?" Sheri said.

Drew moved to the window, dropping the lamp he had been holding. "Looks like sheet metal," he said, and rapped on the black material. It made a hollow, muted bonging. He nodded, then added, "Thick, too."

Jerry turned to the next window. Heedless of the shards of glass in his still-clenched fist, he punched the next window as well. His blood spattered this time, splashing onto his clothes, the carpet, the window pane.

A thick plate of sheet metal behind this window as well. Jerry pushed on it. He didn't feel any give. Not on the edges, not at the center. There was no sense that this was a thin piece of metal that might be forced off. Now he realized why the furniture had been cut apart: even the pieces might break the windows, but they would be useless to break through *this*. And Jerry felt certain that if he rushed at the sheet metal shutter *himself,* the only thing that would happen would be that he would bounce off and break every bone in his body.

"It must be bolted onto the house, or screwed on or something."

He turned back to the family. Sheri looked like she had journeyed to a place beyond terror, her eyes darting from Jerry's bloody fist to the metal, to the broken furniture all around, then back again to the blood coursing off his hand and pooling on the rug at his feet.

And the lights went off again.

30

The lights only stayed off for an instant this time, then they came on once more. But the illumination was short-lived as well. The darkness returned.

The lights flickered. On and off, on and off. Casting mad funhouse shadows that created not mere fear but also pushed Jerry into a place where the barest hint of sanity was a thing of memory, a pleasant remembrance.

"My pills." Sheri's hands were still clutching her shirt, spasming open and shut as though in counterpoint to the silent music of the flickering lights. "My... pills."

She rushed out of the living room.

Ann glanced at Jerry, but then followed the teen out of the room without waiting to see what he would do, Drew at his mother's heels. Jerry ran after them all, and it was as much instinct as thought: *Stay together, stay safe, stay alive.*

No overt threat had come, no direct strikes at their health or bodily integrity. Not yet. But he knew it was coming. It had to be.

The family rushed up the stairs, following Sheri who careened drunkenly down the hall, then into her room. She pushed into her bathroom. The lights flickered in here as well, though no one had ever turned them on in the first place. Someone had their hands on some master switch, and all the lights in the house were alternately ablaze and then dark.

"My pills, my pills," Sheri kept murmuring. She went to the mirrored medicine cabinet that was built into the bathroom wall to the left of her sink. Pulled at it. It opened with a low creak.

"Where are they?"

The cabinet was empty. No toothpaste, no hair care products. None of the things that had stuffed that cabinet since Sheri hit puberty. The glass shelves held nothing, the space looked scrubbed clean.

Her pills were gone.

"Who moved everything? Where are my pills?" She started tearing into the spaces below her sink, the drawers to the side. Jerry could see all were basically empty. Only a few odds and ends, mostly consisting of feminine hygiene products, were left. No medicine.

Sheri stared at the other three family members, all of whom were crowded into her bathroom, staring at her. No one spoke. The teen girl started to shake.

Ann moved. She reached out, but Sheri shrank away as though fearful her mother was going to strike her.

"Calm down, sweetie," said Ann. "I have extras in my bathroom."

Down the hall like a cargo train they went. Only instead of any kind of valuable commodities, all they bore with them was fear.

Through the master bedroom. What Jerry had once viewed as his personal space now felt alien, the property of some invader that had stolen not just his possessions but his sense of self.

The master bathroom. Sheri was there first. As before Jerry watched with Ann and Drew as the teen girl tore into the medicine cabinets. Then she opened the drawers under the sinks, the small linen closet by the tub. Everywhere that might hold her meds.

It was all the same.

All empty.

The lights flickered again. They stayed out longer this time, as though syncopated to the ever-darkening mood that Jerry could feel pulsing through of him and his family.

"My meds. They're all gone," said Sheri. "They're all gone."

And then Jerry had a thought – more than a thought, a *realization*. And it scared him worse than anything that had happened so far.

31

"Medicine," Jerry murmured.

"What?" said Ann. He looked at his wife, but she wasn't looking at him. Her eyes were glued to Sheri as their daughter kept looking through the bathroom, searching and re-searching for her medicine, though it was painfully evident that everything had been stripped out of the bathroom.

Jerry didn't answer. He was thinking of Ann, how she had looked so sick after getting out of bed. Of how he had thrown up, but only that thin trickle of bile had come out, like there was nothing in his stomach. He thought of the kids, both of them blinking and blurry-looking.

He remembered Sheri, looking around at the detritus that had once been their living room furniture and saying, "How could someone have done this? All this? In one night?"

"They couldn't," he said. "Oh, my God."

He pulled back his shirt sleeve. The lights went on-off-on-off-on-off, but he could still see. Could see enough. Could see the crook of his elbow, the small black and purple dot with a dark red center. A needle track.

Now Ann was straining to see what Jerry was looking at. Jerry grabbed her arm. Pulled up her sleeve. A matching spot sat like a tiny tumor in the bend of her arm as well.

"What is it?" said Drew. The boy was craning his neck to look.

Jerry grabbed his son's arm. "Hey!" shouted Drew, and tried to pull away. Jerry's grip tightened, and he pulled his son close, pulled the boy's sleeve up.

Needle track. Several, which told Jerry that they were dealing with someone who didn't know how to place an effective IV – for what good that did.

Drew looked at his arm in horror. "What is it?" he asked. "What's going on?"

Ann's mouth had sagged open. Now it snapped shut and she said, "Have we been drugged?" The words were low, contained, but they sent a shiver through Jerry's frame. "How long were we asleep? *What was happening WHILE WE WERE ASLEEP?*"

Drew joined in as well, both him and Ann pelting Jerry with questions – what's happening, what's going on, when are we going to leave, what's happening, when will this be over? – and all the while Sheri kept tearing through the bathroom. Finally she turned to the water closet off to the side of the bathroom itself. There was another small cabinet in there, where Jerry and Ann kept extra toilet paper.

Drew and Ann were still screaming.

The lights were going on and off, on and off, on and off.

Jerry felt like he was falling apart, pulling to pieces. He couldn't focus, couldn't think.

Sheri reached for the cabinet door.

Opened it.

The lights went off.

On.

Sheri *screamed,* and Jerry had never heard a sound like it before. He knew that this was where it began. Not the fear, not the terror. Not the threat. That was all just in the mind.

No, this was where the danger began. Where the pain would start.

32

Sheri's scream lingered, shredding the air like a sonic chainsaw, but after the first second it didn't even register in Jerry's mind. No, what he focused on, the *only* thing he focused on, was what had fallen out of the cabinet. The thing that had almost fallen *on* Sheri, the thing that now lay in a dark, sodden mass at her feet.

Socrates.

Jerry knew it was the family dog, but only because he saw bits and pieces that he recognized. A trace of fur, a line of the back. Other than that, the dog had been pulverized. Bloody, matted fur stuck up in dark, angry spikes along the misshapen lump of its body. His neck had been broken so severely that his lower jaw – what there was of it – now lay slack atop his back. His legs were all grotesquely broken in multiple locations, yellowed bone sticking out of the fur in spots.

One dead eye stared at the family, looking almost accusing, as though the dog felt vaguely hurt that they hadn't taken better care of him. "Weren't you supposed to keep things like this from happening to me?" the eye seemed to demand.

The rest of the face… Jerry turned away.

Ann found her voice first, after Sheri. She screamed. Drew did, too. Sheri backpedaled out of the water closet, falling against a counter and clutching at her chest. She knocked into her mother, who fell back into Drew. The three of them scrabbled backward, like a bizarrely conjoined triplet, until they hit Jerry.

He stopped them. Didn't want to start moving back. Because who knew what was out there?

He grabbed Sheri. Pulled her to him. Held her against his chest. It was as much for him as for her. He tried not to look at the dog that lolled half in and half out of the water closet. At the mashed face.

What could have done that to him?

A hand touched Sheri. Drew. "Shh... shh...," said the boy. The sound came out stuttered: "Shh-sh-sh-sh... sh-sh-sh-sh...." But Jerry was still touched that the kid was trying to help his sister calm down. She was in the most danger right now, there was no question about that. She could die right here, just die in his arms, and what would he do then?

"Sh-sh-sh-sh... sh-sh-sh-sh...."

Sheri was sobbing, her tears wetting his shirt through in an instant. "What happened to the dog? What happened to my dog?"

Drew stopped stroking her hair. He looked shocked. Or offended. "Who cares about the dog," he managed to say a moment later. "What's happening to *us*?"

And there it was. That was the million dollar question that kept popping up. And it was the one for which there was no answer.

The lights went off. This time they stayed off for a long time.

Jerry stared into the darkness. Stared where he knew the dead dog was laying. And he knew that it was there, not dead, not dead at all, no it was just in some *other* state, some state not alive *or* dead but merely waiting for the dark, for the black time. Then it would move. It would come for them, slithering across the tile floor on shattered legs, snapping at them with a jaw pulled apart and a face that had been removed from its skull.

The lights came on.

Silence. Only Sheri's labored breathing told Jerry that life was still present in this room.

He realized that everyone else was oriented on the dog, too, and thought they must all have been suffering thoughts similar to his.

Sheri turned her face to him. She had a wild gleam in her eyes, like she was receiving all the information around them, but couldn't quite figure out how to process it. "How are we going to bury him?" she said. "We can't get out to bury him!" Her voice rose in pitch and volume, rose until it battered at him, cut him like an axe. "We have to bury my dog!"

Jerry looked over Sheri's shoulder. Ann locked eyes with him. She nodded.

"We have to get out of here. Now," said Ann.

He nodded. He took Sheri's hand in his right. Took Drew's arm in his left.

He started to pull them out of the bathroom. Both of the kids resisted.

"Where are we going?" Drew said.

"We've got to look for a way out."

Drew looked at him with eyes that were every bit as wild as his sister's. "But... *what if there isn't one?*"

Jerry pulled them out of the bathroom. The lights went out again. He kept walking.

Pulling his family into the darkness.

33

They worked their way from top to bottom. First was the master bedroom. Looking for a way out.

The master bedroom had a doorway to a second floor deck. The deck had been a major selling point for Jerry when they bought the house: he had pictured him and Ann, sitting on the deck, sipping drinks and watching sunsets and kids playing in the backyard and enjoying the breeze and all the other things that said life was good. Of course, *real* life intruded quickly, and he couldn't remember the last time he had even set foot on the deck, much less taken the time to enjoy a drink or a good book out there.

The door was sealed. The windows set in panes every few inches along its length were dark. Jerry drew back his fist to punch out a pane, but Drew grabbed his wrist.

"Dad, you're gonna bleed to death." Sheri nodded, and she sat him down on the bed and started pulling out shards of glass from his hand whenever the lights turned on.

Ann kicked out one of the window panes in the door. A hollow *thock* sounded as her shoe hit something beyond the glass, and Jerry knew the upstairs windows were enclosed by metal as well.

Sheri finished pulling the glass out of his his hand. The bleeding had slowed a bit, and Jerry marveled that he hadn't nicked any major veins or arteries. But of course now that the glass was gone it hurt like hell.

Sheri pulled a sock out of one of his drawers. She closed it, and the entire bureau collapsed into pieces. Someone had sawed through this furniture as well.

Sheri didn't say anything, just returned to Jerry and bound his hand in silence. It hurt, but it also seemed to calm her, for which he was grateful. More than grateful. He would gladly suffer a thousand similar wounds to keep his Princess safe.

He smiled at her. She smiled back. The grin was strained, but at least it was present. At least she wasn't hyperventilating, so she'd pulled back a bit from the abyss of an attack.

Something clattered, and Jerry saw Drew pushing all the furniture to pieces. Ann was trying to hold him back, but he shook her loose. "Maybe he missed something," Drew screamed. "Maybe there's something he missed!"

Drew's movements grew jerky. He ran out of the room, the rest of the family on his heels.

Drew's room. Nothing there to help. His furniture came apart with anything more than a few pounds of pressure.

Same in Sheri's room.

There was no way out up here.

Down the stairs.

Drew was snuffling. Trying to hold back tears, like he was attempting to prove to the family that he could be brave, could stand up to what was happening, could be a *man*.

Jerry felt strange, bringing up the rear. He felt disconnected. Like whatever was happening didn't make a difference. As though the family had already been wiped off the face of the earth, and anything that occurred from this point on was superfluous.

The media center. No way out there. The remains of the Chinese food still sat on the coffee table in front of the sofa, and under the still-flickering lights of the house Jerry could see that the food had sprouted hairy green growths. Mold had risen in thick tufts along its length.

He remembered the way the food had tasted. Mealy. Chalky. *Powdery.*

Had they been drugged? he wondered. Was that how this had begun?

The living room carried nothing new. Just the shattered windows and the piled remains of once-exquisite furnishings. A reminder of the dissolution of all that they were.

Kitchen. They found a flashlight, a weak beam that combatted the ever-increasing periods of darkness. The lights were less flickering now than turning off and only occasionally turning on. As though whatever madman was behind this could feel them falling farther and farther into the black pit of their own terror, and simply wanted the ambience to properly reflect the mood.

The flashlight cut a rapier slash through the black room. It reflected off the kitchen windows. No one bothered to check them. No one bothered to knock them out; to find the sheet metal that had undoubtedly been fixed behind the glass.

Jerry felt himself growing more and more desperate. Not for himself, necessarily –

(no, not for you, Jer-Jer, not for the guy who deserves this, not for the one who failed so badly who screwed up who brought this

all down on us because the sins of the father will be visited on the heads of the children)

– but for the kids. They hadn't done anything to deserve this. They hadn't brought this on themselves, and he wanted – no, *needed* – to get them out of here. It was like this moment was the culmination of his existence, the chance he had to prove he was a good father. To save his girl and his –

(*remaining*)

– boy and wake them from this nightmare.

He reached out and pulled on the door that led from kitchen to garage. It had already been tried. But maybe things would be different, he thought. Maybe....

The door was still sealed.

They were still trapped.

Jerry remembered one of his professors in med school defining insanity as doing the same thing over and over, but expecting a different result. If so, then Jerry was insane. Mad as a hatter, standing there pulling at the door to the garage and knowing that this time, *this* time, the door would open.

Because it had to.

Didn't it?

34

"This isn't happening," Jerry said. He pulled on the door again. Pull, pull, pull, pull-pull-pull-pullpullpull*pull*.

Ann said something. It didn't quite break through the haze of terror that had clouded his mind, but something about it must have knifed its way through. Her tone, perhaps, or just a sense of what she had probably said. Either way, Jerry stopped pulling on the door, though his hand remained clamped to the knob in a grip firmer than that of a rigor-stiffened corpse.

"What did you say?" he asked. His voice was just above a whisper. The quiet tone not of calm, but of threatened mayhem.

"I said that saying something isn't happening doesn't make it real."

And he knew, of course. Knew without looking that she was staring at the picture. The damn picture of Brian that hung in the kitchen, just like there was a picture of him in every room in the house.

And Jerry realized that this place had stopped being a home a long time ago. It had become a shrine. And now... now perhaps it was finally finishing its long conversion, finally making the final modifications.

Finally becoming a tomb.

He turned. She *was* looking at the picture. So were the kids, their eyes blank, their mouths half open. Numb with terror present and horrors past.

"It doesn't make it not real," Ann whispered again. And the kids nodded, their heads moving up and down like they were controlled by a single string, a puppeteer who had been dancing them ever closer to a dark abyss for longer than Jerry wanted to think about.

Red rage dropped like a curtain over his eyesight. The lights in the house went on-off… on-off, the darkness coming to stay for longer and longer periods. It wasn't a visitor now, but the lord of the home, and the light a furtive invader that was being thrust out.

But all Jerry saw was that red. All he saw was his children agreeing with Ann as she all but accused him of not doing enough when their son died.

He attacked the door. Because if not he would have attacked something – some*one* – else. He hit it over and over, slamming into it with arms and shoulders and hands and feet. His bad hand left trailing red bloodstains behind, like the last gasps of his existence. Like the only proof that he had ever been alive.

He hit it harder and harder. He felt his elbow twinge, felt his shoulder pull to the side and wondered if he had separated or even dislocated it. A sharp pain barked its way up his side and he couldn't tell if it was a stitch or a cracked rib. He didn't care. He wasn't hitting the door anymore. He was attacking the unfairness of it all. The sadness. The pain. The stress. Trying to kill it. To tear it apart. To break it down.

To destroy his life.

Something crackled. Jerry thought the noise was coming from him. He was vaguely aware of hands on his shoulders, of someone trying to pull him back. He resisted. Hit the door again.

The crackling was louder. It turned into a crunch, then a series of quick snaps like the sounds –

(*like the sounds Socrates' neck probably made when the killer twisted it around when the bastard killed our dog and tore his face of with his teeth*)

– of bones breaking beneath his weight.

The door shattered inward.

And Jerry fell through the now-open doorway, into the beckoning space beyond.

35

"We're through!"

At first Jerry thought *he* had said it, that *he* was the one who had spoken the first words of true hope heard since this had all started. Then he felt hands on his arms, felt those hands clench around his biceps and help him to his feet. "We're through!" Drew said again, and helped Jerry into the garage.

Sheri stepped through what bits of the door still clung to the frame, and joined Jerry and Drew in the garage. Ann, bearing the flashlight like a lance, came last.

"We did it!" said Sheri. Her eyes were aglow with optimism, the promise of freedom clear in her visage. Then Jerry saw her expression fall as her gaze rose up. He followed her eyes, and saw what she saw.

The garage door openers. There were two of them, one for each door in the four-car garage. Both mechanisms were destroyed, the metal-and-plastic casings hammered to bits, wires and cords hanging askew from them. What had once been orderly boxes that would do the family's bidding now looked like grim insects from an alien world, guards that were meant to keep them locked inside.

Jerry walked around the two parked cars. He grabbed the nearest garage door and pulled, but it wouldn't open. He looked up at the garage door opener. "Ann," he said, and pointed at it. "Give me some light."

Ann aimed the flashlight beam at the mechanism, and Jerry felt any short-lived hope he might have enjoyed fade away completely. It wasn't just the machinery of the garage door opener that was destroyed, he realized. The tracks and chains of the mechanism had been bent and tortured as well. There was no way that the garage door could possibly open without the use of some heavy duty welding equipment. And a quick glance at the other track showed more of the same.

The light fell away from the tracks as Ann pointed the flashlight away. Jerry almost barked at her, but caught himself. What good would that do?

"The cars!" said Ann.

Jerry looked at them dully. Had *they* been hammered to pieces as well?

No, they appeared to be fine. He looked askance at Ann. She gestured with the flashlight. "Just drive *through* the door," she said.

A suddenly hopeful Drew turned to the key rack where the car keys hung. The key rack that itself hung beside the now permanently open door to the house.

The key rack that was empty.

All the keys, like all Sheri's medicine, had been taken.

Drew wrapped his arms around himself in a protective coat. He began rocking back and forth and Jerry thought how very young his son looked in that moment. He began weaving back toward the family, but had to go slowly because the lights were out again and Ann had the flashlight pointed well away from him, like she had forgotten he even existed.

"Oh, God," Drew whispered. "Oh, God, oh, God."

"Stop saying that," said Sheri. Her own voice was quavering, a warble that sounded half angry and half steeped in fear. "It's not helping anything!"

Ann joined the fray, speaking quietly: "Stop fighting."

Jerry tripped over something in the dark and went down, banging his knee on the hard floor. He heard Drew speak, ignoring his mother and barking, "Why should I stop, Sheri? It's true, we're going to die in here, ripped apart just like the dog –"

"You don't know that!" Sheri again. Jerry stood in time to see her hold her hands out as she shouted, now angry and fearful and *pleading*. "You don't know *anything*!"

Drew opened his mouth to retort, but was cut off by Ann. "Stop it, both of you! Stop it *stop it STOP IT!*"

Utter silence suddenly reigned in the garage. The kids wore expressions that Jerry had never seen on their faces. Not just fear, more than simple horror. They had never heard Ann yell at them before.

Jerry didn't know what to think of it, either. The family was coming apart, falling to pieces like a building after an earthquake, bits of mortar and brick coming down at first and then entire sections and finally the whole thing would come crashing down.

But at the same time, it was good, in a way, to see Ann actually caring about something again. Even if it was to be angry, at least she seemed… alive. Alive, in a way she hadn't been since Brian died. Like when she buried her son a part of her soul had gone in the ground as well.

Ann stared at her children, then walked back into the house.

The house lights went on as she left.

But a moment later they fell dark again. And Jerry pulled the two kids with him as he hurried after his wife, following her back into the house that had swallowed them whole and seemed intent on destroying them; but that had also in a strange way started bringing Ann back to life.

36

Jerry wanted to take some control of the situation. He couldn't get them out right now, fine. But he didn't have to let them wallow, didn't have to let them continue sliding down the slippery slope of sorrow that they had all been hell-bent on following for the past year –

(and longer, Jer-Jer; don't forget it's been longer for you)

– until they inevitably just gave up and waited to die.

But he could feel the hopelessness around them. It surrounded them like a poisonous mist, bound them like chains that weighed them down and made them slow and stupid.

"We've got to stick together," said Jerry as the family trooped into the hall and then to the living room. "Stay a team."

It was a terrible pep talk, he knew. He was hardly a great orator or motivational speaker. Tony Robbins would probably demand the death penalty if he heard such a stiff rallying cry.

But at least he was trying.

And the lights came on again. This time they stayed on, too, as if the universe – or at least the electric company – had given its seal of approval to Jerry's attempt to provide hope to the hopeless.

Drew stared at the broken windows that lined the living room. He leaned almost casually on the baby grand and said, "We're dead."

He said it in the same tone Jerry might have announced he was going to the store or to work. A foregone conclusion. Jerry's heart dropped to hear his son give up like that. Like he was *already* dead, and had just been waiting for the right time to let everyone else know that it had happened.

"No," Jerry said. "We're not. We're alive. We'll get out of this. We just have to... to *stick together* –"

"And you're the expert on that, aren't you?" said Sheri.

Silence smoldered in the room. Hate was better than despair, but hardly a substitute for hope.

"What now?" said Drew with a sigh. Again, he sounded like he had already decided to die. Like he was really just killing time until the inevitable end.

Ann finally spoke. She, too, was staring at the windows. At the black metal that looked like the inside of a coffin door must look.

"If nothing else, *someone* has got to come looking at us," she said. Her eyes started to shine a bit.

Was that hope? Jerry wondered. It had been a long time since he'd seen it in her expression.

Ann turned to the family, but she was pointing at the windows, at the bank of blank black eyes. "I mean, there's sheet metal over all our windows."

Sheri and Drew stared at her blankly, and even Jerry could feel himself wondering what she meant. Stupidity was often the result of terror and panic, he knew. It seemed he wasn't immune to that effect.

Ann rolled her eyes. "You can see the metal outside our house! That's the sort of thing that people investigate, right? I mean, someone drives down a street and sees a nice house with chunks of metal over all the windows… they call someone, don't they?"

Jerry saw his daughter's face grow taut with hope. Even Drew actually pushed away from the piano, standing straight up as though ready to run to any helping hand that might be offered to them.

But in that moment the lights went off. It had happened before, too many times for Jerry to count. But this time was different. The lights were off, but it wasn't dark. Not completely.

Something else was happening.

And Jerry's stomach clenched, because whatever it was, it wasn't going to be anything good.

37

For a split-second, Jerry thought the light was coming from the flashlight that Ann still held. But that gave little in the way of illumination, just a slim gleam like the reflection off a razor blade, slicing tiny bits from the darkness.

"The televisions," Sheri said.

She was right. The TV in the living room had turned on. Its screen was black at first, but it still spread a subtle glow through the room. Then it brightened to white. And Jerry saw cones of white coming from open doors throughout the house and knew that all the televisions in the place must have turned on.

There was a flash, and they were treated again to a view of the stripper in the pink miniskirt, the one they had seen on the computer before it turned off, the headless woman writhing and grinding the beat of music only she could hear. Then she disappeared into static.

"What's going on?" asked Ann. A rhetorical question that no one bothered to answer.

But in the next second the televisions themselves replied. And it *was* to Ann that they spoke, Jerry realized, as though responding to her statement that someone would see the metal shutters and come to help them.

Onscreen was a closed-circuit video feed. It was a grainy feed, hardly the kind of thing that the manufacturer of the high-def television had intended to be viewed on the appliance. But it was clear enough to recognize.

It was dark outside. And Jerry knew he was seeing a live feed. Even though he'd been operating on the assumption that it was daytime, he knew in his gut that this was *now;* that this was life as the outside world perceived it.

Moon. Stars. Street lights visible as dim glows in the background of the picture.

Mostly, though, the screen was dominated by the view of the house. Their house. The family's house.

Not that Jerry – or anyone else – could have told it was his house. But he recognized the lawn equipment. The trees. The gardens and grass.

The pool.

The house, though....

"No one's coming," Drew whispered.

Sheri moaned, and it was a sound that tore Jerry's soul in two and then ground the pieces under its feet.

"Drew...," Jerry began.

"He's right," said Ann. Her eyes were glued to the TV. It sat on the floor – they had tried to use the TV cabinet to break the windows and it, like everything else, had broken to bits – and now she knelt down before it like a supplicant to an oracular god. "He's right. You don't investigate that."

And Jerry thought – *knew* – she was right.

The house was gone. Gone but there. In plain sight but invisible.

Whoever was doing this had thought ahead. Had done his work well.

The house – sheet metal shutters included – was covered from foundation to roof in the orange and blue striped circus plastic of a termite tent.

38

"You don't investigate houses that have been tented," Ann said again. "You drive the other way! Besides, police in this city barely have time to investigate the murders. What are they going to do about a bug tent, call in SWAT?"

Jerry felt the slim chance he might have had to pull the family together spinning away from him. As a kid he had played Crack the Whip with other kids on his block. You linked arms with your friends in a long line, then the entire line spun as fast as it could until someone at the end got flung off by centrifugal force. Great fun for an eight-year-old. Less fun now. Less fun when he wasn't simply trying to hold onto one of the kids who lived next door, but to cling to hope and survival.

"Ann," he tried, "this isn't the time to –"

He didn't know how he was going to finish the sentence he'd begun. What could he say? "Don't worry, I'm sure someone will find us anyway"? She wouldn't believe that. And he didn't think he would, either.

Sheri stopped him from having to figure out the end to the sentence. "What's that?" she said, and pointed at the TV.

It was dim. It was fuzzy. But it was visible. In the background, to the side of the house, near the garden area, something flew over the privacy wall. Then another thing.

"What…?" said Drew. He leaned in close to the TV, his brows so close together it was like they were getting ready to brawl.

Jerry was standing farther from the TV than anyone, but he was the one who knew what it was before anyone else. Probably because he was the one who had had the most recent contact with what they were seeing.

"It's the neighbor," he said. "It's Ted!" And he gave out a quick bark of joy.

Ann spared barely a glance at his outburst before she looked back at the television. Another branch flew over the wall.

"So?" she said.

"He's always complaining about the dog and the kids' stereos." Now it was Sheri that turned to look at him. Her gaze was a study in blank confusion, "So?" written across it in lights so bright he was surprised they didn't send illumination throughout the house.

"So… he's always complaining about what we're doing in here," Jerry said. Sheri kept staring at him, joined now by Drew and then Ann. None of them got it.

Jerry smiled, the grin feeling almost like an interloper, a stranger that had somehow accidentally made its way to his face and, now here, didn't really know what to do.

But the smile reflected itself on the three faces before him when he explained; when he made them understand:

"*He can hear us.*"

39

Jerry ran to the front door. It was only a few steps, only thirty feet to get from the living room to the sealed portal. Last time he had been here hope had been obliterated. Now he felt it reborn like a phoenix, taking flight as he began battering at the thick wood of the door, screaming at the top of his lungs.

"Help! Help us!"

The rest of the family joined him immediately, Ann and the kids crowding around him and pounding on the door and shrieking as well. Screaming not in pain or panic but for the promise of an end to this waking nightmare.

They kept screaming, screaming, screaming. So loud that Jerry felt like his ears were going to burst, so loud that the idea of Ted *not* hearing them became an impossibility.

The quality of Ann's shouting shifted. It took a moment for Jerry to realize she had ceased her wordless wailing and now shouted something as loudly as she could.

"Wait!"

Jerry stopped screaming, but didn't halt his attack on the door. The kids kept on shouting, kept on beating on the door as though it represented all that was evil and malicious in their world, an enemy that must be destroyed.

Ann was pointing. Behind them. The TV.

"What is it?" Jerry said, shouting himself to be heard over the ongoing din that Drew and Sheri were making.

"It stopped!"

"What?"

"It *stopped*!"

Jerry didn't understand. But as he stared at the TV, he saw what she had seen.

The branches weren't flying anymore. Ted had stopped his bombing assault of Ann's garden.

He was done. He was gone.

But then Jerry spied something and realized that Ted wasn't finished. He had simply paused. Simply regrouped at what he thought was an escalation.

Jerry put himself in the man's shoes: he's throwing branches over – presumably to irritate the irritating neighbors. And as soon as he does, they begin irritating *him* in precisely the manner he most hates: with an increase in noise levels.

So does Ted leave? Does that beautiful, wonderful prick of a human being give up? No way. Not Ted.

No, he goes to his shed or garage, and gets what Jerry was now seeing.

"Louder," he said to the kids.

"What?" said Ann. She hadn't spotted it. She would.

"*Louder!*" And Jerry started screaming again, but did so with an eye on the bigscreen TV that still showed the side of the house. Still showed the termite tent. Still showed Ann's garden. Still showed the wall.

And now showed two pieces of metal, peeking over the top of the wall.

"What's that?" said Ann.

Jerry smiled and motioned her to start yelling. She did.

It was a ladder. Ted was coming over the wall. For retribution, no doubt. But that was fine, because Jerry knew that the man would eventually – if they kept up the noise – have no choice but to call the cops. And the cops would save them.

40

Watching Ted come over the wall was almost comical. Jerry tried to stop the laughter at first, as though his subconscious thought it inappropriate to allow mirth or merriment at a time like this. His hand slapped over his mouth, stifling the panic-ridden laughter. Then he pulled the hand away. Laughter was good. And it could only enrage Ted further. Which was also good.

The out-of-shape man climbed the ladder, his torso well above the ornate metal ironwork that topped the wall itself. He looked at the spikes on the wall, and even at this long angle Jerry could see the man debating whether or not this would be worth it.

"Louder!" Jerry screamed. The kids already sounded hoarse, but they coaxed another decibel or two out of their screams.

That seemed to cinch it. Ted levered himself over. Carefully as he could, but his t-shirt still snagged on one of the spikes on the ironwork. He yanked at it, yanked at it.

"Oh, no," said Ann. But it wasn't fear in her voice. It was the disconnected vocalization you utter when a character in a comedy is about to get smacked in the groin.

Ted's testicles were safe, but his t-shirt ripped a moment later and he plummeted to the ground, apparently having forgotten to hold onto anything while he unstuck himself.

THUD. There was no sound, but Jerry fancied he could almost feel the guy's frame slam to the soft earth of Ann's garden. He worried that Ted might have broken his back or neck – *then* where would they be – but a moment later the guy rolled over to hands and knees. He shook his head, then muscled himself to a standing position.

Jerry saw Drew look at the TV, then redouble his pounding and screaming, spurring his sister on to greater volume as well.

Ted put hands on knees, panting. Then he looked at the house and shook a fist. He screamed at it. Jerry could only imagine he was cursing the family for going on vacation and leaving the television on so loud.

Then Ted began running around in tight circles, doing a small kick-leap in the air every few steps. He looked like a dog that had forgotten where it hid its bone and gone suddenly, starkly insane as a result.

"What's he doing?" Drew said. Or screamed. He was clearly unwilling to let up his vocal barrage for even a second.

Jerry realized that Ann, however, *had* stopped screaming.

"What is it?" he shouted to her. But before she could answer, he realized: the camera angle was shifting. Moving so that Ted was more in the center. Zooming in on him. As it did, Jerry realized that Ted's apparent insanity was mere rage: he was trampling Ann's garden with the intensity of a zealot. But Jerry cared less about that fact than about the question that rose in his mind:

Who was moving the camera?

A moment later, the camera stopped its adjustment. Ted was well-centered in the picture, now, the main subject in a well-framed shot. He had stopped his mad dance and now held a stick he yanked off one of the nearby bushes, and he was swinging it like a scythe at anything over a few inches high. Greenery flew like Ted was some strange new model of wood-chipper. He was laughing.

Then Jerry saw it. And he could tell from the gasps around him that the rest of the family did, too.

Something moved in the background of the shot. Something dark. A shadow with no features, just a dark blot on the larger darkness of the night.

Moving carefully toward Ted.

41

He got there fast. So fast.

That was the first thought in Jerry's mind as he saw the dark form approach the wrath-sodden man in their garden – the man who could be their salvation. It was a sidestepping from reality, he knew, focusing on the fact that their jailor – and he had no doubt that the shadowed form he was seeing was just that – was incredibly fast, since he adjusted the camera and then was behind Ted only moments later.

No, he's just got a remote. Lots of cameras have those. He was probably circling around behind Ted the whole time he was adjusting the camera.

Jerry had to force his mind away from that. It wasn't important. What was important was that Ted, their only real chance at a way out since this had started, was in imminent danger.

Nor did Ted seem aware of the threat. He was still whacking away with his switch, beating now on a small rosebush that Ann had planted and spent huge amounts of time pruning in spite of the fact that it had yet to offer up a single flower.

The form, the shadow, the Stranger – and that was how Jerry was going to think of him, he knew, the foreign being that had forced its way into their lives – flitted forward. Still dark, still featureless.

Within ten feet of Ted.

The Stranger moved, and Jerry saw that their captor was holding something in his hand. A branch? Perhaps a baseball bat? Either way it looked solid and substantial.

The Stranger was only five feet away from Ted.

Ted was focused, utterly and completely, on the destruction of the barren rosebush.

"Look out!" Ann screamed.

But of course, Ted couldn't hear. He swung his stick again. The few remaining leaves on the rosebush erupted upward...

... and as though in counterpoint the Stranger slammed his own club down.

Even with no sound, Jerry could almost hear the crunch. Then the second crunch as the Stranger jerked his club loose from the indentation it had created in the back of Ted's skull.

Ted reeled, his head suddenly concave where all had once been convex. Blood streamed down his forehead and face in crimson waterfalls so thick and dark they seemed almost unreal.

The family was no longer screaming for help. Drew was the only one still banging on the door, but he was doing it mechanically. *Bam... bam... bam....* Like his mind had short-circuited at the sight of what was going on outside and had rebooted to its last command sequence.

Bam... bam... bam....

Onscreen, Ted took a pair of drunken steps. Reaching for the Stranger. Not to attack, Jerry could tell. For support. Ted's brain was shutting down, his legs going limp.

He started to fall.

Bam... bam... bam....

The Stranger caught him.

And dragged him out of frame. Now all Jerry and his family could see on the television were the ruins of Ann's garden, and shadows.

Silence ruled, save only for the muffled sound of Drew's robotic knocking.

Bam... bam... ba –

Jerry reached out and gripped his son's wrist. Drew's arm went limp, as though he had just been waiting for someone to do that, to stop him, to stop the course he had taken but had no strength to step away from himself.

They all watched the television. Jerry didn't know why. It showed nothing but a piece of their backyard. Nothing but empty space where hope had existed only a moment before.

Ann screamed. Then so did Drew and Sheri.

Jerry didn't scream. He didn't know if he had it left in him. Even though he jumped where he stood, even though his skin felt like it was curling off his bones in parchment-ribbons.

Because there was Ted again. His bloody face had dropped into the picture, and the Stranger must have picked him up and carried him closer to the camera, because his battered face took up nearly the entire frame, his jaw at one edge of the viewable space and the now-misshapen curve of his head at the other.

Up close, he looked far worse than Jerry had realized he was. Blood covered his face in a gruesome death mask. His right eye had hemorrhaged massively, only the barest hints of his normal eye color visible through the red that coated it like a Halloween contact lens.

The other eye was unmarked. But it stared at nothing, and somehow that perfect but unseeing eye was far worse.

His mouth moved, and Jerry could see that most of the teeth had been smashed out of his jaw by the Stranger's clubbing.

"What's... what's he saying?" whispered Sheri.

"No sound," said Ann.

But Ted was mouthing something over and over and over as he looked into the camera but saw only dead space.

"Help me," said Drew. Jerry looked at his son. "It's what he's saying."

Jerry looked back at the screen. Drew was right. "Help me," Ted was silently pleading, over and over.

Then Ted's bloody mouth opened even further. His good eye rolled back in its socket.

"What's happening?" said Drew, his voice quavering.

Jerry knew. He'd seen it on patients coming in for emergency operations –

(*though not on her, you never saw it on* her *face, did you, Jer-Jer?*)

– and he knew *exactly* what was happening. But he didn't want to say. Didn't want to say that Ted was screaming. That the Stranger hadn't finished with their neighbor, and must be doing something unspeakably painful to him, just out of sight of the camera's eye.

A new flood of blood erupted from Ted's mouth. He convulsed, moving off camera before a black-gloved, blood-spattered hand pushed his face back into view. The hand kept a hold on Ted's hair so the man couldn't jerk out of frame again. Jerry noticed that the hand was holding not just hair, but chunks of yellowish matter that must be pieces of Ted's shattered skull clinging to his scalp.

Ted screamed his soundless scream again. He coughed. Blood spurted from his nose and his eyes.

Then he was motionless.

A moment later the Stranger's hand jerked Ted out of frame.

The camera angle widened again, moving back to its original shot of the house, the backyard, the trees, the wall.

The pool.

A light breeze rippled the colorful tent that lay over the house, as though a mocking spirit were reminding them all that they were away from the feeling of any such life-giving zephyrs.

Then the televisions – all of them, every television in every room of the Dream House that had become his family's nightmare prison – turned off.

They were alone again. In the dark. And their only small sliver of hope had just been murdered in front of them.

42

Jerry sensed movement beside him and in the dim glow of the flashlight that Ann still held he saw Sheri and Drew clutching at one another. He looked at his wife. Wondered if she would move to him. Wondered if she would seek comfort in his arms the way she had before....

She didn't. She just swung the flashlight back and forth so quickly it looked like an amateur laser show at a garage band concert. She wasn't going to come any closer, he knew. Not now. Maybe not ever.

And that's what you deserve.

"He lives alone."

Jerry jerked, startled by the thin, high whisper that had come from his daughter. She sounded like herself, but also *not.* As though a pale version of his daughter had insinuated itself among them in the past few moments. A shadow, a wraith that was meant to bring to mind remembrances of what was.

Jerry shivered. He wondered if Brian was here, too. Watching on a plane that they couldn't see, couldn't understand.

"He lives alone," Sheri said, and though her voice remained small and breathless, her gaze was rigid, focused. Still, it didn't make her look strong, only brittle – her eyes shifting to shards of obsidian in the pits of her skull, dark glass waiting to crack and splinter.

"Yeah," said Drew.

Apparently Sheri didn't like his tone, because she stepped away from him, and in a weird moment Jerry saw how much Drew and Sheri resembled him and Ann. He wondered if that was something too late to fix.

"You don't get it," said Sheri. "He lives *alone*. No one will look for him. No one is coming, no one will look under the tent...."

Her words spun off into silence, swallowed by the vast sepulcher that had replaced their house.

The gloom and despair that had lifted when the family spotted Ted on the closed-circuit feed now fell over them all again, and fell harder this time. Misery always weighed heavier when hope's corpse had barely cooled.

Jerry searched for something to say. Something to do that would make a difference. That would save them.

Good luck with that, Jer-Jer.

"It doesn't matter!" He blurted the words, less a conscious decision to speak than a need to act, to do. Inaction and despair had brought them here. It had to end. But when the family swung to look at him, faces a mixture of fear and hopelessness and defiance – the last aimed at him, as though daring him to figure something out – he felt his voice choke out. Felt himself wonder what could be done.

He looked at the floor. His shoes. Anywhere but their faces.

He caught sight of Drew's arm. Remembered the needle tracks that had pierced their bodies.

"It's been days!" he said, and a warm blossom of hope bloomed again in his heart. Small, but could he coax it to grow? "We've obviously been in here for a while... maybe a week, maybe even more. People will notice *we're* gone. From work, from school, they'll –"

A sound cut him off.

It was a sound he knew, a sound he recognized. But in spite of its familiarity, he felt his stomach twist anew. Because the one consistency in all this was that the familiar was to be feared above all. A home had become a dungeon, a television had become a doorway to murder.

And what he heard now....

But he still moved closer to the sound. As he had to. And the family followed him, as *they* no doubt had to.

And as the Stranger who was behind all *that* knew that they must.

43

Voices.

He had known that from the first instant. Had known he was hearing words spoken. And had suspected – feared – that he knew where the words were coming from.

It was only a few steps down the hall, past a closet door, his office door… then through the door that led to the kitchen.

The voices grew louder.

It was the phone, hanging on a wall near the basement door. It was active, its answering machine function playing back voice messages received on speaker.

"Who turned that on?" asked Drew in a low voice. No one answered, except for Sheri who said "Shhh!"

The voice was one Jerry knew. He couldn't remember the name, but it was someone who worked at his hospital. Someone in HR?

"… so we're sure you'll call us soon, and this is just a formality, we hope you understand. But if you do *not* return our calls or otherwise contact us, we'll be forced to institute disciplinary actions, Doctor Hughes." The voice paused, sighing. "Call us."

"What did that –" began Ann, but her mouth shut as the phone beeped and another message began.

This voice was high and bright. The kind of voice that made Jerry want to reach through the phone and throttle whoever was speaking. The kind of voice that belonged to the kind of person who had decided she despised the universe and the best way to deal with it was to kill everyone with kindness. "Hi! This is Renee calling from the high school, about your kids. They've been absent since…" and the call paused to accommodate the rustling of pages as though in order to document and prove how hard Renee was working, "… last Tuesday, and we haven't gotten the required absence excuse calls for them. Could you please phone us A-sap?" She giggled at that last word, then hung up.

Beep.

"Doctor, you are to consider yourself suspended as of now," said the voice from HR, no longer careful or worried, only gruff and businesslike. "Please call us immediately, or you will face further action."

Beep.

The family looked at each other. Jerry wondered if they were all feeling what he was: a desire to rip the phone off the wall, to stomp it to pieces and stop it from delivering its messages; and a conflicting *need* to hear. This was part of the Stranger's game, he knew. And he suspected that to survive it they would need to know everything they could about the game and the rules by which they played.

"Hi, this is Renee again!" Still chirpy as a bird. "We haven't heard from you guys yet, and social services stopped by your place and saw the tent." Her voice dropped to a tone that Jerry supposed was meant to sound conspiratorial – just you and me against the world, eh, folks? – but instead just made her sound like she needed to blow her nose. "Now, we know that emergencies happen and you guys probably found out about an infestation and left town until your house can be taken care of. Again, we understand emergencies. But *please* call us and let us know when we can expect the kids back. And remember that the tuition payments you've made are non-refundable."

Beep.

HR. "This is totally unacceptable, Doctor. The board has agreed: if you haven't called us back by five p.m., you will no longer be suspended, you will be fired for dereliction under the terms of your employment contract."

Beep.

"It's one minute after five," said the faceless voice of hospital administration. "You are to consider yourself terminated from our service, Doctor. If you have any questions, please direct them to the hospital's office of legal counsel. Goodbye."

The phone clicked and turned off. Ann snatched it off its cradle, her hand moving so fast it was a blur, then holding it to her ear as though trying to catch it while it still worked. But she put it down a moment later, her frown a clear announcement of the failure of that action.

Jerry barely noticed. His legs wobbled. He felt like his knees had disappeared and been replaced by something with the consistency of Jell-O.

"They cut me loose," he said. His voice was stunned, tired. He had known they were in danger, had known life itself was on the line. But now he realized the Stranger wasn't just after their physical destruction.

He was trying to wipe them off the earth. To erase their existence.

"Welcome to the twenty-first century," said Drew.

"What?" said Sheri.

Drew pointed at the phone. "We send emails and Facebook messages and IMs more than we actually visit our neighbors. America is run by faceless corporations. And if you don't show up, your coworkers don't check on you, you just get a pink slip from HR."

Jerry looked at his son. Knew the boy was right, but didn't want to admit it, not to himself and not to the family. Facing what was inside the house was hard enough; worrying about what might be left for them if they ever made it out would make the night unbearable.

Sheri shook her head like she didn't want to listen to Drew. But the teen boy just opened his mouth as though to resume his tirade.

"Drew," said Jerry, his voice weary but concerned, "stop."

Sheri was gasping. Short, quick breaths. Jerry was reminded of a fishing trip he had gone on once, a "retreat" for the senior surgeons in his department. One of them bagged a real catch, a four-foot yellowtail that took over two hours to haul in. When it finally lay on the deck, hook set deep in its now-shredded mouth, it gasped like Sheri was gasping now, trying to get the air it needed in a hostile environment. And failing.

Jerry wiped his brow with hands that shook. "You're scaring your sister, bud," he said.

Drew nodded, but it was as if he couldn't stop. As if his panic had swollen to the point that at least *some* of it must find egress or he would burst. "No one knows anymore," he whispered. "No one cares."

"Come on, sport, please," said Jerry. He should have hugged his son. Held him. But all he could do was look at the phone. The phone that hadn't worked, that hadn't so much as provided a ring tone before. Not until now. Until the Stranger wanted it.

The damn Stranger.

"No one's coming," said Drew. He breathed out and in, a deliberate moment of preparation, then he said, "We're all going to die." And he said it not as threat or concern, but as prophecy. Like a seer describing a future he had already seen, a course of events that *must* come to pass.

Ann pointed the flashlight at her son. His eyes became dark pits, nothing but the barest twinkle at their bottoms to show he was anything more than a corpse himself.

"We're all going to die," he said again.

And Jerry believed him.

44

He said it again. Standing there in the thin beam of the flashlight, the only illumination in the black cave of their house. Standing like a corpse waiting only for its grave to be dug before it can lie down for eternal peace.

"We're all going to die."

Sheri started to whimper.

"Drew!" Jerry screamed.

Silence fell. Drew turned away from them all, staring at the blank nothing of one of the windows. But other than Sheri's panicked breathing, Jerry thought he could have heard a moth flying through the master bedroom with the doors closed. It was a silence so deep it was nearly fathomless, a quiet so profound it bore with it a special kind of terror. One that Jerry could not bring himself to break.

Luckily, someone else seemed to energize. Ann spoke. "We have to get out," she said. "We have to get out of here." She looked at the answering machine. The phone. Nothing behind it, only another length of the ever-constricting wall of silence and isolation that surrounded them.

"We have to get out. We have to call someone." Ann sounded like she was repeating a mantra. Like she was retreating to rote statements as a way of avoiding thought. "We have to call someone. We have to get out."

Jerry took a step toward her. "We'll get out, Ann. We will." He tried to sound more convinced than he felt; didn't know if he succeeded.

"We have to call someone." Jerry realized that her tone was odd. Not just the repetitious nature of her words, but the fact that it... he struggled to figure it out.

"We have to call someone."

There it was. He understood suddenly: she was speaking as though trying to convince herself of something.

"Ann, we tried," Jerry said. "The phones are all dead."

The lights were off, and Ann's face was behind the flashlight she held, so she was almost totally veiled in thick shadow. Even so, Jerry thought he saw something, saw her face change as though she had just made a terribly difficult decision.

The lights flickered back on. But they were dim, as though the Stranger had put everything on a rheostat and set it at half strength.

Ann looked down, then back up. Jerry saw determination in her eyes. "Let's get out of here," she said.

Then she was gone.

Jerry and the kids looked at each other, and he could see from their expressions that they were as baffled as he by what had just happened.

They heard Ann trudging up the stairs. It was enough to break Jerry's paralysis. And he heard Drew and Sheri rushing after him.

They caught up with Ann at the top of the stairs. She was already walking down the hall, moving purposefully.

She walked past Drew's bedroom.

"Ann?" said Jerry. "What's going on?"

Ann didn't answer. She looked back at him, though, and he saw that her mouth had become a straight, thin line.

She was such an attractive woman normally, but now she had become hard as stone, the small lines in her face deepening under the stress of some decision he didn't understand.

They passed Sheri's door, too.

Reached the master bedroom.

The lights went out again. The family stopped moving, but the lights stayed out. Darkness lay behind them, an inky well that had risen up from a place of nightmare. Anything – any*one* – could be hiding there.

In front of them: the master bedroom.

Ann went in.

Jerry felt for his children. Held Drew's hand in one of his. In the other he held Sheri's.

They followed Ann into the master bedroom.

Her flashlight beam glinted off something. Jerry looked at it, then away. He heard Sheri gasp and figured she must have seen it as well: the huge pool of blood that had seeped out from the bathroom, soaking into the shag that began at the demarcation between bathroom and bedroom. The remains of Socrates.

"Ann?" he said, in a voice that was pleading, practically begging. "Answer me. Please."

Ann didn't speak. She disappeared into the walk-in closet.

Jerry looked at Sheri. She *was* staring at the black-red puddle of gore in the bathroom. Drew was looking into the closet.

Jerry yanked on Sheri. Not too hard, he hoped, but hard enough to jerk her attention away from the proof of violence just feet away.

He pulled on Drew's arm, too. And together, the three of them went into the closet.

45

It was a big closet – so big that Jerry had wondered how they would ever find the clothing to fill it when they had first bought the place.

But with all the clothes, shoes, accessories, and bits of this-and-that accumulated through the very successful years, the addition of two adults and two teens into the space made it more than cramped. Jerry felt suddenly claustrophobic, and wanted to step back out into the master bedroom. Only the thought of the dead dog, the pool of blood out there kept him in the confined space.

That, and curiosity.

What the hell's Ann doing?

She was on her side of the closet. Jerry's side was well-organized, everything in a specific place. Ann's was more of an exercise in barely-contained chaos. It hadn't always been like that, but had started only a few months after Brian's death. She started dropping clothes on the floor instead of putting them on hangers, waiting for Rosa to clean them up or just leaving them there indefinitely.

Ann went to one of the larger heaps, a mountain of shoes that would have put Imelda Marcos' footwear collection to shame.

She dug within the pile. For some reason, the sight of her hands disappearing into the mass of shoes made Jerry's stomach clench. Like she was being sucked into the belly of a freakish monster that had been living under his nose without him noticing.

She grunted. Then pulled something. The shoes scattered, drifting apart almost gently to reveal something that had been hidden beneath them.

It was a box. Wood – mahogany, Jerry thought, though he couldn't be sure. About twelve inches to the side, a few inches deep. Beautiful, obviously antique.

So why was it hidden underneath a bunch of shoes?

What did it need such an ornate lock for?

And why had he never seen it?

"Honey?" he said.

Ann didn't answer. Nor did she look at him as she pushed past the rest of the family and into the bedroom. Still holding the box, she knelt down beside the ruins of a vanity table that – like all other furniture in this house – had fallen to pieces. The contents of the vanity had scattered across the floor like piles of pirate booty. She aimed the flashlight at the bits of jewelry and perfumes, sifting back and forth until….

"Honey?" Jerry tried again. "What's in the box?"

Drew and Sheri were silent, holding hands. They had the same question, he could see it in his kids' faces. What was going on now?

"Honey?" he tried one more time.

Ann held what she had found among the remains of her vanity: a small brass key. She looked at it for a long moment, as though considering one last time whether the course she had determined to walk along was for the best.

Then she moved. She plunged the key into the center of the box's lock, almost stabbing at it like some monster she was worried might come alive at any moment.

She turned the key.

Opened the box.

Jerry stepped forward, trying to see what was inside. Ann moved as well, angling her body in a clear attempt to get between him and the box, to keep him from seeing.

But he did see. And wanted to scream and scream and never stop.

46

Letters. Each carefully folded, each one carefully placed upon the others, then the whole stack neatly wrapped in a looping coil of red ribbon, tied in an honest-to-God bow.

Envelopes – presumably the ones the letters had come in – sat next to the pile of correspondence. They had been ripped open carefully, Jerry could see. Not to be torn, but treasured. Kept secret, kept safe in this cache of secret – hidden – love.

"Where did all this come from?" Jerry said. He could see the kids out of the corners of his eyes, exchanging shocked gazes. He knew, of course. Knew what this had to be, but –

No. Not Ann. She would never –

But look at this!

She couldn't. She wouldn't –

But she did.

Ann must have seen the flurry of emotions that gusted across his face, changing the geography of his visage from shock to disgust to horror and then back to shock once again.

"Now is not the time," she said. Her eyes looked tired.

She put a hand to the letters. Moved them to the side.

"Please, God," she said. "Please let it be here."

Her hand clenched on something. She pulled it out. Opened her hand.

Sheri exhaled explosively.

Ann held a cell phone.

The sight of the phone changed something in Jerry. He didn't know if it gave him courage, if the hope of a possible working phone gave him the strength to think beyond the fact that they were currently entombed in their own house; or if it was merely a sudden bloom of white-petaled rage that pushed at him. Either way, he felt his fists clench into tight, white-knuckled knots at his sides. Felt his breath coming shallow and fast.

"What the hell's going on, *dear*?" he finally managed.

Ann stared at him, a strange look, like she couldn't believe he wanted to get into this problem right *here* and right *now*.

But Jerry did. He did want to get into that. Because as bad as it was to be imprisoned in his own home, it was far worse to find out that he didn't even know his closest cellmate.

"Please, Dad," said Sheri. She was pulling at her shirt again, hands knotting as they gripped double handfuls of the fabric at her chest, then releasing for an instant before she started the process again. "Let's just call 9-1-1 and get out of here."

"If the phone even works," said Drew morosely.

Sheri looked at him in horror. "What do you mean?"

Drew gestured, taking in the whole of the house with the motion. "Whoever's doing this, whoever locked us in here… he kills our dog, he takes your pills, he kills Ted, he takes away every way we have to escape, and now… what? He's just going to leave a phone for us?"

"He didn't know about it," said Sheri, her voice the pitifully small voice of the hopeless.

"*I* sure as hell didn't know about it," said Jerry. He didn't sound hopeless. He sounded, he suspected, like he wanted to kill someone. Probably because he did.

Drew looked around at the mess of the bedroom. "Ten will get you twenty that the phone's insides are missing, just like ours."

And just like that, Jerry felt his attention snap back to the big picture. Whatever secrets Ann had could wait. For now. The important thing was to get out. Survival trumped the need to confront long-lasting lies.

Jerry, Sheri, and Drew all looked down at Ann. She had been looking at them as though waiting for their attention. Now, she moved her finger to the phone's power button.

She pressed it.

47

Nothing happened for a long moment.

Drew made a strange noise, almost a sob. Sheri sniffed.

Then there was a different sound. A tinkling, chirping sound that Jerry didn't recognize, but which must be coming from the phone.

It turned on. The phone was a model that Jerry wasn't familiar with, but anyone who'd been born in the last fifty years would have recognized it as a fully-functioning, *connected* phone.

"Yes!" Sheri shouted. And Jerry felt so good. Not just at the fact that they had a means to call someone outside of this dungeon into which the Stranger had tossed them, but also at the simple fact that Sheri sounded animated again. Sounded like she might actually survive this night... and might actually be happy of that fact.

Jerry watched the phone. "Searching," said the main screen. Then, "Connected."

Ann pressed a button: "9." Then "1."

And in the instant before she touched the last "1," the final number that would get them in touch with someone who could help, the phone rang.

The ring made Jerry feel like he had leapt six feet to the side... or at least like his bones had done so, leaving the rest of him an overly-fleshy bunch of blood and skin. Drew *did* jump a bit, and Sheri barked out something unintelligible.

The ringtone was a song. It took a moment for Jerry to place, but finally he recognized it: Whitney Houston's hit ballad "I Will Always Love You." He had heard it everywhere the year it came out, and though it was a pretty song, by the hundred millionth rendition he was seriously considering carpet bombing both Ms. Houston's home and any nearby radio stations just so he wouldn't have to hear it anymore.

Ann had always liked it, though. The song never grew old for her. She thought it was romantic.

And now it was singing out of the phone.

The screen on the phone read "Private Caller."

The ringtone continued, the first few bars of the song playing over and over and making the dark space seem somehow stranger than it had before.

Jerry glanced at the pool of blood in the bathroom. He wouldn't have been surprised to see Socrates there, tongue lolling through what was left of his jaw, between what few of his teeth the Stranger had left him with.

Nothing. Just blood and tile.

"*Mom!*" Sheri's voice was sharp. "Hang up and call the cops!"

Ann didn't. She looked at the phone. At the children.

At Jerry.

Then lifted the phone to her ear.

48

Even though Ann was the one holding the phone, Jerry was close enough to hear it. To hear the voice.

To hear the Stranger.

But even as the thought entered his mind, he realized it wasn't the right one. Whoever the person on the line was, it wasn't a Stranger. Not anymore. It was something different. Something dark and terrible and deadly. But no Stranger. Because he had become far too intimate a member of the home, far too close to the family. He knew too much to be a mere Stranger anymore.

So what was he?

He's the Killer.

The words came into Jerry's mind unbidden, and he almost rejected them. Almost willed them away as being too much: if he thought of this person as the Killer, then wouldn't he be ascribing too much power to him – or her? Wouldn't he be essentially giving up?

No. Not giving up. Just facing reality. And you have to do that, Jer-Jer. Have to face reality if you hope to survive.

The Killer's voice sounded strange, warped; clearly it had been put through some kind of sound modulator that had rendered it not quite synthetic, but no longer organic, either. The sound of a cyborg, something with all the failures of humanity, but the relentless nature of a machine programmed only to destroy.

"Your secrets will kill you all," said the Killer.

Jerry saw Ann shake, the fist that she had made around the phone growing even tighter as the words were spoken. He didn't know if that was because of the words themselves, or because of the mere fact of how close she was to the Killer. Certainly Jerry felt like giving up, like curling into a ball and waiting for the end. The Killer's voice, even after being electronically altered, had a strange power to it. A siren song, a call to dash your soul against the dark rocks of despair.

"Who is this?" Ann said. "Where did you get this number?"

"What's going on?" said Drew at the same time. Jerry realized that the kids couldn't hear the Killer's words. He wondered if that was purposeful; if the Killer had somehow *known* that only the parents would be close enough to hear his voice. "Who is it?" Drew continued.

Ann didn't seem to hear Drew. Indeed, Jerry suddenly thought she didn't even seem like she was in the same room as the rest of the family. She was there physically, but her eyes bore a faraway look, and Jerry wondered where she was.

And with who.

"I got the number," said the Killer, "from the one other person in the world who knows it."

Ann had been shaking before. Now her entire body seemed to twitch, a giant spasm that ran from her crown to her feet.

"Mom? You okay?" shouted Sheri, terror clear even in the pale beam of the flashlight.

Ann ignored her. Or perhaps didn't hear her at all, Jerry thought. Certainly she wasn't looking at Sheri – or anyone else in the room. Her gaze was faraway. Reserved for the person speaking to her on the phone, perhaps.

"What do you mean?" Ann said into the phone. Her voice trembled, skittering through the room like beads of oil on a red-hot frying pan. She glanced at the family, and Jerry thought he saw something familiar there. The look of a secret long-buried, a truth that refused to die but kept clawing its way back to light.

"Tell the truth," said the Killer, and in spite of the electronic modulation his voice had undergone, Jerry would have sworn he heard a sly, sinister smile in the other man's tones. "Tell the truth, and maybe you'll live."

Again Ann glanced around. Looked at her children. Her husband. Almost choking on the words, she finally managed, "I don't know what you're talking about."

Silence. A long moment of absolute quiet, the complete absence of sound that comes after the gun has been cocked, but before the first shot has been fired.

Then the Killer spoke. "You *disappoint* me," he said. Ann jerked at the second word, and Jerry felt like drawing away as well, as though the phone in his wife's hand had somehow changed from an instrument of salvation to an alien creature that would bring only death. The word "disappoint" was one that meant something to the Killer, Jerry was sure. Something more than the meaning you'd find in the dictionary. And he wasn't sure he wanted to find out exactly what that meaning might be.

The Killer spoke again, his words almost stumbling over themselves as he talked, like he had been holding this thought in for far too long and now that it had started coming out it would come out faster than even *he* could control.

"The man who gave me this number lied, too. He wouldn't tell me his secrets. He was two-faced. Two is too many – if you have two faces you never know whose *turn* it is – so because he had too many faces, I took one of them away. Took one of his faces aw*aaaaaay*."

Ann gasped. Jerry was silent, not sure what he was hearing, but feeling the world start to rock madly below his feet. Sheri and Drew were yelling at Ann, he realized. Telling her to get off the phone, to call 9-1-1, to phone someone to phone the police to phone the fire departments to phone *anyone*....

"Mom, *hang up and call the cops!*" shouted Drew.

The Killer laughed. "And he screamed," he said. "I took his face away and oh, how he screamed!"

Then there was the dry static click of a connection terminating.

Ann looked at the phone with a face that had no room for anything but horror on its features.

"Mom, dial 9-1-1!" shrieked Sheri.

Ann dialed.

But not the three-digit emergency number that would have called cops, fire safety officers, and a broad range of emergency responders to them. No, she dialed a ten-digit number with fingers so shaky it seemed impossible that she would get through the process.

And her children screaming – *shrieking, pleading, begging* – her to hang up and call the cops hang up and call the fire department hang up and call help hang up Mom hanguphanguphanguphangup!

Jerry watched. He felt strangely outside the moment. An observer. No, less than that. He was the man who had come in late to the movie. The guy who had missed the coming attractions, the opening credits, the first half hour. And now he could appreciate the spectacle... but could never hope to connect with the emotion.

Ann punched the last button on her phone. Hit "Send." She put the phone to her ear and Jerry heard the double-beep of a connection.

At the same time....

Whitney Houston began singing again. Singing her hit "I Will Always Love You."

For a moment that was too fast to be an instant, but which nonetheless seemed to encapsulate much of eternity, Jerry wondered why and how Ann had called her own phone. Then that nonsense, head-in-the-sand line of reasoning fled and Jerry realized he must be hearing the phone that was the twin to the one Ann had had hidden in her side of the closet. The phone that was meant as her phone's one and only partner, it's one true love and only reason for being.

Jerry's skin felt cold. But for once it wasn't the cold of fear, wasn't the graveyard-chill of a ghost walking over bones not yet at rest, not yet at peace. No, this was the cold of a star, a deep ball of energy once massive and powerful but now swiftly collapsing into itself, its one remaining reason for being to remove everything else from existence. Other planets, nebulae. Sons, daughters. Cheating wives. And especially any phones that might have the arrogant presumption to sing "I Will Always Love You" while the *husband was right there!*

Everyone had fallen silent as the evocative strains of the out-of-place love song swam through terror-saturated air.

Ann was the first to move. Her motions were forlorn, and she wore an expression bordering on lugubrious reverence on her face. She kept the phone plastered to her cheek.

Jerry wondered where she was going. Then Whitney Houston began playing again and he realized that his wife was looking for the second singer in the strange, secret love song that had been going on without his knowledge.

He didn't know how he'd react when she found the guy. He was pretty sure he was going to kill him. But would it be now or later? Hmmmmm....

Ann suddenly reminded Jerry of Socrates when the pooch was on the trail of a rabbit, or tracking down one of the gophers or rats that managed to get onto the property. He had a weird urge to rub Ann's hair and say, "Gooood girl."

The sound came on again. After only a few repetitions of the eponymous chorus Jerry was more than ready to never hear that song again.

Ann followed the electronic mutilation of the #1 Ballad. The lights still off, of course, so it was only the small flashlight in Ann's hand that attempted to push back the darkness. And largely failed.

The flashlight beam followed the music, stitching a silver pattern through the thick black tapestry that had woven itself among all of them.

Ann was still holding the mahogany chest, the outward evidence of a hidden love. Now she put it on the floor (making sure the door to the chest was shut, Jerry noted) and waited.

The song came again.

Ann followed it with the lance of her beam. A twenty-first century Don Quijote tilting not at windmills, but at something Jerry intuited would turn out to be far more real and fare more deadly. No mythical dragons in this house. No, only lies and secrets and the death they brought.

The song stopped. Ann stopped moving as well. As perfect and pristine as she had been when Jerry married her twenty years before. She hadn't changed.

At least on the outside. Though inside she was someone that Jerry didn't know and might *never* have known.

The music started. Jerry caught a glimpse of Sheri and Drew, silent through all this. Now they shared a quick gaze with one another. And there were volumes spoken in that gaze, though Jerry didn't have the vocabulary to understand the language they spoke.

Ann reached out. Reached for the master bed. Because that's where the music was coming from, Jerry realized.

He also heard something in that instant. Heard the Killer speaking, remembered what he had said on the phone to Ann: "... because he had too many faces, I took one of them away. Took one of his faces aw*aaaaaay*."

He had a sudden unnamed dread, and reached for Ann's arm at the precise instant she took hold of the dust cover, the bit of cloth that hung below the box spring and hid whatever was under the bed from view. As far as Jerry understood purchase of a dust cover was acceptable in forty-eight states as proof you had a vagina. No man he knew had ever stated a preference for a dust cover. Most men didn't even know what they *were*.

Drew must have had a similar feeling, because at the same moment he leaped forward, screaming, "Mom, don't –"

Jerry and Drew were both too late. The two of them moved as fast as they could, but Ann flipped up the dust cover and saw what lay below the bed. She saw, and in the next second her knees buckled and in the second after that she started to scream.

49

Jerry saw it as well. The flashlight in Ann's hand slashed across it, and he was given the thinnest glimpse of a new Hell, one that gaped beneath the one the family presently occupied, but which was no less real for that fact.

Blood had splattered and splashed over all available surfaces below the bed. The bedspread itself was fine, tousled due to Jerry and Ann sleeping in it, but fine other than that. Below that façade of normalcy, that thin veneer of the banal and the commonplace, all was a travesty, an inverted slaughterhouse where blood fell in steady streams.

Ann was still shrieking, the flashlight dancing in her hands like it alone could hear some mad, wordless tune that must be followed until death came to relieve the dancer.

In the mad-flash-streaking light, Jerry saw the blood. Glimpsed the corpse. Saw the body ripped and ragged, the face unrecognizably slashed and battered and cut.

The Killer had peeled the poor victim's face away from his skull in long, careful strips that curled against his neck like a macabre banana peel.

The still-ringing cell phone was jammed in the cadaver's mouth, too-white teeth clamped around it in a death-lock that struck Jerry as horribly obscene.

At the same moment that the phone rang again, Ann screamed something unintelligible. She hurled herself backward, away from the bed, away from the phone, away from the body and the song that came from the dead man's teeth.

She punched at her phone as she slid away from the bed, jabbing at it repeatedly. Jerry didn't understand why she would do that, not at first. Then the ringtone that still emanated from the dead man below the bed cut off suddenly and when the silence dropped he knew. Ann needed to turn off the song every bit as much as she needed to get away from the shredded corpse under the bed. She had to stop the ringing. The singing of the phone.

Sheri screamed, a tiny half-scream that was almost a punctuation mark, the period that delineated the end of the song. And more than that, it seemed to send Ann into even deeper terror, and Jerry saw his wife drop the flashlight.

It spun wildly across the floor, pitching the room from darkness into the lightning storm of a strobe light. Suddenly Jerry could see everything and nothing at once. There was only darkness and the dead eyes of a corpse with a cell phone jammed into its mouth, only darkness and the terrified faces of his children screaming as they saw what monsters had come for them, only darkness and the face of his wife as she looked with eyes that were wide and terrified… and knowing.

Jerry reached for the flashlight as it danced its mad dance across the floor. His hand was shaking. No surprise there: the bigger surprise would have been if his hand *hadn't* been shaking. But in spite of the tremors that gripped his muscles he managed to snag the flashlight. Hefted it. It felt good in his hand. It felt real, a tiny shred of truth in a world that had shown itself to be little more than layer upon layer of thin fantasies created by a delusional god.

Jerry heard screaming. Ann. And not just Ann, but Sheri and Drew, as well. Screaming again... or had they ever stopped? Had they just started screaming when Ann first looked under the bed and kept on until now?

Jerry flipped up the dust cover. The trio of screams behind him rose in volume and in tone, a sudden crescendo that startled him nearly as much as the view of the man below the bed.

Jerry swallowed dryly. He wondered how long it had been since he'd drunk anything. He remembered having that wine with Ann on what he perceived as the night before this. But it really could have been anytime. Days, weeks. A month.

The corpse looked at Jerry with a stare that was impossibly wide. The skin of its face had been peeled away, including its eyelids, so the yellowing eyeballs seemed to hang in the middle of a perfect pit of nothing, suspended in a void for the sole purpose of rendering accusation, of leveling judgment. "I shouldn't be here," the corpse seemed to be saying, "And I certainly shouldn't be dead. Just like Brian, Jer-Jer. You kill everything around you, don't you?"

Jerry gasped and looked away. He wondered if the rest of the family could see what he was thinking. They had to be able to, he reasoned. They had to see his failure, his pain.

His guilt.

Jerry looked away from the staring eyes of the dead man. But he didn't dare look to his family. Instead his gaze fell upon the wooden box that Ann had brought out of the closet.

A fine box. A good box, beautifully crafted. The kind of thing you got because you wanted it to last. The kind of thing you got for a husband on an anniversary.

Or for a lover, just because.

Jerry glanced back at the bed. He didn't lift up the dust cover again, but he glanced back and that was more than enough. Then he looked at Ann. She had finally stopped screaming, she and the kids now pushed against a wall as far from the bed as they could get. The kids were whimpering, crying.

Ann wasn't crying. Wasn't whimpering. She was just staring. Staring at the bed. At what lay below it.

Jerry stepped toward his wife. "Ann?" he said. She didn't look at him. Her eyes remained stuck where they were. "Ann, who is under our bed?"

Both kids heard him. Drew and Sheri both flicked their gazes to him, then looked at the box, then at Ann, then back at the box. He saw comprehension dawn in their eyes.

Ann didn't acknowledge him at all. She just stared at the bed

Jerry took another step. "Ann, who is under our bed?" he repeated. The words came out sharper this time, as though they were knives he was honing to a finer point each time he spoke them. Like they were weapons he intended to use to murder someone.

"Ann, *who is under our bed?*"

He pointed the flashlight at her face, like a cop interrogating a suspect. She didn't even squint, though he could see the kids lean away from light. And he knew he had gone off his rocker. He should be concerned about *whether* what had happened to the guy under the bed was going to happen to all of them, rather than being consumed with *who* it was.

But who it was... that was all that mattered. It was the one question that existed in his mind, the one issue that would drive him past the walls that contained him. Not the walls of the house, but the walls of madness, the walls of insanity that had been pressing closer and closer since this all began.

So close he could touch them now. So close he could feel the moldering paint flaking off like leprous skin. So close that he had nowhere to turn. The madness was everywhere. Everything.

"WHO IS UNDER THE BED?"

He didn't even know who he was talking to. He was alone in a dark place, completely isolated with no company but his blackest fears, his deepest regrets.

A girl stepped into the darkness with him. Illuminated only slightly by the wavering glow of the flashlight he held, at first he thought she was the girl, *the girl* –

(*no, Jer-Jer, no, it can't be, can't be, don't even hope that*)

– until she stepped closer. Threw her arms around him in an awkward half-hug. It was the first time Sheri had hugged him since Brian had died. Maybe longer. Jerry stiffened at first, and Sheri must have felt his body's resistance because she started to move away from him. But then she came close again, as though forcing herself to breach the walls that had sprung up between them. She held him and said, "Dad, please, not now. Please, let's just get out of here. Please."

The world seemed to brighten, and as it did Jerry realized how perilously close he had come to losing his mind.

He wondered if the others were that close. If the others might break as well.

He looked at Ann, still holding herself as she sat on the floor far away from the bed – far away from the flayed man under the bed. She didn't look at him. Her gaze was fixed on the dark slit between the floor and the hem of the dust cover. The doorway between the light Jerry held and the pitch darkness where lived – existed – the literal monster under the bed.

Jerry swung his flashlight to Drew. His son was looking at him with an expression that mirrored the one Sheri wore. What was it? Jerry couldn't place it for a moment, it had been so long since he had seen it on either of his kids' faces.

Then he realized: it was trust. Confidence. The hope that a parent – that *Dad* – could get them out of this. Could make it all better.

Jerry nodded. He pushed Sheri away. Walked to Ann.

She still didn't meet his gaze, but tried to scuttle away from him, like a bug that had been caught in the open and now lurched for the sanctuary of the shadows.

Jerry caught her arm. He didn't do it angrily, or with too much force. "Ann," he said, and his voice was as calm and firm as his grip. His children were counting on him.

She finally looked at him. "Wh-what?" she managed. Her eyes were dark, and he thought he saw in their depths reflections of collapsing walls, of madness drawn near. He hoped it wasn't too late for her. For all of them.

"Let's get out of here," he said, and held out his hand.

50

Jerry was surprised when Ann misinterpreted his movement and reached to take his hand. He wanted to shout, wanted to scream at her, to ask if she really thought he was going to just hold hands and all would be forgotten, all would be forgiven.

He didn't though. He reigned in the urge; just shaking his head and moving his hand out of reach. Now confusion filled Ann's expression.

"Wha...?" she said, then followed his finger as he pointed at what she still held. Her lip curled. "*This* is what you want?"

"It can get us out, Ann," said Jerry. He tried to remain calm, tried not to point out that she had no reason to be angry with him right now, mere seconds after the discovery of an infidelity that looked to be long-lasting and involving not just the body but the mind and the heart.

Ann slapped the cell phone into his outstretched palm. "Fine," she said. Jerry thought for a second she was going to spit at him, but she reined herself in and sat with legs crossed, elbows braced on knees and head resting on her hands.

She looked bereft. Pitiful. In need of comfort.

Jerry turned away from her. Whatever she might need, she would have to get it somewhere else.

He looked at the phone Ann had been using to call... whoever it was. The phone was a cheap disposable model, the pay-as-you-go kind that was favored by terrorists – and apparently adulterers – as being virtually untraceable.

The phone still had power. The orange screen – nothing fancy, just a basic screen – said the name of the phone company and showed that there was phone reception here. Which unnerved Jerry in a way: he had fully expected to see a lack of reception, not the all-clear he was seeing.

"Dad," said Sheri in a "why-don't-you-go-ahead-and-do-it" tone of voice.

He nodded.

Pressed "9"...

(*and this was where someone would jump out of the closet with a mask and a machete and murder them all where they stood, but no, no one came out the closet stayed dark and they all waited waited*)

... then pressed "1"...

(*if no masked man then certainly bugs or rodents or some kind of nightmare creature some beast from the oubliettes of our minds but there was no scrabbling at the doors no scratching at the walls only silence and breathing*)

... then pressed "1."

Jerry felt his muscles relax. He knew how people running from snipers must feel, like every step was a miracle, and when they made it to safety it was like they could see the face of God for the first time.

He smiled at Sheri and Drew. "We're outta here," he said.

He pressed the "Send" button.

But in the instant that he did, the phone darkened. The orange screen went black. The backlit buttons turned off.

Drew said, "What is it?"

Jerry looked at the phone. It had turned off. The call hadn't completed.

He pressed the power button. The phone turned on, but only long enough for the orange screen to blink the words "Charge Battery" at him. Then everything went black again, and when he hit the power button it remained dark.

Jerry cursed under his breath.

"What?" said Sheri. "What is it?"

Jerry looked at Ann. "Where's the charger?" he said. She didn't answer, and for a moment it looked like she was being almost petulant; *sulky*. Like she had been caught cheating at a game and now wanted to take her balls and go home.

Rage flew on red wings in front of Jerry's vision. For her to act like this, now, when everything was on the line, when she was the only one that knew the way out....

You wanna kill her, Jer-Jer?

He forced his hands, which had clenched into tight fists, to loosen, maintaining only enough tension to keep hold of the cell phone –

(*Ann's cell phone, her love phone, don't forget, the phone she's been screwing around behind your back with for who knows how long*)

– and then saying, in words as slow and clear and calm as he could manage, "Where is the charger?"

Ann looked at him, and he thought he saw a flash in her eyes. A number of emotions. Anger, then embarrassment. Then fear. Then terror.

The terror wasn't of the house, wasn't of whoever was doing this. Not in this moment. No, he realized, she was terrified of *him*. And that scared him.

Even more frightening was how much he enjoyed seeing her fear at that instant. How much he thought she deserved it, and how much it refreshed him in the darkness of the home that had shattered around them and reformed to become a rock-solid tomb.

51

Jerry let his gaze fall away from Ann first. He didn't want to scare her too badly; and more than that, he didn't want to give in to the part of himself that desperately wanted to be let loose and become what she feared. Jerry could feel it there, a very real part of him struggling to get out and forget about the problems facing the family and simply solve the one problem at hand, the one problem close enough to deal with, the problem of an unfaithful wife.

Jerry tamped that feeling down. That wasn't who he was. Or at the very least, it wasn't who he wanted to *be.*

Just get out, just get the kids out. Just get everyone out.

So he looked away. Looked away from Ann, and in so doing forced the beast within him to crawl back into the dark confines of his heart, back into the deep places where he hoped it would die and be forgotten.

It seemed to be the right thing to do, because as soon as they had broken eye contact, Ann crawled away. Not far, not beyond the small circle of light provided by the flashlight. Just to the box.

Jerry felt his anger building again as Ann put her hand in among the letters and ribbons, the tokens of love.

Then he realized that her movements were changing. She had grown jerky, frantic. Like the fear that had gripped her gaze had moved now to partial control of her muscles, creating of her a disobedient puppet of flesh and bone.

"Not here," she mumbled.

"Not there?" said Jerry. "What do you mean, it's not there?" He advanced on her again – or on the box. It was hard for even him to tell. They both seemed to be glazed in red, steeped in crimson tones that foretold some horror that would come upon each in turn.

"I mean it's not *here,*" screamed Ann. She cast half the contents of the box out in a large handful. Letters, envelopes, ribbon. No charger. "Someone took it out!"

"Who?" screamed Jerry. He didn't know why he was asking Ann. How would she know? How could anyone know anything of what was happening in here?

Ann looked like she was going to answer him, was going to fight him even. Like maybe she was going to use him as a punching bag to rid her of whatever personal demons had driven her to hide her dreams not with her family, but in a box in the closet.

"Dammit!" he shouted. He threw the defunct cell phone into the darkness that ringed the family. It disappeared into the night-black that held sway over most of the room, thunking against a wall somewhere. Silent. Gone. Nothing. "*Dammit!*" Jerry shouted again. Louder this time. As though by raising his voice he might raise an idea, might bring out some way to escape.

Someone cleared a throat. It sounded almost silly, melodramatic in the terror-filled atmosphere of the bedroom. But it worked, Jerry supposed, because both he and Ann swiveled to look at its source: Drew.

"There *is* another phone in here," Drew said. "One we could use."

"Where?" said Sheri.

Drew looked at the bed. Jerry didn't understand for a moment, then he realized that his son *wasn't* looking at the bed. He was looking under it. At the dark space under the dust ruffle, the black place where a corpse hid. A dead man whose face had been peeled off…

… and a cell phone jammed in its mouth.

Jerry looked at his son. Drew looked half proud of himself, half sick at the idea of what he was proposing. "And we know it works," he said, "we heard it get an incoming call."

Jerry tossed a quick glance at Ann. "Yeah, when your mother called it *instead of the cops*."

Easy, Jer-Jer. Don't let yourself lose it. Not now.

Ann finally wilted under his gaze. Whatever anger had overlain her guilt evaporated for a moment and only embarrassment and a clear awareness of her transgression remained.

Surprisingly, the fact of his wife's apparent understanding of her blame didn't make Jerry feel better. It just opened up myriad doors that led to black places in his own heart. Wondering if he had caused it, if he had driven her to it. If he had, in some way, been more guilty than she.

You already know the answer to that little secret, Jer-Jer.

Jerry looked away from Ann's white face. From the fear-soaked countenances of his children.

He walked to the bed.

And reached under.

52

When Jerry was a little boy, his parents had an attic. Going into the attic had been a treat, an adventure that allowed him to roam through the dust-covered boxes that carried memories of grandparents he had never met; steamer trunks and other containers that seemed to belong to another world. The attic was magic.

But all magic has a price, and for little Jerry, reaching up into the darkness, fumbling until he found the ball-chain that turned on the light... that was his price. For in those short seconds of darkness, anything could happen. Any monster could come for him, any demon could rouse itself from the shadows and pull him into a dark world where all was black and blood.

For years that had stood as Jerry's pinnacle of fear: the idea of reaching into a dark attic, a space full of hulking shapes and looming forms, knowing nothing and only hoping that the light was where it should be.

Now, reaching under the dust ruffle of his bed, Jerry was a little boy again. A child crushed by the threat of the darkness, the promise of what it *held*. Mommy and Daddy had always told him there was no such thing as monsters... but they had never been sealed alive in the tomb of their own home. They had never been shut up tight in a place that had once been a castle but was now become a coffin.

Jerry felt sweat prickle on his brow, felt salt sting his eyes as he reached out. He still held the flashlight in his other hand, but the last thing he wanted to do was shine it under the bed. He didn't want to see those staring eyes, so large and accusing, so starkly white, couched in circles of raw red flesh that had had the skin pulled away in thin strips.

He touched something under the bed. Something rough. He couldn't figure what it was at first, then felt it move.

"Ah, ah, ahah*ahah*!" he shouted, and shoved back.

"What is it?" shouted Sheri. She moved to him. Drew came, too. Only Ann stayed back.

Jerry rubbed his hand against his shirt, against the floor. Trying to get the tiny touches to stop prickling against it.

"Ants," he said.

Sheri gasped, and Drew made a strange sound that was half gag, half hiccup. Jerry felt like throwing up, too. But he couldn't. They had to get out.

He pushed his hand back under. The moving carpet of insect life had been invisible under the quick flare of light they had seen the man with before, but now each scavenger felt huge under Jerry's fingers, the size of a cockroach as his hand quested over the unnamed corpse's clothing, to his neck.

Wetness. The ants were thinner here, but the wetness was worse. It felt like banana peel, and Jerry felt his muscles lock. He tried to convince himself it was just like any other surgery, just the feel of moist flesh under his hand.

But that's not true, is it. This isn't a patient. This is a murdered man under your bed.

He shuddered. Felt a damp knot of slime that he knew must be the putrefying remains of the cadaver's flayed skin, peeled back from his face. His fingers pulled back again, but he forced them to return. Back to the cool wetness, to their search for the phone. He tried to think of what he was feeling in clinical terms.

Sternal head. Scalene muscles?

Flesh of the neck. Wet and red and cold and dead.

Masseter.

Cheek. Flayed and tissue thin. Peeled back from teeth that grimace in a fleshless smile.

Then he felt it. The welcomingly inorganic angles of the phone beneath his fingers. He pulled.

It didn't come out.

Jerry heard a noise, a sound that was half sigh, half sob. He opened his eyes – realizing only when he did that they were so tightly shut he had a throbbing headache – and looked around.

Ann, Drew, and Sheri all looked at him. Close-mouthed, silent as terra cotta warriors. He realized the sound had come from him.

He pulled on the phone again. Harder this time. It still didn't come. He twisted, yanking the thing back and forth.

A rasping slide whispered out from under the bed: the sound of a corpse being pulled along by the phone clamped in its jaws, like a strange fish caught by an even stranger lure.

A part of Jerry's mind, perhaps insane – or perhaps the only remaining *sane* part of his brain – whispered that it was appropriate. That a shiny cell phone was exactly the perfect lure to fish for and capture a man. He could almost hear Drew commenting on it. Drew, with his teenage certainty about the evils of corporate impingements on everyday life, the horrors of technological dehumanization.

He laughed. The sound was sick and wet.

Sick as an ant-covered shoulder. Wet as a flayed face.

Jerry felt vomit bubbling at the back of his throat. He threw back his head and cried out. Twisted again.

A pop sounded from beneath the bed. He suspected he had just dislocated the dead man's jaw; had just widened the body's already immense smile.

But the cell phone came out.

Something came with it. A gout of liquid. Jerry cried out, thinking it was blood. But then a wave of foul air rolled out from under the bed.

Drew put his hand over his face. "Gah, what is that?" he said. Sheri's face scrunched up as well.

Ann remained impassive, as though she wasn't even in the room.

Jerry didn't answer. Didn't tell the kids that they were in all likelihood smelling the partially-digested remains of the dead man's last meal, knocked loose by Jerry's struggle with the phone and by internal gas buildup. He just wiped his hand and arm on the carpet, and then pulled himself out from under the bed and brandished his prize as proudly as King Arthur holding aloft the sword pulled from the stone.

He had their means of escape. He had the dead man's phone.

53

The moment of triumph lasted forever. Forever, and at the same time no time at all.

Just like life, Jerry thought in that moment, that bright spot in the darkness that had pulled them into its deep maw. The good moments should last forever, and somehow they feel like they do. But then you blink and they're over.

He thought of Brian. Of his son, floating.

Then he brought the phone down. He hit the "9" key. The others lit up as he did, and Sheri muttered, "*Yes,*" at the sign of the phone's functionality. "1" was next.

And the phone rang. That damn song. That song that matched the one on his wife's own secret phone. "I Will Always Love You."

He glared at Ann, like the song was her fault.

She wasn't looking at him. Wasn't looking at anything. Just stared into space.

Jerry thumbed the red button in the corner of the phone's keypad that would ignore the call. As he did he remembered that Whitney Houston hadn't actually written the song. Nor had she been the first to sing it. She had just been the most recent singer to remix the ballad into a hit. He also remembered that Whitney Houston was dead. Died when she OD'd on drugs and drowned in her hotel bathtub. The thought sent a shiver down Jerry's back, a quick shock of frozen electricity that ran from the nape of his neck to his buttocks.

He started calling the cops again.

And again the phone started ringing. "I Will Always Love You."

He glanced at the caller ID. "BLOCKED NUMBER."

He hit ignore. Started calling 9-1-1.

The song started once more.

"Call the cops," someone shouted. It was Drew, but his voice was so high and crackling it could almost have been Sheri speaking.

"I can't while it's ringing," said Jerry. Or better said, he shouted it, his own voice rising more than a notch or two.

He kept hitting ignore, kept trying to get a call out. But it wasn't working.

And after a few more tries, almost of its own accord his finger hit the green button, accepting the call. He held the phone to his ear.

"Hello, Jerry," said the Killer. As before, his voice was electronically shifted, warped and modified to something less than human. But at the same time, Jerry suspected that this was the real sound of the man's heart: alien and ugly. "Put your wife on the line."

"Who is this?" said Jerry. He tried to sound brash and strong. And tried to ignore the quaver in his voice when he failed. "You let us out right now, or so help me I'll –"

"*NOW!*" shrieked the Killer. The single word came out so loudly that Jerry shouted as well, and almost dropped the phone. The word was a window: a clear view into the madness that held them. For an instant it was as though Jerry could read the book of the Killer's mind, and in that moment he teetered on the edge of insanity himself.

He walked to Ann, feeling wobbly and only partially in control of his actions. With every step what little sense of control he had maintained fell farther away.

We're never getting out of here.

He looked at Ann. At her gaze into nowhere. He wondered what she could possibly be thinking of at a time like this.

The man under the bed.

The thought came like a crash of thunder that split his mind still further. Despair and hopelessness were now joined by rage. It was her fault. It was all her fault. It had to be.

Had to be.

He jammed the phone against her cheek, smearing the blood and gore of a dead man against her face as he did so. And as soon as he did the Killer's voice rang out, again clear and loud enough that Jerry could hear it, though he doubted Sheri or Drew could.

"I left your phone with enough juice to make a call after talking to me," said the warped voice of the Killer. "Just one call. You could have called 9-1-1 and been done with this. But you didn't call 9-1-1. You didn't choose your family, you chose your *secrets*. You chose the man under the bed. And the result? Your phone is dead." There was a stretch of silence. A moment of deathly quiet long enough that Jerry wondered if the Killer was done. But then their captor spoke again. Four more words that felt like a knife to the gut, twisted and pulled back and forth for maximum effect:

"And so is his."

And with that, the phone Jerry was holding made a sound like a cap gun going off. Ann jerked her head away with a cry, and Jerry saw a curl of black smoke writhe through the air, a dark curve that dissipated almost instantly but left behind an acrid smell that made him wrinkle his nose.

A moment later another sharp sound, the twin of the one that had just issued from the cell phone, came from the other end of the room. Something flashed in the darkness, and Jerry realized that was where he had thrown the first phone, Ann's secret cell phone. So whatever had just happened was happening to both of the phones.

He looked down at the phone he still held, the phone of the dead man. The LED screen was dark, and a large crack ran down its center. Smoke still curled up from the edges of the phone's seam, and parts of the plastic looked melted.

An explosive, he realized. And also realized that if the Killer had wanted, he could have been looking at the stump of his arm instead of the broken phone right now.

"Dammit," he whispered.

He hurled the cell at the wall. It broke into four pieces.

"What now? What now?" Sheri was saying. "What now? What now?" She whispered the words over and over, a litany repeated to whatever god might reach into the abyss of their damnation.

Drew had his hands over his eyes. "This isn't happening," he said. Tears shone on his cheeks and Jerry was transported to the days when his little boy would run behind the couch and giggle, secure in the knowledge that if he couldn't see Daddy, Daddy couldn't see him. But he knew that whatever was happening to them would come for his son whether his son watched or not. Whether his son *saw* or not.

He turned, finally, to Ann. And as he did so the fury he had felt before rose up again.

This is her fault.

No, that's ridiculous. What did she do?

What did she do? *Who's under the bed?*

You think that's what did it?

Her fault.

Come on, Jer-Jer –

HER FAULT.

Ann looked at Jerry. He could see terror in her eyes. And guilt, shame for what she had just done. The Killer had been right: she could have gotten them out. She could have saved them. But she killed them instead.

"Who's under the bed?" Jerry said. His voice rasped out, snake scales across a bed of jagged rocks. "Why did you call him, Ann? Why in God's name did you call him? *WHY DID YOU CALL HIM*?"

Ann started to cry.

Jerry looked at her and for the first time he could remember, he didn't see his wife; didn't even see the memory of her. He didn't know *what* he saw. And didn't care.

He turned away from Ann, from the stranger in his bedroom, and walked out of the room alone.

54

"Dad!

"Where are you going?"

Sheri's and Drew's cries followed Jerry out of the bedroom as he stomped into the hall, moving like a Sherman tank toward the stairs. He didn't stop. Wouldn't stop. The anger had him right now, and if he let it release him all that would remain would be the terror that he could feel pressing at him. Pushing him. Forcing him back.

He kept walking. A moment later he heard the light sounds of his kids' shoes as they sprinted after him. He had known they would –

That's a lie, Jer-Jer. If you knew they would follow you, why are your shoulders unkinking, why are you letting out that breath you've been holding?

– but he still didn't stop walking. Nor did he stop when he heard a third set of footsteps. Ann. No, he *especially* wouldn't stop for her. Not now, perhaps not ever again. You stopped for family, you helped your friends. But Ann was neither of those things. Not anymore.

Halfway down the stairs now. The bright circle at the center of the flashlight beam bounced on the stairs before him as he moved at a pace that was nearly a jog.

Easy. Don't want to break an ankle.

But he didn't slow down. Couldn't. For the same reason he couldn't let go of the anger. Movement was survival. The one thing every dead man and woman had in common was this: they all were still.

He had to move.

A hand touched his shoulder. "Daddy," said Sheri, "What are you doing?"

"I'm going to the garage," he said, biting off each word. Almost off the stairs. "I'm going to my tools."

He was in the hall now. He turned toward the shattered remnants of the garage door, the still-open frame beckoning. "I'm going to get my skill saw, and I'm going to cut a big hole through the wall."

"What do you –"

That was Drew. Jerry cut him off. He stepped over the remains of the door. Into the garage. Darkness, broken only by his flashlight, which glinted off the cars' chrome and the waxed floor. "And after I cut the hole in the wall," said Jerry, "I'm going to get the hell out of here because *I'M DONE PLAYING THIS GAME!*"

He screamed the last. Shouted it at the ceiling, hoping that the Killer heard him. Hoping that the sonofabitch heard and knew: he had lost. Jerry was leaving. They were *all* leaving.

Jerry got to the tool closet. He pulled the latch open. Yanked the door back.

And in the instant before the scream tore loose from his throat, he knew the Killer *had* heard. That the Killer was everywhere and knew everything. He knew, but did not care. He was a dark God who could not be beaten, a creature with all power, holding fate in his merciless hands. A deity who existed only to destroy, to maim, to kill.

Jerry screamed at what he saw. Screamed, and heard the children and Ann scream, too, a profane hymn sung not to the heavens, but to the darkest pit of Hell.

The Killer had won again. He had known they would try this, just as he had known everything else.

He knew everything.

Everything.

55

The tools were gone. Gone, but the tool board that had once housed enough tools to start a small hardware store was not empty. No, far from it.

The screams petered out, but even the silence seemed to shriek, the nothing-sound battering at Jerry's ears until he wanted to curl into a ball and put his hands over his eyes and disappear.

But he didn't. He couldn't. He was locked into place, the silence battering at him, his flashlight pointed at the grotesque sight that had greeted them when he opened his tool board.

Rosa.

The maid hung from the board, and Jerry could see what looked like thick loops of copper wiring wrapped tightly around her wrists and ankles, suspending her above the floor in a crucifixion pose. The wires bit deep – some of them disappearing into her flesh completely for an inch or more before resurfacing like some strange sea serpent in an ocean of flesh – testament to the fact that they were all that held the woman aloft. Blood caked the wounds in lumps that seemed black and insectile in the darkness, as if the body had vomited forth scavengers to devour itself in death.

Her chin tilted up. Far – too far. It was at an angle that only someone in severe traction or perhaps a professional sword swallower could have achieved, and Jerry saw why a moment after he registered the fact that her face was partially covered.

"Dad, what's that on her face?" asked Sheri in a voice that shook so much she was almost incomprehensible. Then she apparently realized what she was looking it, for she began screaming again.

The ladle. The one that Ann had said Rosa tried to steal on the night this horror all began. It was jammed down Rosa's throat, the stem of the ladle pushed completely down her throat and straightening it beyond human capacity. Only the bowl remained outside of her mouth, partially covering it and her nose like a futuristic mask that might protect her from anything but itself.

Rosa's eyes could not be seen. She was too high up. But rivulets of blood ran in thin streams down her temples and into her sodden hair, and Jerry suspected that if he were to climb up on a ladder to look, he would see only empty and ragged pits where her brown eyes had once been. As though she had looked upon a deity of fearsome darkness, and like the people of the Old Testament, she could not be suffered to look upon her god and live.

"What is that?" said Drew.

Jerry looked at his son. Drew looked pale, whiter than Jerry had yet seen him, and so fragile. Jerry wondered how much of this kind of thing a person could put up with before their heart would simply stop, before they would just crumple or blow away like a dandelion seed in a hurricane.

Drew was pointing at something. Jerry followed his son's gesture and saw that blood had pooled below Rosa's wired feet. The blood was black and brown, mostly congealed into a scabbed mass that looked worse than a wet red pool would have.

Something – the thing Drew was pointing at – was in the center.

"What is it?" Drew said again.

"I don't –" began Jerry.

He looked closer. He twitched, and knew he was in shock. *Don't look at that, get the hell out of here!*

Where you gonna run, Jer-Jer?

He leaned closer. It was a white and gray rectangle, maybe six inches to a side. Looked like it had been dropped in the blood, or perhaps dropped on the garage floor when the blood began to flow. Either way, there were streaks of brown-black-red crusted across it.

Jerry leaned still closer.

What the hell are you doing?

I have to know.

You already *know.*

And he did. But he had to look. Had to see. In this place of darkness, he couldn't stand to be blind.

He saw.

It was a photograph. Blood-streaked, gore-covered, but he could make it out, could make out enough. It was a beautiful woman, barely more than a girl. She looked to be in her mid-twenties –

Twenty-three, in fact.

– and was very clearly pregnant.

Third trimester, Jer-Jer.

Jerry was almost kneeling before Rosa, like a penitent before a dark Christus, a statue of rent flesh and flowing blood rather than cool, comforting marble. Now, looking at the picture, he felt his balance leave him. He reeled, the world spinning around, and almost fell forward. He put his hand down, barely avoiding putting it in the middle of the blood, dropping the photo into the gore, then pushed himself away.

He was no longer aiming the flashlight and the beam whirled in the dark garage. A light that spun without rhyme or reason and turned already-fearful into still greater terror. He saw Drew and Sheri, terrified at his reaction.

He saw Ann, and her face bore an expression for the first time since they had left the master bedroom. Her eyes drew together, twin pits of darkness. She had been distant, hiding from her guilt in some kind of shell she had put up in her mind. Now....

Hands came under his armpits, steadying Jerry. "What is it?" said Drew. The boy – the young man – helped his father up.

"Who's that woman, Dad?" said Sheri.

Jerry thought about denying he knew who she was.

They won't believe you, Jer-Jer. This was going to happen someday. You always knew it would.

"Yeah, *honey,*" said Ann. "Who is that woman?"

Jerry stared at her. He couldn't believe the expression on her face. The rage, the *betrayal*. As though it wasn't her who had been cheating on *him*. As though it wasn't her who had brought a man into their home. As though it wasn't her who had *killed them all* by calling her lover. She was accusing *him*?

It's the nature of people who are guilty to find others with blame. It's the nature of humanity, all of us fallen and evil to some degree, that we seek a sinner upon whom we may cast the stones otherwise destined for us. Jerry knew that. But still, to feel it directed against him like this....

"Who is she?" Ann demanded.

Jerry felt... *away*. Like he was viewing all this on a closed-circuit TV camera. Like he was watching this the way the Killer must be watching it, close but outside of things. Someone who knew everything that was happening, but perhaps didn't truly *understand* any of it.

"I... I don't know what's happening," he said. His mind felt fuzzy, like the gaps between the axons in his brain had expanded, inhibiting his thinking. He looked at the picture –

Don't lie, Jer-Jer, you know what that is.

But how did it get here? *What's going on?*

– and then back at Ann in a motion that seemed to take years. She had her arms folded across her chest now, her eyes almost flashing in the darkness.

"You don't know what's happening?" she said. "Isn't *that* an easy answer." She paused, then spat, "Just the way you like." The fire went out of her eyes, and now they were flat and soulless as those of a serpent about to strike. "Do you think we're stupid? That we can't guess?" She looked at him. Waiting. Then screamed, "Answer me!"

The noise echoed through the garage, and in his mind Jerry heard the creaking of the wires that bound Rosa's wrists to the tool board. Heard her dead flesh struggling against them as she strove to rise in the darkness.

He turned the flashlight on the maid. She didn't move. The bowl of the silver ladle flashed brightly in the permanent midnight of the house.

The ladle....

A horrible thought struck Jerry. Too horrible to be true.

And yet what was this night, if not just that?

The ladle shone as it reflected Jerry's flashlight beam. He started to shake.

Too horrible. Too horrible.

And yet....

56

Ann was screaming at him. Screaming *now,* screaming *then.* In the *now* she was screaming at him to answer, to speak to her, to answer damn it because she deserved that much so *answer.* In the *then* she was screaming about the maid, about Rosa stealing and about the ladle.

The *now* faded from Jerry's consciousness.

Only *then.* "I shoulda jammed this thing down her throat," Ann screamed, waving the ladle around in the kitchen while she raved at a level that frightened Jerry.

Back to the *now.* Ann was still screaming, but he wasn't listening. He looked at the ladle, the bowl covering poor Rosa's face like some strange offering to Charon as passage to the underworld.

"It happened," he muttered. He felt the words fall into cracks between Ann's shouted questions and epithets and demands, into a silent moment where they could be heard.

Ann quieted. He turned to her. "It happened just like you said. Like you threatened."

Ann blinked, visibly taken aback. She clearly didn't know what he meant by that, and Jerry wasn't sure himself. He didn't mean Ann had anything to do with this... did he? No. That was nonsense.

"Don't change the subject," Ann finally growled. "Who *is that woman*?"

Jerry felt the world snap back to full speed, and with it came rage. "Why should I tell you?" He stood, and moved to

Ann, looming over her. "Why should you be the only one in the family allowed to have secrets?"

Ann shrank away from him, which surprised Jerry, until he realized that he was holding the flashlight above her.

Like a club.

Jerry lowered it. Ann's lip trembled, though whether from a return of the feelings of guilt she must be feeling or from fear he couldn't tell. And he didn't much care, either. The anger had fled as fast as it came, and now he felt strangely numb.

He turned his back on Ann. "Why should you have secrets?" he mumbled again.

And because he turned when he said it, he saw what happened next.

Drew and Sheri had pulled closed to one another as though lashed together by a shrinking noose of terror. They had been watching their parents, Jerry was sure, but when he said, "secrets," they stopped looking at Ann and Jerry.

Instead, the teens looked at each other. A silent communication passed between them and a new kind of fear dropped over their gazes. Not replacing the fear they already felt, but rather adding to it.

"Secrets," said Drew. He said it so quietly it was less than a whisper. But Jerry heard it. Or maybe he just read his son's lips in the shaking beam of the flashlight.

Sheri's face bunched up. Concern. Fear. Other emotions that Jerry couldn't read.

And then Drew darted forward. Whatever was happening was strong enough to cut the noose that held him close to Sheri. The teen threw himself at Jerry, so fast that he thought his son was going to attack him.

Drew didn't have mayhem in mind. Jerry felt his son's touch, and though a bit violent it was far from vicious. Drew moved faster than Jerry had ever seen his son move before, yanking the flashlight out of his father's grip and then running out of the garage before Jerry had time to more than half-register that his son was gone.

In the next moment he felt a blast of cool air in the now complete darkness of the garage. Sheri. She was running, too.

His children were going back into the house.

57

It seemed like a fully minute, but it couldn't have been more than a half a second before Jerry coaxed his feet into movement. Then he was after them, following the bouncing – and rapidly diminishing – light that signaled his son's location. He heard the thud of footsteps behind him and knew Ann had taken up chase as well.

A silhouette in front of him. Sheri. Running up the stairs. He followed.

Second floor. Hall.

Where was Sheri? Drew? Jerry felt panic draw tightly around his heart, compressing it down to what felt like a tenth of its normal size, before he realized that Sheri was standing in Drew's doorway.

He joined her there. Ann was behind him, he knew. He could feel her, and suddenly realized that he was more aware of his wife than he could remember being. Ironic that the affection might die just when attention began to be paid again.

Jerry looked into his son's room. "What's going on?" he said.

Sheri ignored him. She was sweating, terror etching lines on her face that didn't belong there, making her look much older than her years. "Hurry," she stage-whispered.

Drew ignored both of them. He was rifling through some of the drawers in his desk. Then, apparently finding nothing, he bent down. Jerry though he was going to open the bottom desk drawer, but Drew kept bending, kept reaching. The teen pried a loose floorboard up, revealing a void below, a black patch that was barely visible in the darkness that clutched them all.

"What's that?" said Ann from behind Jerry, and her voice sounded surprisingly normal and "Mom-like," just a shocked parent finding her son's secret stash. "What's in there?"

Drew aimed the flashlight down into the space. He put his hand into it, feeling around vainly.

"Well?" said Sheri.

Drew shook his head, rocking back on his heels as he almost moaned, "Nothing. Nothing. Whoever's doing this knows *everything about us*."

Sheri rushed into the room. She snatched the flashlight out of her brother's fingers, almost knocking him flat on his rear in the process, then shoved past Jerry and Ann.

"Where are *you* going?" said Ann. She still sounded oddly normal. Like she had finally defaulted to a mode beyond panic, past terror. As though her baseline reset was "Mom Mode," and she was now acting in the only way her programming permitted.

Sheri didn't answer. But Jerry knew where she was going.

Of course he did.

58

Sheri tore between Ann and Jerry, then took a quick few steps through the hall, past the bathroom door, then to her own room. Just as Jerry had known she would. Drew had gone to his stash, and part of Jerry had been waiting for Sheri to do the same.

Ann followed their daughter immediately. Jerry didn't want to split up the family – he knew he was in shock, and not in full command of his mental facilities, but even so he wasn't going to commit that classic bit of horror idiocy – so he darted into Drew's room and grabbed his son's collar, practically yanking his son with him as he followed after Ann.

Drew didn't make a sound. He looked like he was in a fugue.

Jerry got to Sheri's room just as his daughter was pulling a framed picture of some rock star away from her wall. Behind it, a section of the drywall had been hacked away, making a small hidey-hole.

It was empty.

"Oh, God," said Sheri, with the same moaning inflection Drew had just used a moment before. She looked at her brother. "Everyone's secrets," she said.

"What secrets?" said Jerry. He looked back and forth at the kids. They didn't speak. Neither did Ann when he turned to her. She just glared, dropping back to the defensive posture that she had taken ever since seeing the picture of the girl –

(*So clinical, Jer-Jer, like you don't know her*)

– frozen in blood at Rosa's feet.

"What was in your room, Drew?" asked Jerry.

"Personal stuff." Drew's voice was low, sliding into the darkness and disappearing.

"Like what?"

"Does it really matter right now?" said Drew. He lifted his chin and stared at Jerry, and his gaze was the mirror of Ann's. Anger masking guilt, guilt blanketing terror.

And what was below that? Was there anything? Or were they all just empty husks at their center?

Maybe the Killer *couldn't* kill them, Jerry thought suddenly. Maybe we're already dead.

"Tell me," he said to Drew. Drew was silent, defiant. "Tell me or I'll –"

"You'll what?" Drew laughed, and it was a sound wholly unlike the usual chuckling that characterized his son's merriment. The laugh was all hard edges and hollowness, the signal of a final attempt at self-defense; a last stand. "Ground me? Not let me go outside for a week?"

Jerry opened his mouth, though he didn't know what to say. The house, once his home, once his refuge, had become a place of terror and threat. His family had transformed to a group of strangers, alien and cold.

Then he didn't have to speak. Because the lights in the house, which had been dark for what seemed like days – months, *years* – suddenly flickered on.

Sheri gasped, and Ann put a hand over her mouth.

The lights went off. Then on again. Off. Then on. And they stayed on.

And then Jerry heard a sound he had heard before, had heard a million times. But he didn't recognize it, because it was a sound that belonged to the real world, not this halfway place of shadow and death. He looked around and saw the same confusion he felt reflected in the eyes of the others.

But then his feet moved. He took a step, then another. Then he was running, his body moving before his mind really realized what was happening, as though his muscles knew what was going on, recognized the noise jangling through the blackness the salvation it brought.

Jerry ran. Ran through the hall, down the stairs. He heard the others behind him, and saw the flashlight bobbing along on floor and walls close to him, though the houselights stayed on and made the flashlight unnecessary for the time being.

The sound came again. And this time Jerry recognized it, not just with his body but with his terror-soaked, fear-shocked mind. Sheri was saying something under her breath, and he realized what it was, and that she must know what the sound was, too: "Please, God, please, God, please, God, please, God...."

The sound came a third time, and they were almost to it. It was coming from the living room.

It was the phone. Ringing.

59

A moment later they were all standing in a rough semicircle around the phone. It was on the floor where it had been discarded, and it rang again as they watched.

The lights were still on, but darkness gnawed at Jerry. He had run here like his feet had known that the sound of the phone heralded deliverance. But now that he was here, he hesitated. Nothing had been as it seemed in this nightmare so far. The furniture had been pieces of wood held together only by the memory of what it once had been. The safety they had felt behind their gates and inside their walls had really been the false security felt by animals caged in a slaughter house.

The people he thought of as family were really just stangers, secret-keepers who happened to live near to one another.

So what of the phone?

Jerry could tell everyone else was thinking similar thoughts. Because the phone kept chirping like a computerized cicada, kept calling for their attention, kept crying for them to answer… and no one moved.

"I thought the line was dead," Sheri said.

The phone rang again as if to reply, but no one else spoke. Then it rang once more, and Drew stepped forward. He picked up the phone and hit the intercom/speaker button.

Silence. Then the sound of slow, measured breathing, rendered strange and threatening by the voice-altering hardware that the Killer was using.

Jerry felt like crying. Whatever hope he had been nurturing in the back of his mind that the phone had been calling in from the world outside this prison shriveled and died.

"Please," Drew said. A tear pushed its way down his cheek. "Please, let us go."

Breathing.

Then a single word: "Disappointments."

"Please," whispered Sheri, and she began to cry as well, "help us."

The lights in the house began flickering. Not the slow, almost languorous on-off-on-off that they had started with; they flashed so quickly it was almost painful, like an eon's worth of lightning compressed into this room, this instant.

He's angry, Jerry thought.

"What's your secret, Drew?" said the Killer, his words coming out slowly and evenly against the violent backdrop of the lightstorm.

Jerry looked at his son and knew that Ann and Sheri were doing the same. Drew backed away a step. "I don't... I don't know what you're talking about."

Breathing.

Breathing.

Drew looked at them all. At the phone.

"I'll kill you, Drew." The voice was still strange, altered, but Jerry got the feeling that the person behind it spoke these words happily. With a wide smile on his face.

Drew started crying. In earnest now, not a single tear but a flood of them pressing through eyes half-squeezed shut by guilt and fear.

"The house was so empty," he said. "It's always been so empty." His voice hitched and he sobbed. Jerry could see the violence of the night and the sour memories crashing on the teen almost visibly. He put an arm over his eyes, and Jerry couldn't tell if his son was wiping away the tears, or hiding from everyone's gaze.

There was a snap. Jerry turned around. The TV behind them had turned on, just as it had to show them that they were trapped in a termite-tented house. But this time it didn't show a close-circuit live view. The feed was grainy, but it was a recording.

The angle was strange, high up and cornered oddly, but Jerry could see that he was looking at his son's room. At his son. At Drew, with tubing around his arm, getting ready to inject himself with a hypodermic needle.

Jerry glanced at his son. He felt as though he'd been kicked in the stomach. A dull ache settled into the center of his body, the center of his soul. Drew? A drug addict?

A knock sounded from the television. On the screen, Drew sprang into action, wrapping all his paraphernalia into a tight bundle and then tossing it into the space below the loose floorboard beneath his desk. "Yeah?" he said as he put his gear away.

"It's me," came a voice from the television, and Jerry almost didn't recognize it as his own.

The onscreen Drew threw the loose board back into place, tamping it down, then whipped out a textbook and sat down at his desk. He opened his window and fanned fumes away before finally shouting, "Come on in!"

The camera angle didn't show the door to Drew's room, but there was the sound of a door opening, and then a moment later Jerry saw himself stepping into the room, standing beside his son, his perfect, good, innocent son.

"Hey, kid," Jerry heard himself say.

"Hey, Dad," the television Drew answered. "What's new?"

"Not much," said TV-Jerry, "just a long day of 'stickin' it to the man.' You?"

The dull throb at Jerry's center heightened; became an almost knifing pain. *This had just happened.* It had happened the night before all this began.

The Killer had been watching them. And Drew had been lying for… how long? Since Brian? Since before then?

He remembered looking at Ann's and Drew's arms in the bathroom while Sheri looked for her medicine. Ann had a needle track in the crook of her arm. So did Jerry for that matter. Drew, however… Drew's arm had been riddled with marks. Jerry had thought that whoever was doing this just placed bad IVs. But now he understood.

The TV turned off. Black and empty.

The phone clicked. No more breathing, no more nothing. Silence.

Jerry looked at Drew. So did Ann and Sheri.

The house lights flashed. Faster, faster, faster. Like they were racing to a place where light died, a place where time ended and all was nothing and nothing was all that mattered.

Drew was backing away from them. "What?" he said. Jerry thought he was trying to sound defiant, but instead he just sounded damaged. Broken. "Why are you looking at me like that?"

He backed away from them, step by step. A stranger among strangers. Framed by the dark hallway, the lights that came on and off transforming him into a range of shadows and light, a caricature of himself.

Then the lights slowed down as though exhausted. From onoffonoffonoffonoff to on-off-on-off-on-off to on off on off on off to on… off… on… off… on….

"STOP LOOKING AT ME LIKE THAT!"

… off…

… on…

And Ann shrieked.

"DREW!"

Because behind Drew, in the hall behind the teen… was someone else.

And the lights went off again.

60

Darkness is a funny thing, Jerry thought in the timeless forever between the end of Ann's scream and the moment the lights came on again. It covers us, and we fear what it conceals. Then it comes away, and all too often we find that the light is far, far worse.

There was a thud. A strangely wet sound, one familiar to Jerry but he couldn't place it before the lights came on again.

And everyone was standing where they had been only moments before. Ann and Sheri beside Jerry.

Drew, still framed in the hall. The dark shadow that had been behind him before now gone.

Jerry heard Ann heave a sigh of relief, and was almost surprised to hear it, almost surprised to hear evidence of caring that had survived the night.

Drew smiled at his mother, a lopsided smile that conveyed his own surprise to be standing after the lights turned on.

Then Drew held up a hand.

He touched his throat, and his lips puckered in confusion. His hand moved away, and Jerry saw it was stained red in the instant before a red line appeared on his son's throat.

The line only remained for an instant, an instant in which Jerry placed the wet noise he had heard, the familiar sound he now recognized from his own operating room as the sound of flesh being cut. Deeply. Then the red line disappeared in a gout of blood that geysered so far that Jerry knew there was nothing that could be done.

Drew fell.

Ann rushed to her son. Tried to catch him. Didn't make it. Drew crashed to the floor.

Sheri backed away from the hideous tableau, from the blood that was reaching crimson tendrils across the floor to her.

Jerry didn't move. He couldn't. This wasn't real. If he moved, he thought it might *become* real, but for now, as long as he stayed put, there was a chance it wasn't, there was a chance it was all a dream, a horrible dream –

"Drew!" screamed Ann. She clapped a hand on her son's throat, a hand that almost instantly disappeared under the flow of red.

"Oh, God," said Sheri, her eyes darting up/down/left/right as she tried to take in as much of her surroundings at once as possible. "He's inside. He's *inside* with us!"

"Help me!" Ann screamed. "Help me!"

Who's she screaming at? thought Jerry.

You.

Not me. I can't move. If I move it's real.

He'll die.

Jerry felt his feet move.

You've killed him.

He tried to ignore the voice – the voice of impending madness that sounded so very much like *his* voice – and ran to Drew. To his son. Two steps, and he was running through sodden carpet.

He knelt. Moved Ann's hand away and clamped his larger one over the gaping gash that separated one part of Drew's throat from the other. He tried to push the two halves together, knowing it was hopeless, knowing that there was nothing he could do and would have *been* nothing even if he had been in a fully equipped operating room rather than kneeling in the debris that had once been a living room in a locked-down home, but unable to stop himself, unable to stop trying to halt the bleeding, unable to stop looking at his son's eyes as the teen thrashed under his hands, as the blood pumped out fast and fast then slow and slower then slowest of all then nothing and Drew was still, too, his eyes looking up at nothing, seeing nothing in this house, seeing darkness in darkness, and there was nothing left of him but a shell, just like there was nothing left of Jerry but the shell of what he had once been.

Drew's feet twitched.

Jerry covered his son's blood-spattered face with his own blood-covered hand. Closed the boy's eyes.

Ann fell away from Drew's side, like his life had been a strange sort of gravity that had kept her clinging to him. As she fell she began weeping, and by the time she hit the floor her entire body was shaking with sobs.

Jerry reached out to touch her. But his hand stopped in mid-air. There was no wall between them, no unpassable crevasse. There was just too much time. Lack of care had become something tolerated, then expected. The norm, and then habit. The empty space between them had filled with secrets that were now more comfortable to bear than the affection they had once had.

Love doesn't die all at once, or in big steps, he thought. It dies in tiny pieces, with daily decisions that nip off bits of it like the edges of a living branch until you've cut away to the heart of the trunk and then that, too, is gone and there's nothing left.

He let his hand fall.

Just as well, a part of him thought. Your hand was bloody. Wouldn't want to get her shirt bloody, too, would you?

He knew it was ridiculous, but he took a strange comfort in the thought. He would keep her as clean as he could.

Jerry looked away from Ann. He couldn't spot Sheri, and a new panic attacked his terror-seized heart. Then he realized she wasn't where she had been because she had backed away from her brother –

(*her brother's* body, *not Drew, not anymore, just an empty costume that he used to wear*)

– as far as she could, pushing herself into the far corner of the living room, half crouched beside the sealed door to the backyard that might as well be another dimension. She was shaking, her face white. She looked like she wasn't seeing anything in the room, like the horror of what had just happened may have snapped something small but terribly important in her mind. He thought there was a good chance she would never return from wherever she had gone; that she might be the only member of the family who had found a way to escape the house, if only mentally. And having done so, she might not be able to find her way back *in*, even if that meant she floated forever in a pleasant space beyond reality's touch.

I've lost *all* my children, thought Jerry.

61

As if she had heard this thoughts, Sheri's eyes refocused the moment Jerry worried she might be gone for good. Refocused... and looked right at Drew, still laying as if afloat in a dark pool of twilight.

Jerry almost jerked at that, flinching at the realization that this was the second son he had seen like this, body afloat, to be found and fished out by family. At least this time they knew what had happened.

Small comfort that turned out to be.

His thoughts turned away from his son when Sheri started to shake. She looked eerily like Ann in that moment, both writhing with the pain of the loss they felt. The difference with Sheri, though, was that Jerry could still go to her.

He moved quickly, almost dancing over and around the debris and detritus that had once been the furnishings of their lives, jumping over to his daughter and grabbing her shoulders, forcing her eyes away from what lay behind him. "Don't look," he said. "Don't look, Princess."

"We're going to die," she whispered. He didn't think she was talking to him – or anyone in particular – and that added another layer to his fear. How far gone was Sheri? Her hand moved to her collar, and her breath hitched.

"Easy," he whispered. "Easy. We won't die, sweetie. I won't let anything happen to you." Her hand was rubbing her chest in circular patterns now, and the last time he had seen that happen, she had ended up in the hospital. He had to get her out of here. Had to get them all out of here.

"We're already dead," Sheri whispered.

"No, we're not."

"We are –"

"No –"

"Already –"

"No –"

" – dead –"

" – we're *not*."

Her hands tightened into fists, still at her chest. "We're *already DEAD, ALREADY DEAD!*"

Jerry reached out and touched her hands. He could feel heat pouring off her. She clenched further at his touch and he thought she might run off, might take flight into some other part of the house.

He held her hands. Kneaded them, slowly opened them from fists and turned them flat. "We're not dead," he whispered.

She looked at him, her eyes piercing, her terror insisting on hopelessness even as she asked for some hope. "Then what are we going to do?"

"I...." He looked for something. Some way out. Some way to escape this trap, this prison. "I don't know."

Ann was no longer sobbing. She was now crying more quietly, holding her motionless boy in her arms. "My baby," she wheezed. "My baby, my baby boy."

For some reason, the sight of her mother's despair was able to do what words of hope could not. Sheri stood up all the way, seeming to step out of herself as she stepped across the room to her mother. She held Ann. One of Ann's arms remained holding Drew, but the other left the cold comfort of her dead son to hold onto Sheri.

Jerry watched them, feeling glad that they found solace in each other, but also strangely jealous. His wife preferred the arms of a corpse to his own. His daughter would rather succor an adulterer than stay with a father who had remained faithful.

No, you can hardly play the guiltless card, Jer-Jer. Remember the girl. The pregnant girl.

He looked down the hall. Partly to make sure no one – say, a madman with a razor sharp knife – was sneaking up on them. Mostly to silence the voice in his mind. There was nothing. No movement in the still-lit corridor.

Sheri must have caught him looking and gotten spooked, because she drew away from Ann and looked down the hall as well. Still nothing.

Nothing. But the lights went out again. Darkness, broken only by the flashlight that lay on the floor near Drew. He had been holding it when he was killed. It must have rolled away.

Jerry reached for it, and his hands trembled. For some reason the fact that he was going to touch the flashlight that his son had been touching felt like conspiring to murder him. Like Drew might not really be dead, if only they didn't have to take the flashlight that he had been holding.

Jerry's hand closed around the flashlight. He turned it down the hallway, suddenly sure that the Killer would be there, would have come in the darkness, come for Sheri or Ann or him. And the panic he felt was wonderful, was *delicious,* because it freed him from the grief that had threatened to overwhelm him. It blanketed the sorrow, covered and hid it. Later he would feel it. But now, now the fear was almost welcome.

No one was in the hall. Just an endless well of perfect black, and then the flashlight beam illuminating a thin spear and leaving the rest in darkness that danced and writhed before his eyes.

The lights came back on. The shadows fled, but who knew for how long? Jerry left the flashlight on, and his grip tightened around the heavy metal cylinder.

Ann was still crying, still holding Drew. Jerry looked at her, then locked eyes with his daughter. Sheri nodded. She pulled gently at her mother. "Mom," she said. "Mom, we have to go."

Ann didn't answer.

"Mom, we can't just stay here." Sheri took her mother's arm and pulled on it gently. Ann wrenched it away, but wiped at her eyes and Jerry could see her visibly trying to pull herself together. She laid Drew down. Looked at him one last, long time. Then let Sheri draw her away, toward Jerry, as though seeking safety in numbers.

Yeah, right.

"What now?" asked Sheri.

"I told you, I don't know," said Jerry, and suddenly *he* was the one struggling to maintain control, struggling not to think of his boy – his dead boy – laying only a few feet away. "I don't know, *I don't know.*" He stopped speaking. Shut his mouth and ground his teeth together hard enough that he thought he heard a molar crack. "Why is this happening?" he finally whispered.

"The basement," Ann said.

The words were so quiet Jerry felt like he might have imagined them. "What?" he said.

"The basement," she repeated. "One way in, one way out. Supplies. We barricade ourselves in there. Wait until someone comes for us. Until someone comes to help."

As if to answer her plan, a creak sounded from somewhere upstairs. Jerry couldn't place it, not exactly. Fear and grief had stolen his ability to tell with any certainty.

"What if no one comes?" asked Sheri. The question that Jerry didn't want to hear, but the one that he knew everyone – even Ann, who had proposed their only plan of action – was thinking of.

So connected. Facebook. Twitter. Google Plus. A hundred other ways to stay in touch with a hundred thousand people you'll never see. But when the lines are cut, when the doors are shut… no one comes. The connections aren't real. The friends are a lie, the followers fade.

Almost as clear as if it was recorded in his mind, Jerry heard Drew saying, "Welcome to the twenty-first century."

The lights went out. But it was different this time. Where before they had extinguished all at once, the entire house falling instantly into darkness, now the darkness seemed to be moving from one end of the house to the other. Moving toward them in an expanding cylinder of darkness, a stygian serpent swallowing the universe from the inside out.

Click. The far hall fell dark.

Click. Upstairs bedrooms that had thrown cones of light into the hall only a moment before now grew cold and dim.

Click. Offices and media rooms disappeared into void.

And then Jerry thought he saw something. Just a spot in the darkness, the huge black eye of the serpent. Sheri gasped, and he knew she had seen it as well.

The Killer.

The lights flickered on and off, and then the patch was gone. The Killer was hidden. But still there.

Still coming for them.

"Dad," whispered Sheri.

"Go," he said. "Go, go."

No one moved. He thought Ann and Sheri might actually be petrified by panic. He had to lead.

He moved. Ran. Trusting that they would follow. Because they had to.

A moment later, he heard footsteps, running after him as he sprinted for the basement. Hiding, gone to ground and hoping. A pitiful plan, he knew.

But it was all he had. All any of them had.

62

He waits and watches and then he watches and waits. A time for everything, and everything in its time. Taking turns, because to do other would be chaos. Not everything can happen all at once. So he seals them in, then he shuts them down. One at a time, any who won't play the game properly.

"My turn," he says, in a voice so quiet it travels barely past the steady thump-thump-thump of his heart. Which is important. He has to be quiet, has to listen. That's the important thing about his turn, about *this* turn.

Listening. Listening in his small dark space.

He likes the darkness. He grew up in darkness, grew up in the black, spent enough time in it that he finally learned that it was – and always had been – his friend.

Sometimes he even closes his eyes when in the light, just to be closer to the dark. Because it is his friend. Because it reminds him of home. Of his life before he came outside, and found the world filled with madness and chaos and secrets and lies.

He stiffens. Sound. There was the sound of the voices, that had always been there. The three voices that were left, their words rising and falling and falling and rising like a symphony orchestrated by the greatest musical genius the world had ever known. Maybe that wasn't too far off.

He frowns. That thought smacks of hubris. He might have to beat himself for that later. Perfection is order, and order can never be achieved when one person steps ahead of another. All must be equal. All must know what their brothers know. No secrets, no differences.

Yes, a beating. But later.

Another sound. Footsteps. Running.

He tenses. This is it. His time. His turn.

He cracks open the door. Just a bit. Just enough to see the nothing beyond. All is darkness. And that is right. That is what he planned.

Then a quick ray of brightness chases away his friend the dark, pierces it like a needle, poisons it with flashes of quicksilver and pushes the black away.

He frowns. He considers taking the flashlight. But then he worries they might simply fall to pieces. It is a delicate line to be walked, trying to teach a lesson without having them tumble into madness.

The flash passes him, along with the heaviest footsteps. And then another set of footsteps.

And then he hears the third set. Light, quick. They can only belong to....

"Sheri," he breathes in that same sly voice.

The footsteps hitch, as though maybe their owner hears him, hears the name whispered in dark, or simply senses... *something*.

That is when he moves.

He is fast. He's always *been* fast. So fast his father joked he could outrun himself in a footrace. So when he throws open the closet door and grabs Sheri she doesn't have the chance to make a single sound. Silver needles of light from her still-running parents illuminate her terrified face, darning fear-lines across her beautiful forehead.

She can't scream. Can't even breathe, because he has a hand clasped over her mouth and her nose so hard he thinks he might have broken something. Her eyes roll back.

The light fades.

His friend the darkness comes and hides them both.

And with it, he disappears, his now-unconscious prize under his arm

63

Jerry hit the kitchen running, and the sound of his feet as they hit the tile floor made him feel like he was a pilgrim entering a promised land. He didn't realize how much he had pinned his hopes on Ann's plan to stay in the basement until that moment, but his heart skittered a few beats, then sped up as he ran to the basement door. He could hear Ann at his back. How long had it been since he felt her behind him – figuratively or literally? A long time. A long time, and it felt good to have her here.

He allowed himself to dare that they might make it. That Drew might be the last one to die.

And even as he thought it, he realized how dangerous the concept was. Realized that if his life had taught him anything, it was that prosperity brought suffering, that any promised improvement would hide threats and danger. Life was never a garden paradise, and anytime it seemed to be, it was time to walk carefully and check for hidden traps.

Even so, he reached for the basement door. Even so, he gripped the doorknob. Even so, he looked at Ann.

Even so, he was for some reason surprised that Sheri was not with them.

Ann saw it at the same moment. "Where's Sheri?" she asked. Her voice was low, absolutely no fear, no strain. Passionless to the point of sounding robotic, and Jerry knew she was close to breaking.

Jerry whipped the flashlight around the kitchen, even though he knew it was a useless gesture. What, did he think she'd run ahead of them somehow, and then chosen the world's worst moment to play hide-and-seek? Still, he couldn't help himself. Like a sense of hope wasn't just mental, it was built into humanity's bones and muscles, drilled into their DNA. He couldn't *help* but hope, no matter how futile it might be, no matter how much it might kill him when the hope turned to hopelessness.

"Princess?" he said. The shadows made in this room were worse than the rest of the house. The kitchen island seemed made to hide things. Perhaps his girl. Perhaps the Killer. And what about the pantry? The copious spaces under the sink and counters?

Ann didn't seem to suffer from the indecision that had suddenly cut off Jerry's will. She stepped toward the hall. Back where they had come.

"Sheri!" she shouted. And kept moving.

Jerry snapped out of the near-coma that held him. He almost jumped to Ann's side, grabbing her arm and jerking her back into the kitchen.

"Let go," Ann said. She batted at his hand. "Let me go!"

Jerry bore down harder, pulling his wife closer. "What are you going to do?" he demanded.

"Find her!"

"How? By running as fast as you can into the dark? Into who knows what kind of trap?"

Ann twisted and yanked at the same time, pulling herself away from him. He felt his nails scratch her skin and knew she was probably bleeding, but she didn't seem to notice or care.

"Coward." She practically spat the word at him.

Jerry shook his head. "Thinking before doing something stupid doesn't make me a coward."

Jerry flashed his light over Ann's shoulder, checking the hall to make sure no one was sneaking up on them. But he still saw her face, saw the rage and revulsion that now fought for exclusive control of her expression. "And saying you're 'thinking' is also a nice excuse, isn't it? An excuse to do nothing, see nothing, *feel nothing*." She paused, then seemed to shrink in on herself. Her hands went over her stomach, as though feeling for something that was gone. "No matter how many children you lose," she said, and she was looking over his shoulder now.

He knew what she was looking at. What picture, what face she stared at. And he suddenly wanted to hit something. Now this was about *Brian*? With all that was going on, she wanted to rub dirt in that old wound?

He raised the flashlight. She flinched, and that just made him angrier. He'd never hit her, so why did she get off –

"Come on in here, sexy."

63

Jerry froze. So did Ann. In fact, she looked positively stricken.

Jerry was confused. "That was...."

He turned around. There was a TV in this room, as in every room: a small eighteen-inch LED screen on the counter nearby. As he turned he heard a sound he knew well, even though he hadn't heard it in a long time: a low, throaty giggle. Ann. Laughing the way she did when they were....

The TV showed grainy video feed, the same way it had before, showing Drew shooting up. This time, though, it showed a recording of Jerry's own room. He felt something dark writhe inside him, something hidden and sleeping. Something he had known was there, but had ignored for a long time.

Now, it was moving. Awakening.

Onscreen, Ann appeared. She was dressed in the lingerie she had gotten dressed in for him last night – or rather, the night before they were drugged and all this started.

But what if she didn't *get dressed in it for you? What if she was wearing it the whole time?*

In the kitchen, Ann tried to pull him away. He shrugged her off.

And as if watching a synchronized twin, the Ann on the television also pulled at something. A hand. An arm.

The dark thing in Jerry rolled. Roiled.

Jerry felt his knees go weak. He recognized that arm. And the shoulder. He recognized everything on the man she was leading forward but the face, because that face had been pulled off the skull. But the body, the hair, the clothes... it was the man under the bed. The corpse that had held the cell phone in its teeth.

Onscreen, the man handed Ann a letter, wrapped in ribbon. She read it, then bent over seductively and dropped it in an open mahogany box. The box she had brought out from the closet.

Jerry was horrified, both at the sight of the box actually being used and at the view his wife – his *wife* – was presenting to some stranger.

Apparently the stranger didn't share Jerry's feelings. He attacked Ann, grabbing her and flinging her on the bed –

(*on my bed*)

– their passionate kisses muffled. Grabbing, groping.

Jerry felt the thing inside him roaring. But he was reeling. He didn't know what to do. He couldn't look at this anymore, but he couldn't look away, either. Because if he did, he might see Ann – the real Ann, the *here* Ann – and that would be far, far worse.

New sounds came out of the TV. Socrates. The family dog, still hale and energetic, barking at something. Ann jerked off her lover, sitting upright. "He's home," she said.

Her lover leapt to his feet, pulling his clothes back on. "I'll go out back."

Ann shook her head. "Sometimes he comes in that way."

"Where do I go?" said the man. Jerry could see him clearly. He wasn't particularly handsome. Just a man. A normal person. A normal person who was screwing his wife.

Onscreen, Ann pushed her lover –

(*good to admit it, Jer-Jer, good to say it, her lover, the man she chose over* you)

– under the bed. "Stay here for a minute," she said.

He resisted. "What? I've got to get *out* of here."

The onscreen Ann looked over her shoulder, as though afraid Jerry might burst in on them at any second. "We have a minute," she said. "I jammed the gate shut."

And now the black thing in Jerry *was* Jerry as he remembered; as he realized. The rake that had been rammed in the gate's mechanism. No accident. A stall. An escape tactic.

Onscreen, Ann kissed her lover, and a chill skittered up the darkness at Jerry's center as he realized that she was pushing the man under the bed in the exact position where the Killer later placed him. As though the Killer were avenging the infidelity. And Jerry wondered suddenly if he should be thanking their captor, at least for that.

The TV. Ann speaking: "When you hear me hollering, it'll be safe to go down the front stairs, out the front door. We'll be in the kitchen."

Another moment of black realization. Of dark memory. Ann screaming: "Bitch was *stealing* from us." Just part of the ruse. Jerry wondered if Rosa had even *been* stealing at all. Probably not. Nothing was true. Everything was a lie, so why not that?

The TV finally stopped running. It went black, and Jerry felt like a mortally wounded man, held up by what he had been seeing. Now it was gone he sagged. The darkness inside him reared up, but he felt curiously weak. Barely enough strength to look at her. To look at Ann. The woman he had thought was his wife; had thought he had known.

Ann backed away, her hands in front of her. She looked terrified, again as though he might hit her. "Honey, it wasn't what it looked like, it –"

Jerry felt strength flood his muscles. "It wasn't what it looks like?" he said. He laughed, a single bark of a laugh. He had thought people only said things like that in movies. Then he returned his eyes to her, and felt hatred pouring through his gaze. "In our house," he said, his voice low and almost deadly. "With our children down the hall –"

Then Ann stood up, fighting back, and he saw a year's worth of stored anger and grief finally finding egress. "Yes, in this house!" she shrieked. "This *tomb* you've made of our home, this wall you've built between us. Between you and me… between you and the kids."

That stopped Jerry's righteous rage in its tracks, faster than any attack by the Killer could have done. He stared at Ann, aware that she was far from being in the right, but just as aware that wherever she was, she had plenty of company.

He didn't know what to say. Now didn't seem like the time to tell her what had really begun the family's dissolution. Not the time to tell her that it hadn't begun with the Killer, or even with Brian.

He turned away.

Now was not the time.

Later. If there was a later.

64

Jerry began throwing open drawers, moving around the kitchen as he did so and quickly verifying that all held the same thing: practically nothing. A few spoons, but not much more. Certainly nothing to threaten a madman, nothing that could be used to reclaim his daughter, the only person he felt like he had left in the family.

"Shit," he muttered. He looked at the spot on the kitchen counter where a knife block had sat since they had lived in this house. It was empty. Of course. "Shit shit shit."

He felt something on his arm and jumped. Looked over and saw Ann. Her hand on his arm. Her face was tear-streaked, and there was something new in her eyes. Contrition? He wasn't sure. Didn't care. Sheri. Sheri was all that mattered. He tried to shake Ann's hand off his arm, but she held tight.

He wondered how differently this nightmare would have played out if she had held to him this tightly before.

That's neither here nor there, Jer-Jer.

He tried to shake her hand off once more. And once more she wouldn't budge. "Jerry," she whispered urgently. "Jerry, he's trying to get between us so we can't help Sheri, so we –"

"Shut up," he said. The words came out between gritted teeth. He opened the cabinets beneath the sink. Empty. Not even dish soap. "My daughter is out there, and I don't have time to deal with you right now, you two-faced…."

He stood up and walked away without finishing the sentence. Part of him whispered that was just because he had looked everywhere that weapons might be found. Time was ticking. They had to look for Sheri, prepared or not.

But the rest of him – most of him – knew the truth. Knew that he couldn't yell at Ann, or even get too angry at her for her betrayal. Because he had caused it. He had been the one who betrayed *her* first.

That girl, Jer-Jer. Just tell her about the girl in the picture.

No time. Gotta help Sheri.

He could almost believe it was true.

He walked out of the kitchen. Ann followed, her footsteps light behind him. He was glad to have her there, at his back. Glad as he hadn't been for a long time. She was watching, helping. There were problems, there were lies, but in this moment at least they had a single common purpose.

It felt good.

Jerry walked into the hall. It felt like the darkness had weight and presence, like he had to physically push against it in order to proceed. He wondered how many steps he would be able to take, how many feet he would be able to walk, before he just collapsed in exhaustion from the stress and strain of holding the darkness at bay.

You'll go as long as you have to. As long as it takes.

He thought he heard something. Glanced back at Ann. She looked askance at him; she clearly hadn't heard it.

He swung the flashlight back in front of them, realizing as he turned what the sound had been.

When Brian was born, he and Ann had been the typical, nervous first-time parents. They ran to him at every sound, at every cry. And after a while they both started hearing him cry even when he *wasn't* crying; when he was playing quietly or fast asleep. They laughed about it, about the "ghost cries" that were nothing more than the anxieties of new parents manifesting themselves in sounds that weren't really there.

Now, the ghost cries weren't of a baby that needed feeding or changing. They were of a daughter who was being tortured, maimed, raped... the list went on and on. His Princess, violated and demeaned and ripped apart

Ghost cries.

He heard another one as he completed his turn. And managed to ignore it, managed to recognize it for what it was.

I'm going crazy. Going mad in my own home.

But though he could ignore the sound that wasn't there, the face looking at him was real. The face that his flashlight found, looking at him in the darkness of the hall. No ghost cries.

Someone was with them.

65

Jerry's breath solidified within him. It felt like icicles, pricking at his lungs, scorching them and piercing them and filling them with blood so that he froze and burned and drowned at once.

The eyes that watched from the end of the hall didn't move.

"What is it?" whispered Ann.

Jerry almost jumped in place, and only that strange sensation that still clenched at his lungs kept him from screaming in terror. Instead a strange choking sound issued, and the flashlight – still aimed at those staring eyes – quavered in his hand.

Why isn't Ann scared? She has to see it.

Then he realized: there was no one else in the hall with them. The flashlight beam cut razor-thin shavings out of the darkness, almost useless as illumination in their near-mansion of a home. And it had illuminated nothing more than the staring eyes of a portrait, the subject of an expensive oil painting Ann had bought him for an anniversary five or six years ago.

Jerry felt the frozen/heated/drowning sensation leave him as he exhaled, trying to do so quietly but only half-succeeding.

"What is it?" said Ann. He shook his head, but she must have seen the flashlight beam still aimed at the portrait and intuited what had happened. She snorted under her breath, a sound that communicated perfectly her disgust at his weakness, his fear.

The great advantage of marriage is that you have someone who understands you. The great *dis*advantage of marriage is that you have someone who understands you. And even on the ropes as their marriage was, Ann knew his feelings, knew his terror, and obviously despised him for it.

It shouldn't have mattered. But it did. Shame writhed through Jerry, and he felt like he had failed his family anew. He swallowed and pressed forward. The dark didn't seem any lighter, but he pushed it back more easily somehow.

They reached the other end of the hall. He didn't know how to conduct a proficient room-to-room search – it wasn't like he was an ex-cop or a retired SEAL. He was a surgeon. A good surgeon, even a gifted surgeon, but his recon skills were lacking. So he was glad when Ann said, "One of us should keep watch on the hall while the other looks in here."

Jerry nodded. Then nodded again. And again Ann understood the meaning behind the gesture: "You or me?"

"I'll watch the hall," she said.

Jerry entered the room.

Ann was no longer right behind him, and he felt her absence starkly. He felt naked.

The room wasn't huge, but it was big enough to hide a thousand things. Easily big enough to hide Sheri… or the Killer.

He took a breath. And started to search.

66

So… much… *fun*.

The man watches from just far enough away that he is sure they can't see. He has to clap his hands over his mouth to keep from laughing.

They're looking in all the wrong places, in all the wrong ways. Which is typical. They haven't done anything right since this whole travesty started. He had real hopes for Drew, had real hopes that the boy would make it, but… not to be. It just wasn't Drew's *turn* to make it, that was all.

The man watches for a bit more, then withdraws. Jerry and Ann see themselves as the heroes, perhaps. Maybe they're still *that* deluded, in spite of all he's shown them. But they're not the heroes. The only hero in this fairy tale is *him*. He is the only One.

And now he's got a mendacious Princess waiting for his ministrations. After all: it's his turn, and he owes her his fullest attention.

67

The coat rack that scared Jerry so badly before was still there. And even though he knew it was just a coat rack, it seemed to have a demonic presence to it. He thrust his hand into the coats, just to be sure no one was hiding there, and fully expected something to bite him. Like they had stepped out of the world and into some outer ring of Hell.

And that wasn't too far off the truth, he supposed. The Killer was almost certainly a demon, if not the Devil himself.

He checked under and around Ann's sewing desk, the boxes and file cabinets that cluttered the room.

Nothing.

There was still the closet.

He pulled open the doors – French doors that opened with a slight squeak of hinges that sounded louder than a landmine going off. He looked at Ann automatically, as though the sound *must* have drawn the Killer – then realized that doing so left him totally vulnerable to attack by anyone in the closet, and whipped back around.

He felt dizzy. He needed eyes in the back of his head.

The closet was dark, even with the flashlight aimed at it. Full of coats and games and the clutter of life.

So much here, thought Jerry. And I can't remember the last time anyone used any of it. Why do we even have it? Why do we have this huge house for that matter?

He suddenly hated the life he had led. Hated not just his mistakes, but his successes. Because his successes had made this possible.

Could this have happened if we had lived in an apartment, two bedrooms? Cramped but happy? he wondered.

There was nothing behind the coats and clutter, just like there was nothing behind so much of what he owned, he was realizing.

He left the closet, and sensed movement to his left.

The curtains.

At first he thought automatically that they were just moving in the breeze. But how was that possible in a house that had its windows covered over in sheet metal and a bug tent?

Jerry crept to Ann. Touched her shoulder and pointed at the curtains that flitted like restless ghosts in the corner of the room.

She put a hand over her mouth, managing to keep her silence but obviously needing to make some show of her fear.

Jerry pointed at himself: "I'll check," the gesture said. She nodded. Understanding. Marriage.

Jerry geared up to move into the room again.

He reached for the curtains....

They still moved, just enough to accommodate someone breathing slowly, gently.....

He yanked the curtains apart, ready to beat whoever was there with the flashlight, ready to beat him until he told Jerry where his daughter was.

But it was nothing. An air conditioning vent on the floor, blowing cool air into the room, the draft moving the curtains.

Jerry relaxed. He felt strangely like laughing and weeping at the same time. Once again it reminded him of his children's infancy, when they would color on the walls or wreck the television or do something else that drew out his ire. And then in the next moment they smiled, or kissed him, or laughed that beautiful baby-laugh that sounded like a piece of Heaven given voice and his heart would swell with so much love it was almost too much to endure.

One of the hardest parts of being a father, he had found, was not the highs or the lows, but the fact that they came so close together. Sometimes he felt like his heart wouldn't be able to handle it.

He felt like that now. Laughing at his own foolishness, crying because his baby was still gone, still held by a madman, a murderer.

Then he realized: the curtains had been *open* before. They had been open in the whole house. So the Killer had been here. The question was simply when? Was it recently, or long ago? Was he playing with them again?

Jerry heard something. He glanced at Ann and saw she heard it as well. No ghost cries, this was something real.

There was something moving.

Something near.

68

Jerry couldn't figure out what the sound was. That scared him. But worse than that was the fact that he had no choice but to investigate. Another aspect of their new Hell: they had no personal volition. Couldn't leave, couldn't call out, couldn't turn on the lights. Now they couldn't even ignore strange noise: they had to find out what it was, because what if it was something awful happening to Sheri?

He had never realized what a blessing it was, simply to choose whether to ignore something or not. Simply to be able to turn on a light.

He and Ann reentered the hall, moving toward the noise. It was rhythmic, low then high then low again. It sounded like one of Jerry's tools –

(*another blessing, the ability to just go and get a tool and trust that it would be there instead of finding a dead body hanging in its place*)

– and that thought led inexorably to thoughts of his electric sander, his circular saw. He felt himself moving faster, fear mounting as he saw an image of Sheri, her flesh being pulled in moist patches off her body by a madman holding Jerry's own tools against her skin.

Ann kept pace with him, her hand on his back as though to let him know she was with him.

The sound was growing louder.

They were getting closer to it.

But that's not it. It's almost like it's *coming closer to* us.

Then Ann screamed as the sound burst into brightness, and something came into the hall.

This time it was Jerry's turn to be amused and a little disgusted. "It's the vacuum cleaner," he said.

The Roomba floor cleaner was what was making the noise. It was an automatic vacuum, a computerized disc about four inches tall and twelve inches in diameter that scooted around the downstairs rooms every night and cleaned up without needing much in the way of human oversight. It was just doing its job. Just cleaning.

He felt Ann bury her head in his back, felt it shaking. He moved to the Roomba and kicked it against the wall, some of his pent-up frustration and fear coming out in the form of this small violence against the appliance. The Roomba hit the wall and flipped over, a few bits of plastic exploding off it and disappearing into the darkness before it went silent.

Ann was sobbing.

"Just the vacuum," he said again.

At the same time, though, another sound could be heard. This one louder than the others, and there was no mistaking what it was. They had been walking around blindly, looking for their daughter without any clue as to how to go about doing so. Now an answer presented itself.

Because the whimper they heard, muffled and strangled thought it was, was definitely Sheri.

69

The whimper came again a second later. Louder. Loud enough that Jerry could tell where it was coming from: his office. They had walked right past it earlier. Would she have been there if they had looked?

No way to know.

He flitted down the hall as quickly as he could, Ann behind him, hoping against hope that the Killer didn't know they were coming. But at the same time he was aware that this was just one more choice that had been made for him, one more path that he was taking whether he wanted to or not.

Jerry flipped the flashlight to an overhead grip, holding it cop-style so he could use it as a club if need be.

Ann was still behind him. Her hand on his back.

They passed through the entryway, the foyer with the high ceiling that Jerry had once been so proud of. And why? He couldn't remember. It was just one more empty trapping.

Jerry heard another sound. Not in front of him. Above him. He wanted to ignore it. Sheri was in front. He and Ann had to get to her, he and Ann....

Where was Ann's hand? She had been touching him constantly. Where was her hand?

He turned.

Ann wasn't there. She wasn't *anywhere*.

Jerry flicked the flashlight upward, following the beam with his eyes, knowing somehow what he was going to see.

Ann's feet.

Ann's body

Hanging.

"Ann!"

He jumped up, trying to grab her. She was too high.

Ann started to kick.

"Ann!" Jerry screamed again, and ran to the stairs, taking them two and three at a time.

How could this have happened? he wondered as he ran, a portion of his brain seizing on the question as being of critical importance, even though the only real issue was whether he could get her down. And that same part of his brain knew that the noose must have been there, ready for them to pass by. The Killer waiting at the second floor, dropping the loop precisely as Ann passed under, then hauling her up so quickly and quietly that Jerry didn't even notice her absence at first. Not until –

Too late?

– that sound had alerted him.

He was on the second floor. Ann was kicking and squirming, her fingers working to get between the noose and her neck and clearly failing. And Jerry saw something tied to the banister ten feet away: a thick rope. It was tied to the balustrade, then looped over one of the exposed ceiling beams and then down it went to the noose that was rapidly choking the life out of his wife.

Jerry was there in an instant. He tried to untie it one-handed, but it was impossible. The knots were too thick, too tight.

He put down the flashlight, kept trying.

Ann was still kicking.

Jerry kept pulling at the rope. But now, though he had two hands to work with, he was basically working in complete darkness. And the rope was so… damn… *tight*.

He finally abandoned the knot and picked up the flashlight again. Started to hammer at the knot and banister with the flashlight, thinking – if what his panic-soaked mind was doing could be called thinking – that he would loosen one or the other.

Nothing.

He turned the flashlight on Ann. She was dying. Her face and lips blue, her eyes bulging and her tongue starting to protrude. Kicking, trying to get her fingers under the rope. Frantic, but even the level of frantic energy was lessening as the oxygen was cut off.

She abandoned the attempt to get the noose off and reached for Jerry. He reached out for her. Grasped only air. He leaned over the banister, forcing himself so far over that he was only inches away from overbalancing and falling.

Ann was still too far. Her fingers scraped the air only centimeters away from his own outstretched hands. He tried reaching with the flashlight, hoping that she would be able to grab it. Her fingers brushed it. Touched it more solidly.

The flashlight illuminated her face. He saw hope. He smiled at her. She couldn't have seen his face, not behind the flashlight, but she smiled back.

Then her eyes widened. Not in happiness, not due to lack of oxygen.

Fear.

Jerry, still leaning out over the railing, glanced back to see… the Killer!

It was just a shape, just a dark shadow in the hall behind, but there was no mistaking who it had to be.

Jerry shrieked and arched his back, trying to pull himself to a more solid position, but he had no time.

No time.

The Killer ran at him, and Jerry felt two strong hands seize his legs and flip them up. Over.

Jerry was weightless. His fingers, still outstretched, finally brushed Ann's hands.

Then the moment of zero-gravity ended.

Jerry fell. He fell forever. Fell and fell and fell, and finally hit bottom and was enveloped by the softest sense of silence he had ever known.

70

Jerry's eyes fluttered open and for a single, glorious moment he knew – *knew* – that it was all a dream.

Then that moment ended. Oddly enough it was the memory of the picture, the pregnant girl, that reminded him where he was and what was going on.

The house. Confined. Sealed with the family, like a premature tomb. Drew. Sheri. Ann –

He bolted up, sitting up though every bone and muscle in his body shrieked at the motion. He realized that he was somehow still holding onto the flashlight.

Unless the Killer *put* it in my hands, he thought. Unless it's part of the sick bastard's plan for me to have a flashlight.

That made sense: certainly everything else of use in the house had been either removed or destroyed.

Jerry shook his head. He was getting sidetracked. Concussion? Probably.

He looked at the flashlight. The bulb was still lit, though considerably weaker.

How long was I out?

How long was she hanging?

The last thought seemed to come from someone else, as though a psychic watcher had injected the idea into Jerry's mind, but with it a wave of panic seemed to wash away his confusion, leaving him in pain, in terror, but clear of mind.

He looked up.

Ann hung above him. She had lost a shoe in her struggles, and Jerry cast his light about and saw it a few feet away.

She was dead, there was no question. She wasn't moving, not even swaying.

She'd been dead for a while. A long time.

Just me, he thought. Me and Sheri.

Sheri....

He stood, holding onto the wall and the banister when his legs threatened to give out from under him. He felt his head, and his fingers touched hard, crusted matter that could only be blood. It felt like a shattered helmet all over his head. He must have bled copiously, and when he shined the flashlight at where he was laying, he saw the outline of his head and right shoulder in a coagulating puddle of blood.

He was no stranger to blood, but he suddenly felt nauseous. Another symptom of concussion, he knew. But he also knew that the Killer was hardly likely to call a timeout on whatever devious game he was playing in order to let Jerry seek medical attention, or even have some time to recuperate.

And sure enough, as soon as he thought that he heard that same sound, that same whimper that had drawn him and Ann down the hall in the first place.

He wondered if it was always the Killer's intention to murder Ann in the hall, or if he was simply going to kill whoever went second.

Jerry thought for a moment he was just wasting time thinking this, either because he was afraid to continue his search for Sheri or just because his concussed brain was incapable of concentrating on a single issue. Then he realized that no, it was far from a waste of a time. He had to figure out how this maniac ticked, didn't he? Had to figure out what was happening if there was any chance of getting his family through it.

What's left of my family.

The whimper came again. Louder, more urgent.

Jerry forced himself to stand up unaided. His daughter was all he had left.

He walked down the hall. The office was only twenty, thirty feet away, but it seemed to recede as he approached it, like he had suddenly found himself in the darkest part of Alice's Wonderland. A fantasyland where physics did not rule, where the darkness was king and if you took a single misstep… off with your head.

He felt something on his side and almost spun into it before he realized it was the wall. He had veered into it. Jerry pushed himself away and shook his head. A new surge of nausea came with the movement.

Don't turn your head like that again, Jer-Jer.

The sounds were coming from the office, louder and louder. And again Jerry knew that this had all been predetermined, that he was without volition, a puppet being operated by the hands of a dark puppet master.

But knowing this did not change anything. Did not change the fact that he had to get to the office. Had to open the door. Had to see.

Jerry waited until he was fairly sure the nausea had passed. Then moved as quietly as he could to the office. At least it wasn't moving away from him anymore. The door just stood in the jamb. Waiting.

He eased up to it. Reached out. Gripped the knob. Slowly. Didn't want to make a sound, not even shaking the knob in its own housing.

He turned the knob. Prayed for hinges that had been oiled.

Then pushed the door open.

71

The door swung open. Slowly, quietly.

Jerry had thought maybe he would rush in. If Sheri was there alone, he'd free her and they'd get out somehow. If the Killer was there with her, he'd rush the bastard, get the upper hand.

But of course, those were the actions of a *man*, not a puppet. Not a marionette with strings far too short for even the illusion of freedom.

So the door opened.

And Jerry stood.

After a moment, he stepped in, the flashlight held slack in his hand. He could feel his face rippling under the combined weight of the shock and horror he was feeling.

His desk had been pushed aside, leaving a large clear space in the center of his office.

An arena. Like the Roman circus.

In the middle of the space, Sheri stood on a short footstool. Her ankles were tied together, her hands bound behind her back. A rope went from her wrists to a heavy ceiling fan above her.

"Daddy," Sheri whispered.

And behind her: the Killer. He was holding a bulky flashlight that he had pointed straight at Jerry, so he wasn't much more than the outline he had been throughout everything that had already happened. But he was *here*. Not running, not attacking. Not killing. Just standing.

Though Jerry noticed at that moment that there was a glint in the Killer's free hand: a knife. Probably the one he had used to slit Drew's –

Don't go there.

Still, the thought pushed enough anger into Jerry's veins that he was able to take a reasonably straight step toward Sheri.

The Killer reached out. Pushed his knife against Sheri's upper arm, and she gasped as a trickle of blood appeared. Jerry froze.

"I've been watching you," the Killer said.

As he spoke, the TV in the office flicked on. Jerry heard clicks behind him and knew that, again, all the televisions in the house were coming to life. As though the Killer wanted to drive his message home not just to the family, but to the house itself.

The television in Jerry's office was medium-sized but big enough to clearly show hidden surveillance shots of the family. In the house. The shots were quick, cutting from shot to shot so fast Jerry barely got a sense of what he was seeing. But it was enough.

Drew playing video games in his room....

Sheri brushing her hair in her bathroom....

Ann talking on the phone....

Jerry reading a research book in his office....

And on and on and on. Scenes of weeks – months – of surveillance played in a disorienting series of flashes.

In the office, the Killer shifted his knife away from Sheri's arm, now pressing on her back with it. She tried to pull away from it, but could only move a few centimeters forward before her feet were hanging off the edge of the stool on which she stood. She groaned, and Jerry could see that as she shuffled away from the knife her arms were being pulled higher behind her. Too high. If she fell off the stool, the weight of her body plummeting could pull her shoulders right out of her sockets.

"Tell us about yourself, Sheri," said the Killer.

"Daddy?" said Sheri. She didn't know what to do, he could tell. Jerry moved toward her.

"Tell us, Sheri, or you won't like what happens."

She shook her head. Started to cry.

Jerry took another step toward her. His Princess. In the movies, things like this were shaken off, no big deal. In real life, he was looking at a truly devastating injury. If Sheri fell hard enough, she could be looking at years of surgeries and therapies before she could use her arms or shoulders again… and even then, they'd likely never be the same.

"Daddy?" Sheri whimpered. There was a wealth of meaning in the words. *Daddy save me, Daddy help me, Daddy are we going to get out of here, Daddy I'm afraid to die, oh Daddy.*

"It's okay, baby. It's okay. We'll be okay," said Jerry. Another thing no one told him about parenting: how much of it involved lying. *Yes, there is an Easter Bunny. Yes, Santa exists. Yes, I'm sure everyone will treat you wonderfully at the new school. Yes, the other kids will all like you.*

Yes, we'll get out of this alive. We'll be okay.

Still, he continued the lie. "We'll be okay. I promise, we'll get –"

The Killer moved, shifting behind the light he held.

The televisions all changed. And suddenly they no longer showed random flashes of the family's life. No, they showed something much more frightening.

And once again, Jerry felt a part of his universe pull apart and spin away as he watched the TV screen.

72

At first it was nothing unusual. Just another surveillance camera view of the house, this time of Sheri. She was in her room, seen from the back as she typed on her computer.

She spoke. "Come on, pervo. You want it, pay up."

The computer beeped. "Goddam right, payment approved," said the stranger on the screen, the girl masquerading as his daughter.

In the office, Jerry looked at Sheri, at his *real* daughter. She was crying. "Princess?" he said in confusion.

On the TV, Sheri adjusted a webcam attached to the top of the computer. A webcam Jerry couldn't remember seeing there before. Then, after adjusting it, Sheri stood. She was wearing a pink miniskirt. So short it was almost a belt. And then she started writhing and dancing in front of the webcam. Stripping.

Jerry remembered the headless girl, the stripper they saw on the computer when this all started, when they tried to use the internet, and again when they had first seen the video of the outside of their house. He remembered Sheri's face. The shock when she had first seen it.

Because it was *her*.

He looked at Sheri. His Princess? Doing… *this?*

He wasn't going to watch. Drugs, even infidelity were one thing, but he couldn't stand this.

Then there was a knocking at the door. Coming from the TV, and Jerry's already fallen stomach spiraled even lower.

On the TV, Sheri looked at the door in fright. "Hold on, I'm not dressed!" she called. She killed the computer screen, then quickly shoved her stripper outfit and the webcam in the hidey-hole behind the picture on her wall, then darted into her bed. She pulled the covers up around her neck. "Okay, it's safe."

And just as with Drew, just as with Ann, Jerry had to suffer through the realization that he was watching his daughter the night before this had all started. Which meant that either the Killer had waited for a night when lightning struck thrice and everyone was involved in their secret sins, their secret vices... or it was just something so normal, so literally *everyday* that he could have started any time and gotten the same result.

Jerry thought it was probably the latter.

"Hey, Princess," he heard his own voice say on the television. "Hitting the hay early?"

The Killer muted the scene, but allowed it to continue playing, forcing Jerry to bear silent witness to the rot that had crept into every room of his once-perfect dream.

The Killer leaned in close to Sheri, though still hidden behind her, still cloaked by the glare of his light. "Not a princess at all, are you?" he whispered. Sheri whimpered but didn't answer. The Killer moved, and must have pressed against her with the knife again, because she cried out and shuffled another millimeter forward on the stool, shrieking again as the strain on her arms increased. "*ARE YOU?*" shouted the Killer.

"I'm... not... a princes...," Sheri gasped between sobs.

The Killer moved again. Sheri swayed forward, clearly being pressed by the knife, but just as clearly having nowhere else to go. Literally at the end of her rope. She started screaming, not stopping this time as whatever infinitesimal slack that remained ran out and the pressure on her arms became both unending and unbearable.

Jerry watched dully. He didn't know what to do. He felt slow, stupid. He was suddenly catapulted back to the first year of his residency, a week he had been on call more days than he could remember, a day he suddenly found himself staring at a patient, a syringe in hand, weaving on his feet and no idea what he was supposed to do next. Too tired.

He wanted to lay down and sleep. Just sleep.

The Killer slashed Sheri across her arm, a long vertical cut. Blood flowed.

"Stop!" he shouted.

At that moment, as if waiting for his voice to trigger it, the TV screen changed. A new scene appeared. And Jerry's stomach clenched even as his bowels suddenly felt loose. Because there was only one more image, one more memory. The one he didn't know if he could handle. The one that would break him.

"No," he whispered.

73

The pool.

It was a silent green gem, its surface rippling in a gentle breeze that made moonlight dance across it, one of those moments where nothing could possibly be wrong with the world, nothing at all.

Nothing but the body. Face-down on the deck beside the pool, the body of a young man, a teenage boy.

"Brian," whispered Jerry. He wanted to hide his eyes, to look away, but he couldn't. He was paralyzed. Nothing existed in that moment but him and the vision of his long-gone son, like a ghost come to mock him from beyond.

He realized that his son was not the only one in the scene. There was someone else, standing in the foreground of the shot: the Killer. Still in shadows, Jerry couldn't make out his face, but it was him. Of course it was, who *else* would it be?

How long has he been watching us?

The Killer was staring at the body. And as he stared, blood started to seep from below it, a widening pool of darkness that ran along wood and concrete in lines and puddles until it dripped off Brian's feet which hung over the edge of the pool. The red blossomed in the green pool, reaching bright crimson tendrils out that trailed off into obscenely beautiful patterns in the water.

The Killer watched, then turned and walked away, gone from the scene, gone from the shot.

But not gone from the family's lives.

Jerry felt himself return to the office with an almost audible *snap*. Sheri was still screaming, moaning, crying, and he hardly noticed. He looked right past her, past the light being shined in his eyes, to the darkness where lived the Killer.

"It wasn't an accident?" he said.

The darkness said nothing. Jerry looked back at the screen. Back at the silence, at the rippling pool.

At the body.

He acted. Moved so fast it shocked him. "No!" he shrieked. Dropped his flashlight.

And threw himself at the Killer.

74

Jerry wasn't the only one shocked by his sudden movement: no one in the room was ready for it. Sherry's non-stop scream spiked in volume, and she shuffled backward on the stool at the same time.

He only noticed these items as superficial information, though, because he hit the Killer at that instant. The Killer wasn't expecting his sudden motion any more than was Sheri, and Jerry heard an "Oof" as he hit the man's mid-section.

He fully expected to go right through him, to find that the Killer was in fact a supernatural demon that would dematerialize when threatened, but the man was solid, and so was the knife arm that Jerry grabbed.

They both went down in a muddled pile. Jerry still couldn't really make out the man's features; it was as though darkness clung to him like a second skin. But that didn't matter. All that mattered was the knife.

The Killer's flashlight went flying, spinning into a corner of the room, sending wild shadows everywhere, like a visual counterpoint to Sheri's screams. Jerry felt suddenly like he was in some insane version of a dance club, a place where the damned might dance to siren songs of the suffering, might writhe to the sweet strains of death come a-calling.

Then the Killer was suddenly on top of him, and all thoughts were of survival. The knife bore down on him, a glittering scythe emerging from the darkness.

The Killer was silent.

Jerry's knee went up, almost a spastic movement, certainly not a result of training or practice. Regardless, though, the Killer seemed to crumple in on himself, and then *Jerry* was on top, and had the knife. He pushed down with it. Bore down on the Killer, on the man who had taken his family, his home, even his *illusions*.

Everything.

He was going to kill him. He was going to kill the man without even seeing his face. Pushing the knife into the darkness, aiming by feel, slaying the demon.

Then the Killer moved. Jerry angled his hips away reflexively, thinking the other man might be mimicking his groin shot, but there was no danger of that. No, the Killer wasn't even trying to touch him.

There was a solid thud. Then a scream that made the others pale in comparison.

Jerry looked over. Saw, in the pale light of the TV, in the spinning glare of the flashlight, the shaking form of Sheri. His once-Princess, his daughter.

The Killer had kicked the stool out from under her.

75

Sheri's screams ended, and Jerry took this as a bad sign: she must be in too much pain even to breath.

He looked at Sheri for the barest fraction of a second. Just long enough to process what was happening. The next fraction was dedicated to wondering if he had long enough to kill the bastard below him before his daughter's arms ripped out of their sockets… and in the next fraction of a second he found himself reeling, a white-hot pain in his head.

He rolled across the floor, wondering what had happened, realizing at the same moment what it was: the Killer had used his distraction to good effect. The man had grabbed *Jerry's* flashlight from where he dropped it and used it to brain him.

The Killer was up in an instant, running out the door even as Jerry struggled to his feet, the room spinning around him. Part of him wondered how much more of this kind of punishment he could take – the general stress of the situation, plummeting over the second floor balustrade, being hit by the flashlight.

The answer came immediately: *You'll take as much as you can. And then you'll die. So if you're not dying now, get the hell up, Jer-Jer.*

There was a ringing in his ears. A moment later he realized that it wasn't ringing, but screaming. He turned slowly. Saw something blurry that he didn't recognize. Blinked.

Sheri.

He hurried to her. She was screaming again, her arms pulled up unnaturally behind her. He reached for her.

And stopped.

Saw again, the image of her bumping and grinding in front of the computer.

It wasn't that he thought she should suffer. Wasn't that he wanted her to be in pain. He was just seized by the sudden certainty that this wasn't her. It couldn't be Sheri. Not his Princess. This must be an impostor.

She screamed again.

He shook his head again. Reached for her. As with the Killer, he almost expected her to puff away to nothing, a succubus come not to assault him sexually but mentally, to batter away the last of his internal walls and leave him a shadow of himself, good for nothing but an asylum.

If you're not in one already, Jer-Jer.

But no, she was whole. Solid. He lifted her up high enough that the strain was off her shoulders. She collapsed against him, weeping. He realized he was still holding the Killer's knife, and used it to slash the rope that tied her to the fan, then put her down and cut the bindings at her wrists.

Sheri's arms fell loose at her sides and he thought he might have acted too slowly. She might have had her shoulders pulled out of their sockets, or at least separated. His fingers went to her shoulders automatically, the doctor in him surfacing of its own accord.

Sheri gasped as he checked her. "Stop it," she moaned between sobs.

"You'll be okay," he said. His voice was gruff, gruffer than it should have been. Shouldn't he be holding her? Stroking her, saying *shhh, it'll be all right*? "Maybe minor separation, but you got lucky."

He turned away from her. Away from the TV with its still image of his son. His only son, he reflected. The only one he really knew.

"Where's Mom?" Sheri said.

"Dead," he said shortly. "He killed her."

Sheri made a noise Jerry couldn't interpret. But he couldn't look at her. He was still reeling with the many different revelations that had been pushed onto him. Still struggling to come up with a framework for dealing with it all.

"How?" she said.

"He...." Jerry's voice caught. He didn't even know what *he* was feeling. Grief? Anger? Fear? Certainly all those, and more. "He hung her. In the foyer."

Silence. Jerry almost ached for Sheri to ask him for help, for her to ask him to make it all better, the way she had when she was a little girl and came to him with a boo-boo. But he knew he couldn't. He didn't even know the extent of the wounds among the family, so how could he possibly hope to fix them?

What was left of them.

Sometime later – it could have been a second, or it could have been minutes, he somehow lost track of time in there, in the office with the ghost-image of his first and last boy behind him – he felt a hand on his shoulder.

He turned. Looked at the stranger behind him. He wanted to help. Wanted to be caring and helpful, but instead he just felt the horror on his face as he saw the strip-show in his mind. He wondered why that would bother him so much, why it would be worse than drugs, worse than what Ann had done.

She was my Princess. Every man with a daughter has a Princess. And when you put someone on a pedestal, it's just that much farther to fall, and that much greater a crash.

"Dad, I –" said Sheri.

Jerry found himself shaking his head emphatically, averting his eyes.

Don't want to hear it don't want to hear it don't want to hear it.

"Please, Daddy."

Sheri sank to the floor and started to cry. Jerry didn't go to her. He turned and aimed the flashlight out the office door.

Wouldn't do to let the bastard get you now, would it? Not now that you're all alone?

His thoughts were falling apart. Fragmented. Out of control. He was going crazy. Madness teetered. People always talked about madness like an abyss that you fell into, but he realized that was wrong: madness was something that fell *onto* you. Like a mountain, or a train, or….

Or a house.

He heard motion behind him. Sheri getting to her feet. He flicked a quick glance over his shoulder, checking on her. She was glaring at him, which he thought was odd. Leaning on his desk for support and glaring at him, *angry*.

She caught his gaze. "Don't pretend you're better than me," she said. "Don't pretend you're perfect."

She was standing now. Standing in her fury, looking like his Princess, but she wasn't. She wasn't, she couldn't be and never would be again –

"Who was the girl?"

Jerry blinked. Realized that he had lost himself in a spiral-spin of half-finished thoughts again.

"What?" he said.

"Who was the girl?" Sheri repeated. "The girl in the picture?

76

Jerry suddenly wished to go back in time. Not long, he didn't want much – nothing so grand as a trip back to a time when he was actually happy and life made sense. Just a few seconds. Just back to the comforting moments where a shadowed madman was trying to stab him to death. Anything to avoid this moment.

"Come on, Dad," said Sheri. She was advancing on him now. "All those late nights, all those 'long work days' where you came home so late.... We all just thought you didn't want to be here. To be around the memories."

Jerry wanted to run. To flee. But where? Into the dark house? No, not there. The house offered no safety. He had nowhere to go. Nowhere to hide. Nothing was his, not even this room, not even this moment. No freedom, not even in his words.

"But that's not it. You weren't hiding from the memories. You had your *own* secret." Sheri looked at him with the loathing that had made its home on his own features a moment ago. Destestation, then revelation. "You slept with her, didn't you? Just like Mom did! You're no better than she was!"

No choice. Have to hide, it's the only thing.

Then he realized he did have a choice. He always had. There was always choice, even when the choice was between awful options, between two things that seemed worse than death. Because sometimes the true choice wasn't in the decisions presented, it was in the way they were faced.

Jerry screamed. Not in anger, not in fear… it wasn't even madness finally crashing down on him and crushing him under its dark weight.

It was simply *time.*

It was the years of hiding, of pretending. Years of covering what had happened, of becoming what he wasn't by trying to excise a part of his reality. He screamed and buried the knife down on the desk, embedding it deep in the wood as he shrieked:

"I didn't sleep with her!"

The silence after his words was total. Jerry felt like he should have heard himself perspiring, but he was cool. Composed. His thoughts coming back to themselves, reversing the outward spiral that they had been embarked on during the entirety of this travesty.

He looked at his daughter.

She stared at him blankly, just as he stared at her.

He didn't hate her. Nor did he love her. Maybe later he would come to do so again. But there was not time to repair things now. No time to reclaim trust, no time to locate lost love.

From somewhere upstairs: a thud.

And Jerry knew that they didn't have much time.

There was still a Killer among them.

He shook his head. "Why is he doing this?" he asked. He said it to himself, still pulling his thoughts together like they were strands that had come unraveled and he was reweaving, desperately shaping them into something that could save them.

Sheri answered. "Secrets," she said.

"What?"

"All our secrets," she said. "He found them out, somehow. Like we're being punished for them. Whatever they are."

She looked at Jerry intently, clearly waiting for him to reveal *his* secret; obviously believing his was merely an issue of adultery.

More creaking upstairs. Another thud that could not portend anything good.

"What now?" asked Sheri.

And a thought-thread came to Jerry, woven into a pattern that had long been lost to him. It was still fuzzy, still faraway. But he was finding it again.

"What do we do now?" she asked again.

Jerry grasped the thread. Held it. "He came in," he said. "That means he knows the way out." His face grew grim. He stood a bit straighter, and it seemed suddenly that some of the pain he had been feeling left his body. There was nothing left. Nothing but truth.

Perhaps that would be enough.

"And he's going to tell us."

77

The man takes refuge. He knows he has at least a minute or two before Jerry gets his daughter down and they figure out what to do.

"What happened?" he asks himself. Not much more than a whisper, but he can hear the shock and anger in his voice. They weren't supposed to do that. Weren't supposed to *fight*. "They didn't take their *turn*," he answers himself.

Hearing his own voice, even whispered, calms him. It always does. He is the only reality that he could count on, the only person who will never lie to him is... him. And so talking to himself always soothes. Reminds him that there *is* goodness in the world. He is proof of that.

Perhaps the One proof. But proof nonetheless.

"Besides," he continues, "maybe they're not cheating, maybe they're just doing something you haven't seen before."

That gives him pause. Even a bit of hope. "Maybe," he says. "But they didn't take their turn."

He shakes his head.

"No, they didn't."

Taking turns is important.

If you don't do it, you get punished. On that, he always agrees.

78

They looked through the house.

They had done this before, the entire family. But that family had been a family of liars, and so by extension was a lie itself. What was left now was a pair of strangers. But at least there was no lie holding them apart, burdening them, weakening them. And it seemed to Jerry that they were more in sync as strangers than they had been as family; more aware of one another as unknowns than they had been as "Daddy" and "Princess."

They still didn't find much. The Killer had been thorough in removing everything that could be used as a weapon. No utensils – nothing metal that was over a few inches long – certainly no bats, no sticks. The curtains could be pulled down, but they had no rods, only a complex system of chains and reels that were sewn into the heavy fabric itself.

Sheri found a lighter in one of Drew's pants pockets. Jerry tried not to think what his son had used it for. Then gave up the effort and found that the reality of his son's addiction hurt a bit less than it had.

Still, the lighter wasn't much as a weapon until he suggested adding one of Sheri's hairsprays. She found an aerosol hairspray under her sink hidden below a box of tampons and held it like a flamethrower, one thumb on the hairspray discharge button, the other on the lighter wheel as they moved from room to room.

They had been looking for weapons before, and still were. But now that they each had *something* – they were also looking for more.

They were looking for the Killer. For the only way out, the way he *would* reveal to them.

The tension was almost unbearable, pushing down on Jerry's head like a heavy hand. He could feel his heart thudding against his ribs as he went from place to place, and wondered if Sheri's own heart would be able to bear up. He looked at her. She didn't so much as glance at him. Her eyes remained locked on the flashlight beam, looking for any hint of movement.

Living room… nothing….

Media room… empty….

Jerry stepped forward, one foot half in the garage –

"*Hsst!*"

He froze as surely and securely as if he had been about to step on a landmine. "What?" he whispered.

Sheri was at his shoulder. "Thought I saw something."

Jerry nodded. He swept the garage with his flashlight. And though the safe thing – the *sane* thing – would be to walk away from possible contact, they had to find the killer. Had to force him to get them out of here.

How you gonna do that, Jer-Jer? How you gonna force him?

Jerry clenched his jaw. He'd deal with that when they came to it.

They went into the garage. He forced himself to look at Rosa. Just in case there was some way to hide behind her.

Nothing. She was still dead, still hanging with her chin to the sky, the ladle jammed fatally down her throat. The pool of blood under her was now black and brown, a grotesque scab on what had once been the flawless floor of his garage.

The photo, the picture of the girl, was gone.

Jerry swept the flashlight away, but he knew Sheri had seen its absence and would be looking a thousand questions at him.

He looked under and around the locked cars, behind the few things large enough to hide a man.

There was no one in the garage.

On to the rest of the house.

79

Footsteps.

The man waits until he hears them die away, wondering if they will find him.

They might, he supposes. But probably not. They have no real way to get at him in here. And even if they do… he can't be captured by them. Not completely.

He is, he supposes, *magic*. At least to some extent. No locked door can hold him unless he wishes it, no jail can contain him completely unless he allows such to occur.

He hears the steps recede. No door shutting – they are leaving doors open behind them as they go, and besides, they already destroyed the door to the garage.

He waits, then presses the button on the fob in his hand.

There is a click and he climbs out of the trunk of Jerry's car. He has to stop himself from giggling.

"Hide and seek," he whispers.

Then he glides out of the garage after the last two people, the last two pupils, the last two who have to be taught the lessons they have refused to learn.

"Ready or not, here I come," he says, and creeps into the darkness.

80

Up the stairs.

Jerry tried not to look at his wife's body, hanging to his right as they took the gentle curve up to the second floor. He glanced back at Sheri, though, realizing that this was the first time she was seeing this.

Sheri stopped for a second. The hand holding the hairspray went to her chest as she stared at the body.

For some reason, Jerry focused on Ann's single missing shoe. As though the entirety of the vision was made endurable only by the fact that the hanging body had one bare foot.

He did not look at his wife's face.

Sheri's breath hitched. And though the love between her and Jerry was gone, still there was… something… and he took a step down to her.

She waved him away, waved him on, waved him to continue.

He did.

Drew's room. Not *too* many places to hide, but some. Enough. Sheri pushed through and looked while he aimed the light, stopping every so often to point it in the hall behind him.

Sheri went into the closet and was gone from his sight for a few seconds. Jerry's heart sped up in that instant, and he almost darted after her, but then she reappeared and shook her head.

Nothing.

81

The man waits. Listens.

His turn to hide. Theirs to seek.

So much fun.

They rummage through the boy's room, then move out.

He moves from the jack-and-jill bathroom into the boy's room as they go… and touches Sheri's hair as she passes into the hall.

She shivers and turns, but he darts out of sight behind the wall of Drew's room.

Did she see him?

Apparently not. A moment later he hears the click of them entering her room.

Too much fun too much fun too MUCH FUN!

82

By the time they got to the master bedroom, Jerry felt like he was on the verge of a heart attack. Sheri clutched her chest and bent over beside the bed. The stress was literally going to kill her.

He stepped toward her. "You okay?"

She forced herself to stand up straight. Or almost straight. She veered a bit to the side, as though gripped by a low-level scoliosis. But she waved Jerry off again. "Don't worry about me," she said in the same gruff voice he had heard coming from his own mouth a short time ago. No love lost from her, either, apparently.

She took a single, faltering step. Then another, with a look of determination he had rarely seen in adults, let alone teens locked in such a nightmare.

No love lost, perhaps. But admiration…?

"End of the road. What now?" she said.

"We look again."

There was nothing else *to* do. They would look until they found a way out, or found the Killer, which amounted to the same thing. Jerry had briefly considered Ann's old plan to hide themselves in the basement, but then discarded it. Their tormentor knew everything about them, and had apparently planned for just about every contingency. Jerry doubted he would be stymied by a locked basement door.

No, the only way out was through whoever was doing this.

Room by room by room, top to bottom this time.

Sheri was close on his heels for the whole search, but she started gasping by the time they reached the stairs. She didn't look at the hanging form of her mother.

Jerry did, though. And was unsettled by the fact that she was swaying as if in a breeze. There was no air movement, though – at least none sufficient to swing a one hundred and ten pound body back and forth.

He's been playing with her.

He swallowed away a scream, gagging it down and trying to remain silent, afraid that if he made so much as a whimper he would finally give in to the madness that had been pressing in on him, threatening to destroy his mind and leave behind nothing but a hollow shell of sense and self.

In the media room, the big-screen television was silent and dark. Television screens always seemed gray to Jerry when they were off. But in the darkness this one seemed black, like a bottomless hole to nothing, a tear in the universe through which they had all fallen.

Jerry looked away, entering the room to glance around while Sheri waited near the hall to make sure no one could sneak up on them.

Sheri hissed. He turned to her. She was waving him over, facing down the hall.

"What?" he whispered, stepping toward her.

"Kitchen door just swung shut," she whispered back.

He took another step.

Something huge swung at Jerry. He jumped back, but the thing collided with him and he felt something heavy and cool and wet. Sheri cried out and he realized it must have hit her as well; must have swung down from the balustrade above the media room.

Then he realized what it was. What had hit them, what had knocked them both back into the media room. And he screamed himself, loud and long.

83

Jerry fell back, flailing at the thing, struggling to keep from falling down, struggling to keep from grabbing onto the monstrosity for support.

It was Ted.

Their neighbor had been trussed and tied so much that he resembled a cocoon as much as a man, only this cocoon was pierced all over with the very same branches that he had consistently thrown onto their side of the wall, dozens of rough shafts of wood jammed into his body every few inches. His feet were tied so that he hung upside-down from the second-floor balustrade, swinging like a gory piñata with his head dangling a few feet above the floor of the media room.

It came to Jerry as he slowly managed to calm himself down that their persecutor was not without a sense of irony, if not a kind of twisted humor.

Then a click interrupted both his thoughts and his continuing attempts to get himself under control. He turned, but knew what he would see. It was the same click they had all heard before. The televisions.

The TV in this – and every – room had come to life. Like the tear in this reality had been illuminated, showing what lay beyond.

"What is this?" said Sheri. She pushed herself against Jerry – or better said, she pushed *away* from Ted, who was staring sightlessly at them from a face that itself had been perforated by no fewer than a dozen sticks, as the dead man swung back and forth, back and forth.

The screen showed a man, his face just offscreen, dressed in a TV repairman's uniform, placing surveillance cameras through the house. They were already live as he placed them, hiding them in each room.

Jerry focused on the uniform. The repairman outfit.

"Oh, my –" he began.

"What?"

"This is how he did it. He's the reason our cable keeps going out."

"What do you mean?"

Jerry thought about the dozen or so times the television had switched to snow over the past few months. He pointed at the repairman uniform on the television. "We've let him in. Over and over." He shivered, his eyes glued to the television. "He must have been spying on us for… who knows how long?" At the same moment he also realized that he had heard the Killer's voice before: on the phone to the cable company.

We never called out, he realized. He rerouted our calls somehow. We've been living in a closed circle that he created.

The screen flickered. The scene changed to shots of mundane things a "perfect" family would do:

Goodnight kisses.

Hello hugs.

Brushing teeth.

Combing hair.

Then the TV flickered again, and now it showed the Killer in the kitchen, his back to the camera. He held something high over his head: a silver ladle.

Jerry cried out, reaching out as the Killer slammed the ladle down, knowing he couldn't stop what had already happened but helpless to stop himself from trying.

Rosa's feet flopped into view, twitching as blood dripped down her legs.

The scene changed again. The master bedroom. Now not merely fear but revulsion curdled Jerry's guts.

He saw himself asleep in the bed, asleep next to Ann. Or no, not asleep: drugged. As he must have been when Rosa was killed in their home. And now the Killer dragged a screaming, shrieking mass into the room. It was Ann's lover.

"I didn't, I swear," the man cried. The Killer slammed him down on the bed, right across Ann's and Jerry's feet. The man struggled, but couldn't break free.

The Killer's face was still away from the camera.

"I didn't!" screamed the man again. "I don't know who they are, I've never seen these people before!"

The Killer's knife came out. He started carving at the man's face, inches away from Ann's and Jerry's own faces. Blood dripped directly on them, and they didn't so much as twitch.

Ann's lover was flayed alive. Face peeled right off before he was murdered.

Ann and Jerry slept on. Slept through it, and Jerry felt like he must have been sleeping like this for most of his life, through all the secrets his family had kept. He looked at

Sheri, gasping beside him, nearly choking, and felt empty inside.

There was nothing left.

The scene shifted. Now he saw what they had gone through, from the eyes of the cameras hidden in the house. The family waking, finding themselves trapped. Finding Socrates maimed and dead. Finding Ann's lover, finding Rosa.

Drew's death.

Ann's death.

The Killer had clearly been watching every second of their suffering and pain. Reveling in it.

On and on went the replay of their excruciation, louder and louder and faster and faster until it all dissolved in a blur of cacophonous white noise. Jerry screamed, but couldn't hear his own voice. He clapped his hands over his ears, but it didn't help. He felt like he was dying, dissolving, disintegrating with the force of the static, the sound of chaos.

And then, just as it became unbearable, just as he felt like he was going to – like he *must* – simply fall and surrender himself to the hammer blows of the sound and light, the televisions all died.

Silence. Silence like slamming tidal waves in his skull.

Jerry turned to see if Sheri was okay.

And the Killer was standing right beside them.

84

"Secrets can kill," said the man.

Jerry barely had time to process the words, because an instant later the man flew at them. Pure madness, pure evil. Punching, gouging, kicking, biting. He fought like it was *he* who was trapped, like *he* was the one who had to win or face a painful death at the hands of a nightmare made flesh.

Jerry stabbed out with the knife, but knew he couldn't kill the man. They needed him to tell them the way out. Likewise, Sheri had moved away and was circling them, but she didn't let loose with her makeshift flamethrower. He could practically hear her thoughts: Where do I hit him, where can I hurt him without hurting Dad?

Jerry bashed at the other man with the flashlight then followed the move up with a backhand slash and the Killer backpedaled into the hall. He tried to take advantage of the moment, but Sheri bounded forward and put herself between him and the Killer. She raised her jury-rigged flamethrower, obviously trying to take advantage of the space Jerry had opened up between them, but the Killer didn't do the logical thing. He didn't fall back and give her the room to wield her weapon. Instead he flung himself at her.

The madman hit her. A single hammer punch that landed on the top of her head. She fell.

Jerry dove over Sheri while she was still falling. He thrust the knife into the Killer's shoulder.

The Killer roared. Threw Jerry away with strength that seemed beyond what should have come from someone his size. Jerry let go of the knife and hurtled into the wall headfirst. Sparks flew behind his eyes.

When they cleared, Sheri and the Killer were gone from the hall. Jerry heard noise in the living room and tried to stand, but his feet kept sliding out from under him.

He switched to a half-drunk crawl, and got far enough into the living room to see Sheri, her hair in the Killer's grasp, thrown to the floor.

She screamed with the impact, but also seized the moment. Spun and let loose with the flamethrower. The Killer barely managed to get his right arm in front of the sizzling tongue of flame. He screamed as his arm alighted, then he rolled along a wall, trying to put the flames out.

The wall caught fire.

But now the fire on the Killer's arm was out. He rounded on Sheri. She tried to blast him again but this time the cigarette lighter didn't even spark. Out of juice? Malfunctioning?

It didn't matter. The Killer hit her again. Hard. She didn't go down at first, but rolled backward as though she had been hit by a vicious riptide at the beach.

Jerry was still struggling to get to his feet, still failing. Reaching out, wondering why his hands weren't working either.

Sheri rolled back toward the Killer, and Jerry thought the man was going to hit her again. He didn't, though, and after a second Jerry saw why as his daughter dropped both lighter and hairspray and her hands went to her chest and she crumpled to the floor.

No, no, no, not now she lasted so long not now, not now.

The Killer loomed over her.

She was helpless. Jerry thought the man might stamp a foot on her neck, might break her back or simply chew through her throat like the animal he was. And Jerry would simply have to watch it happen, drunkenly maneuvering as he was through the hall.

But the Killer did none of that.

Instead, he pulled something out of his pocket.

A remote. A TV remote.

He pushed the button.

85

Click.

Such a small sound, but to Jerry it had come to represent the sound of a world crumbling down, piece by piece. It was the sound of atoms crashing, the sound of fission in the moment before oblivion.

No, not oblivion. Oblivion would be a gift. This is something worse. This is what Adam and Eve were cast out of Eden for seeking. This is the damnation of knowledge.

And Jerry understood *why* God might have taken such a tack, understood why knowledge might have turned Eden into nothing more than a pile of weeds. Contrary to the saying, knowledge was not power.

It was dissolution.

The TV came on.

Brian. Alive and –

"No," he breathed. "Please, no."

– healthy and whole. Darkness in the background. Jerry couldn't see where the boy was.

Then the darkness around his son seemed to leap from the screen, seemed to wrap itself around Jerry's sight and create a dark tunnel with nothing but a pinpoint of light at the end. He hissed, realizing that he was falling, and managed to right himself in the last instant before gravity would have dashed him to the floor.

The pinpoint widened. Became a smile. The Killer.

Jerry realized he had never seen the man's face before. Not really. And he was startlingly... ordinary. Just a man, brown hair that was receding a bit at the temples. Five o'clock shadow that clung to a chin that was rather weak.

But there was nothing weak about the mad light in his eyes.

The tunnel that had encircled Jerry's vision widened more, and Jerry saw the television again, where his dead son was standing, looking down at something. A paper.

The scene widened, an invisible cameraman allowing Jerry to see that Brian was standing on top of the family's home. The roof of the dream house.

Brian looked at the paper one more time, as though he had secluded himself on this manmade mountain so as to find the perfect spot to memorize the words he found there. Then he held his arms out wide. The paper fluttered in his hand like a bird, wishing to be free.

And he jumped.

He hung in the air for eternity, arms out, legs together. He looked like an artist's vision of an angel. Then he crashed to earth, slamming headfirst into the deck beside the pool.

There was a sickening thud and his body crumpled into itself, then lay at length, feet hanging out a few inches over the water of the pool.

The body twitched.

The camera shifted, the angle lowering. Being put down. And the Killer walked onscreen.

Brian was dead. He had to be. And yet... his arm moved. Not just a post-mortem spasm, he was reaching. Like he had changed his mind, like he was repenting of his decision.

Help me, the gesture said.

Jerry tried to look away. He saw Sheri, clawing her chest. Gasping. Saw the Killer. Smiling.

He looked back at the screen. The angle had widened a bit, sharing the screen equally between both Killer and suffering penitent.

The Killer on the TV picked something up. The paper that Brian had been holding. He read it. Glanced at the teen....

And then he turned Brian over and began administering CPR.

Nausea reached greasy fingers into Jerry's stomach. The sight of the madman, mouth to mouth with his son, was almost an abomination. That Brian should commit suicide was one kind of horror. That he should be murdered would have been shattering in a different way.

But to see this murderer trying to save his firstborn? It was wrong. Not just wrong, it was... *blasphemous.*

Jerry tried again to stand. To walk. He still couldn't.

Sheri. Gasping.

The Killer. Smiling.

And on the TV, the same Killer – the then-Killer – stopped breathing life. Brian was motionless. The Killer watched the spreading blood around the youth. Then the boy himself.

Then he held up the note and Jerry realized he was seeing something that had been cut out of the version he had watched earlier. Like the Killer was showing them only a bit at a time, only what he judged them ready for, like a teacher of a macabre subject bringing his students to understanding as fast as he believed them able to handle it.

The Killer read the note aloud to the camera, as though recording a last will and testament for posterity.

"Dear Mom and Dad. I'm sorry. The house is empty. We all live in it, but it's empty. No one knows what anyone's really doing. No one but me." The Killer's voice broke, as though he were trying not to weep. "But I've heard Dad talking to Socrates about what he did. I've come home early from the movies that Mom sent us on so that she could have her… visits. I know how Sheri makes money, and what Drew does for fun." Again the Killer paused. He drew a trembling hand across his eyes, then finished, "I don't know you. I don't want to know you. And you'll never know me."

The Killer stood in front of the body. Then he folded the paper, put it in his pocket, and walked away as blood dripped off Brian's feet and reached long red tendrils into the perfect green of the pool.

The TV turned off, and in the room the Killer, the real Killer, the one of flesh and blood they had to fight *now*, turned to face them. He said, "You killed him."

And Jerry's heart clenched.

Because it was true.

86

The Killer's eyes bored into Jerry, as unfocused and unsteady as Jerry felt himself. Then the murderer looked back at the still-dark television as though looking for the secrets of a suddenly confusing universe.

Sheri's gasping turned into a light panting. She didn't have much time.

Jerry forced himself to take a step.

He thought of Brian. Flying. An angel.

"Your secrets," said the Killer.

An angel coming down.

"Your secrets killed him."

Crashing down.

"They destroyed him, then they killed him."

The Killer reached for Sheri, who was now almost completely still.

"*NO!*"

Jerry felt his feet moving under him. Felt like he had felt through all of this: like he wasn't controlling himself. Like he was a puppet. But now he was a puppet in the hands of someone he was grateful to dance for. Because this puppet master wanted what Jerry did: for the Killer to pay.

He reached out. The knife he had stabbed into the Killer's shoulder was still there, and he twisted it. The Killer screamed and fell. Jerry went down as well, his strength subsiding as suddenly as it had risen.

But at least he fell on top of the madman. He felt like an ant taking on a lion. All he could do was hold onto the knife and twist it and turn it and grind it against the bone of the Killer's shoulder.

He saw Sheri in the tumult. She was staring at him. It didn't look like she was breathing.

The Killer stood and now Jerry was hanging onto him like a man riding a rogue tiger, hoping that the beast would tire and fall before he did. Knowing that was an impossible hope.

But still, he held.

Smoke started to billow through the room. The fire the Killer had set. It was growing. It pushed its way into the kitchen. Parts of the hall.

The Killer slammed Jerry into another wall, and he felt a pair of ribs crack. His head flipped into the wall as well, and everything went sideways again. Not just his sight, but his thoughts.

He thought of Ann, bringing a lover into the bed he had shared with her for twenty years.

Of Drew, shooting up in the room while Jerry stood in the hall.

Of Sheri, dancing naked for pawing perverts who paid to see her body.

Of Brian… the angel brought crashing to an earth that would not bear his existence.

Each of the images flashed in his mind as the Killer crashed through the room, slamming Jerry against walls, onto the floor, battering at him in an effort to dislodge him. Each of the images speared through him. Each of the moments sapped what strength Jerry had.

But they brought something with them. Not the strength that he had been relying on for so long. Not the lie. The something beyond it. The truth that was all that was left, the honesty that was awful, but somehow sustaining.

He hung on.

And suddenly the Killer fell.

Jerry rolled on top of the man. Grabbed his head. Slammed it into the floor. Once. The Killer bucked at him. Twice. The Killer tried to turn away.

Three times.

The Killer was still. Silent. The rogue tiger slept.

87

Jerry looked at the man. He was a surgeon. He had extensive medical training. He was almost certain the Killer was out cold.

He had also seen too many movies where the bad guy came lurching to life to trust what he saw.

So he grabbed the Killer's head and bashed it against the floor again a few more times. He didn't want to kill him, but wanted him jumping up and attacking them again even less.

Jerry looked at Sheri. She was quivering, tiny shivers running up and down her frame. She didn't have long.

And he just... *looked.* At his daughter. The girl he'd known all her life, but never known at all. He felt like he was taking a test, not a school test, not his licensing exams. Something much more important.

He saw his daughter. Not his Princess. Not the fiction she told him, not the things he had always hoped or believed.

Just her.

He crawled to Sheri and cradled her head. He rubbed her shoulders, trying to calm her down. "It's okay," he whispered. "We got him." He rubbed her temples, drew his fingers through her tangled hair. "We got him, Sheri. Calm."

He kept whispering, keeping an eye on the motionless figure of the Killer as he did so, until finally Sheri stopped shivering. She started breathing more regularly, then closed her eyes a moment after he whispered, "It'll be okay, Sheri."

She opened her eyes again, and he thought she might be looking at *him,* just like he was looking at her.

They smiled.

Jerry held the moment as long as he could, but finally had to look away. He felt stronger. Strong enough to do what came next.

He sensed Sheri tracking his gaze. Looking at the fire that had made its way into the kitchen. "We're going to burn alive if we can't get out of here," she whispered. But she sounded calm. Like the worst had already happened, the storm had already passed.

Maybe it had.

Jerry helped Sheri up. She was wobbly, so he leaned her against the wall before going to the Killer's still form.

"What are you going to do?" asked Sheri.

Jerry felt his countenance harden. He wondered if he would actually be able to do what he was thinking about.

He thought so.

"We're going to get as far away from the fire as we can… and we're going to make him tell us how to get out of here."

88

Jerry tossed the Killer to the floor of the master bedroom and looked around as the madman moaned and Sheri, still feeling the aftereffects of her near-brush with cardiac arrest, leaned against the wall.

Smoke filled the room. He knew that conventional wisdom was to go under fires since smoke and heat rose, but the flames Sheri had set and the Killer had spread had gone into the kitchen, cutting off the basement and the garage. The master bedroom was the farthest they could get from the flames' leading edge; and gave them the most time to do what they had to.

Can you do this, Jer-Jer?

Watch me.

The Killer moaned again, more stridently this time. Jerry strode to him and yanked the knife out of his shoulder. A gout of blood and some dark clumps of clotted gore came rushing out and the monster's eyes fluttered.

"Dad…," Sheri said, her tone indicating clearly that she had seen the movement and was worried about the man's impending consciousness.

The monster was wounded, and would wake angry.

"Watch him a sec," said Jerry.

"What do I do?"

"The second his eyes open, kick him in the head."

"How hard?"

"Break your foot."

Then he turned to the bed. He didn't look back at Sheri, trusting she would do what had to be done. Indeed, she was already stumbling over to the man and he had no doubt a glance in her direction would reveal her getting herself in field goal position with the Killer's cranium for a ball.

Jerry used the Killer's bloody knife to cut the sheet on his bed into strips. The cuts were ugly and irregular, and for some reason that bothered him immensely, as though all could be forgiven save the sin of slipshod craftsmanship. He didn't know if this represented a newfound pride in self or a continuing trip into lands darkened by madness. Perhaps both.

Regardless, though, he had a few long strips of cloth in moments, and he hurried back to Sheri. As he had imagined, she was standing next to the Killer, one leg actually cocked back for a kick.

He smiled at her.

She smiled back.

Jerry flipped the madman over. The world swum as he did it and he prayed that his reserves of strength and/or adrenaline wouldn't run out before he finished his work. He tied the Killer's wrists and arms tightly behind him.

He heard crackling as he did it, and thought for a moment he must be breaking bones. But no, the sounds were too small, the sounds of a squirrel's bones perhaps. Not those of a grown man. Then he realized that the noises were the sound of the fire, slowly consuming the house around them.

"Wake up," he shouted. The Killer moaned again. Jerry punched him in the mouth. It was the first time he had ever punched someone in his adult life and he thought he did it wrong. Maybe broke a finger. But at least the Killer woke.

Jerry realized he was sweating, wetness slicking his forehead and cheeks and running down the back of his neck. Nervousness? Pain?

Or the heat of the fire?

The Killer made a noise. Not a moan or a groan. Jerry couldn't place it, then realized: the man was *giggling*.

"My turn is *so much fun* this time," rasped the Killer. He spat at Jerry's feet, and Jerry was absurdly proud to see blood trickling from the madman's mouth: his punch had done some damage.

"How do we get out of here?" Jerry demanded.

The Killer laughed again. Spat once more. This time a tooth came with the blood, but Jerry felt no pride this time. The room was definitely getting hotter and starting to grow hazy with smoke.

He stared at the Killer. Gearing up.

Just do it.

This is not what I'm about.

You're about survival. Do it.

I can't.

DO IT.

Jerry kicked the Killer's prone form. The other man's body was wracked by automatic spasms of pain, but Jerry ignored his distress, though it went against everything he had ever trained for in his personal or professional life. Instead he just jerked the other man half-upright, pulling him by his hair alone across the floor and leaning him against the bed.

Then he slashed the madman's own knife against him, dragging it against his chest, scraping it deep enough he felt it jitter along the other man's ribs.

The Killer screamed.

"You know everything about us, right?" said Jerry. He turned the knife, running another furrow along the lunatic's ribs. "So you know I'm a surgeon. I know how to do this for a long time without killing you."

And the Killer started to *laugh*.

89

The laugh was one of the ugliest things Jerry had ever heard, a rasping, madly dancing thing that brought to mind the image of a prima ballerina set ablaze in the middle of a performance, twirling madly into the most painful of oblivions. Sheri grabbed her chest again, as though the sound alone might drive her into another attack. Jerry held her arm, trying to impart a calm he did not feel.

"You can do this a long time?" said the Killer, jerking his chin in the direction of the knife that still rested against his chest. "I don't think so. None of us have long. Not long at all."

He nodded over Jerry's shoulder. Jerry didn't look, but he realized: the room was *growing brighter*. Sheri was holding the only flashlight to survive the melee in the living room, but the illumination wasn't coming from its weakening bulb. No, the brightness entering the room was a flickering, flashing, yellow-gold light.

The fire. Here already.

Out of time. What do we –

Sheri erupted in a shriek, rushing at the Killer. Jerry had a horrible vision, suddenly fearing that this was part of some master plan on the part of the madman and that in a moment Sheri would be in his clutches. He tried to stop his daughter's mad attack, but was too tired, too spent, too slow. She ripped past him and hit the lunatic like a bullet train gone off its rails, knocking the Killer down and bashing his head against the floor as Jerry had done only a few minutes before.

"How do we get out?" she screamed in a voice that Jerry hardly recognized. *Slam, slam, slam.* "How do we get out, you sick bastard, *HOW DO WE GET OUT*?"

Jerry tried to stop her, but he could barely reach past the flailing mass of movement she had become. As though his daughter had ceased to exist, replaced by a creature with no mass, only heat and kinetic energy.

Then she stopped. So suddenly it looked painful. Her eyes rolled back, the whites showing. She slumped. Jerry caught her.

And the Killer laughed again. He propped himself back up against the bed, smearing blood from the back of his head against what remained of the covers. He wasn't trying to flee, Jerry could tell instantly. He just wanted to see. Just wanted a better view.

He was enjoying this. Savoring their pain. Luxuriating in the desperation of their destruction.

Jerry turned his attention to Sheri. He moved her to the opposite edge of the bed, out of the Killer's immediate line of sight. Her eyes rolled forward again… and she yanked out of his grasp.

"Get away from me!" she shouted, as though he were nothing but a stranger in a bar who had invaded her space.

For a moment Jerry wanted to strike back, to scream at her, to ask why it mattered if he held her and brought her to safety when she had –

(*say it, Jer-Jer, WHORED herself out*)

– allowed so many strangers so much more intimate access to her. He even opened his mouth to say it.

And the Killer laughed. Enjoying their continued dissolution. Jerry didn't know whether it had been part of the madman's plan to be captured. He didn't think so – he *hoped* not, or God save them, because nothing else could. But if he kept carping at Sheri he'd certainly be playing into whatever part of the Killer's game called for them to be at each other's throats.

Crackles. The dry decrepitation of wood and plaster heated to a thousand degrees and beyond. The sounds of a house in distress.

Sheri was weeping, not pushing him away anymore, but not letting him draw closer either. "What are we going to do?" she was murmuring. "What are we going to do?"

Jerry listened to the sounds. A wall of noise washing over him, making it hard to think, to feel.

He touched his daughter's shoulder. She pushed him away again. "Don't touch me! I don't even know you!"

Another long moment passed. Something popped below them as the heat burst it open. Sweat pooled on Jerry's brow then ran in a thick line down the bridge of his nose, to the tip. Drip, drip. He wiped it off.

The Killer laughed. Like he was winning.

Because he was.

"I was driving," Jerry finally said. "I was driving."

90

Jerry didn't know if Sheri was listening or not. It didn't matter. All that mattered was that he was saying it. Was saying the words that he had never said to anyone (save only Socrates on one drunken night). He was opening a part of himself that he had kept sealed tight for so long.

So long....

"Your mother and I had been fighting," he continued. "I don't remember about what. Something stupid. We always fought a lot, but we always made up. At least before...." He drifted off. Almost didn't start again. Made himself continue. "Anyway, I drove forever. Just clearing my head. And I fell asleep. Hit something." His breath hitched. He inhaled deeply, coughing as a thick cloud of smoke moved into his lungs. "It was a woman. Out walking. Pregnant." He coughed again, though this time it was as much to cover up the tears that threatened as to clear his body of smoke. "I left. I ran. But someone saw. I never found out who, but I've been paying blackmail since then. Trying to keep it secret."

Jerry paused. The heat was wafting in from the hall in dry waves, flickering tongues licking into view. He felt like he was at the edge of a furnace, the edge of tolerance. "What's my secret?" he said. "Nothing much. I just killed a girl."

He closed his eyes. He had nothing left. No ideas. No family. No will to survive. All was gone. He was dry and empty, a parched husk that would burn well in the coming flame.

Annihilation would be a relief. Nothing to give meant nothing more to take. The Killer's hold over him was gone. He would embrace the flame and smile.

Then, a feeling. A touch.

Jerry opened his eyes. Sheri had rested a hand on his. And as he watched she reached out with her other one and did the same. Her fingers curled around his.

The fire peeked in at the doorway. The sound of wood splintering surrounded them. The entire structure of the house seemed to groan like an old man getting ready to lay down one last time.

Jerry looked from the smaller hands that had curled around his own to the fingers of fire curving through the doorway of the bedroom.

He was a husk. He would take the flame. But could he do more in his last moments than simply expire?

Yes.

91

Jerry's own fingers responded, gripping Sheri's. Not like he was holding onto some possession – she was not his, never had been – but like he was protecting a rare and fragile object before handing it off to its rightful owner.

Something fell in the hall. Glass tinkled. Metal buckled.

Jerry looked at his daughter. "Sweetie, the fire is almost here. When it gets in the room…." He took a deep breath. Could he do this?

I have nothing left to give. And so nothing that can be taken from me. Not even my fear. Not even my pain.

"I want you to lay down in the bathtub, and I'm going to lay on top of you. And no matter what you hear or see or smell, just don't move. Stay beneath me. And maybe you'll survive."

Sheri stared at him blankly, as though he had suddenly begun speaking ancient Greek. Then: "What…? *No!* That's insane! That won't –"

"It might. It happens in forest fires all the time – baby animals covered by their parents until the fire burns out." He closed his eyes. "Please don't argue this, Sheri. There's not a lot of –"

"No." Her voice was firm. She looked around the room, her eyes searching. "There has to be… the fireplace!"

She got up and stumbled to the small fireplace at the wall. Jerry shook his head. "It's ornamental," he said. "You know that."

"So? Maybe it's enough." Sheri pulled the grate off the fireplace and looked in. Jerry knew what she would see: a small flu, really suitable only as a vent, maybe fifteen inches square. Still, Sheri reached in. And then yanked her hand out with a yelp, sucking at her fingers. The metal must have superheated from the house fire already. Going in would be suicide.

But Sheri squared her shoulders. "I can get through. I can get us help," she said. "I can save you." She took a shaking breath then added a single, musical word: "Dad."

Jerry could see that she knew. Knew going in the flu would be a painful death. And that she didn't care; was still willing to try.

For her family.

His vision blurred. Smoke all around them, sweat dripping from the heat.

And tears.

I do *have something to give. I* do *have things that can still be taken.*

Jerry took his daughter in his arms. Coughing, choking, they stood together in the face of the flame. And there was nothing between them.

They would die together, but at least they would never again be alone.

92

The fire was loud now. It sounded strangely like a thunderstorm, like the *tic-tic-tac-tic* of huge drops of water pounding on a roof. Jerry held his girl and tried to empty his mind of the fear that was creeping up in him.

"Let's move," he said, wondering if he would really be able to do what he had said he would and hold his daughter beneath him while he cooked alive.

Then his eyes opened so wide he felt like the eyeballs might drop right out of their sockets.

"What is it?" said Sheri.

"There's a place we never looked."

Sheri's eyes lit up.

"Where?"

Jerry grabbed her hand. "Come on!"

He pulled her toward the walk-in closet. Then in. Started throwing things out of the way, moving toward his goal. He did so one-handed for a few seconds, holding to the knife with the other, but then abandoned the weapon, dropping it at his feet so he could work faster. Shoeboxes and clothing got thrown haphazardly over his shoulder as he moved in like a burrowing tick. Some of it hit Sheri but there was no time to worry about that.

"It's got to be here."

93

The man watches Sheri and Jerry disappear, and he frowns. What's going on in there? He didn't expect to be captured like this, but he can adjust. He can adapt. He can *roll with it*. Especially since capturing him – *truly* capturing him – is impossible. He's here because he wants to be here. Because he is curious how this will play out. But he just has to say the magic word and freedom will be his immediately. So nothing has really bothered him so far.

Until now. He doesn't like seeing Jerry and his daughter go into the closet. Doesn't like them out of his sight.

He thinks about saying the word. The magic word.

But then he realizes he doesn't have to. The fire is here. Fire is help enough. He prefers to do things himself if he can. Because if he says the magic word, he'll have freedom, but then… his turn might end.

The fire has rolled in through the door, and now curtains one of the walls. The man rolls over to the wall, tumpety-tumpety-thump, each roll over his slashed chest causing stinging stitches to weave across his front, each roll over his side causing agony to roil through him as his body shifts the deep knife wound in his shoulder.

He ignores it all. Pain is nothing new. Pain is how he was taught. How he learned that there is a place and time and turn for everything.

How he became *who he is*.

Finally he is at the fire. He manages to stand, then thrusts his still-bound wrists and arms behind him into the fire. He hears something sizzling and realizes it is him only an instant before the smell of scorched meat wafts up to his nostrils.

He is suddenly very concerned that the burns on his arms will cause them not to match. This makes him angry.

He feels the sleeves on his shirt burn away. Something flitters to his feet, a long sheet of black. He thinks it is another piece of his shirt, then realizes it is not. Nor is it the bedspread with which Jerry bound him. No, it is his flesh, his skin.

His arms are definitely not going to match now.

He is *very* angry.

He pulls at his bonds. They have not burnt away. Not completely.

But soon.

94

Jerry pulled down a final trio of hatboxes, standing on his tiptoes to do so, and revealed what he had been looking for: a small attic hatch. He let go an explosive breath, wondering how long he had been holding it, then turning to Sheri.

"We have an attic?" she said incredulously.

"Not really. More just a storage space. I'd forgotten about it," he said. "Most of the house is loft ceiling, except this one small spot."

Sheri looked suddenly terrified, staring at the two foot square hatch as though it were a ticking time bomb. "Wouldn't... *he*... know about it?"

Jerry shook his head. "I doubt it. It's never been used, as far as I know, so it wouldn't have been on any of the surveillance videos he took. I mean... none of *us* even really knew about it. The only time I ever saw it was the day we were shown the place by the realtor, years ago."

"Is there a way out through there?"

Jerry shrugged. "I don't know. But we have to try."

He swung back to face the hatch. It was in the ceiling of the closet. There was no way he could reach it. Problem. There were a few shelves under it, but they weren't going to be sturdy enough to support him, not even Sheri.

He turned to face his daughter and bent down, making a cradle of his hands, then nodded to her to climb up.

"What about you?" she said. She still looked like she didn't trust this option.

"We'll figure me out in a second."

Sheri bit her lip, a curiously childlike gesture that made Jerry feel sick. She shouldn't be here. She should be with friends or at the mall or a movie. Anywhere but here.

Sheri stepped forward. At the same time a cloud of thick smoke rolled in the room behind her, forcefully reminding him that they didn't have much time. She put a hand on each of his shoulders, then her foot in the stirrup of his hands. She stepped up, and he hoisted at the same time.

His vision swum spectacularly, and he felt like he might vomit. His body clearly didn't want to keep doing this.

How about a nap, Jerry?

Just a little longer. Just a little longer and then you can lay down as long as you want. Forever.

His vision cleared. Sheri had her hands on the attic hatch and was pushing. Terror seized him: what if the attic door was locked somehow, or even simply nailed shut?

Then those concerns evaporated as Sheri pushed the beige-painted board that served as the hatch's door up and over. She hoisted herself up a bit and looked around.

"What's in there?" said Jerry.

"Lots of dark."

"Good enough."

Jerry lifted with all his strength. His vision swam and then blurred. Fireflies gathered at the edges of his sight, then were joined by strange insects he had never seen, a kind of bug that brought an *absence* of light with it. Sparks and darkness mingled and soon he could see nothing but a dizzying display of flashes crawling across a black background.

Don't need to see to lift. Just keep lifting, Jerry.

Sheri groaned. As she pulled herself up, Jerry could feel her bodyweight diminishing. She coughed: the attic must be full of smoke.

As her weight went to the floor of the attic instead of his own overstressed muscles, Jerry's eyesight returned. Though at first he didn't even realize it because the closet was so dark, so thoroughly choked with smoke.

He looked up and could vaguely make out his daughter leaning out, reaching down for him. He jumped. Missed. Jumped again. Grabbed her hands. Held.

He heard Sheri grunt in pain as he began to kick frantically, his body searching for some foothold that would allow him to push up, to get to his daughter.

His foot found something to push against. He didn't know what. Didn't care. He pushed. Pulled on Sheri, pushed on his feet. Sheri groaned. He pulled harder. Managed to let go of one of her hands and in the same jittery movement slap his palm down on the edge of the attic entrance hatch. The wood bit into his palm, and the pain was sweet.

Sheri switched her now-free hand to his back, yanking on his shirt while continuing to pull on his other hand. Jerry kept kicking. Felt his shoe smash through drywall. Didn't care. The house was doomed already. Had been for a long time, whether he realized it or not. He wedged his foot into the drywall and levered up, up. Wiggled higher. Now Sheri had two hands on his back and he was a third of the way into the attic. Daring to hope he would make it in. Him, a surgeon who hadn't done a pull-up in probably twenty years, and he was going to make it.

Halfway in.

Inching higher.

Almost far enough to throw a leg over the lip of the hatchway, and then he'd be home free.

Then his eyes widened.

"What?" screamed Sheri.

Jerry didn't answer. Couldn't.

Something yanked him down, out of the attic, and he plummeted away from Sheri and back into smoke and flame.

95

"Run, Sheri, get out!"

Jerry felt like the words almost disappeared behind him, he was pulled away so fast. He slid out of the attic, the rough edges of the hatchway digging deep scratches in his belly and chest, then fell. But before he had even hit the floor below it felt like he was being yanked out of the closet by the seat of his pants, like a toddler being hauled ignominiously out of a supermarket while in the middle of a tantrum.

He found himself in almost total darkness. Not the same inky black that had followed the family through this ordeal, but a new kind of blinding force. This was a cloying, choking darkness. A darkness that forced its way down your throat and yanked the air out of your body in superheated blasts that left you feeling cooked from the inside out.

All this was Jerry's impression in the instant before something whipped around him. It went around his shoulders at first, and Jerry felt something hot and somehow wet and dry at the same time. Pieces of it sloughed off on his shirt, leaving black and red trails behind, then the thing moved to his throat and tightened and Jerry realized it was an arm and that arm was choking him.

Then the arm yanked back and Jerry was hurled backward, thrown down with stunning force to the floor and he felt hands around his neck. But the hands were wrong somehow. Too short, like the fingers ended halfway to the first knuckle.

The Killer looked down. Hazy, wreathed by smoke and firelight like a demon come to herald the final Apocalypse.

"I don't match," he said, his voice so calm it was jarringly at odds with everything else going on.

He slammed the back of Jerry's head against the floor and Jerry felt his eyes cross even as the Killer began choking him in earnest.

There was no question of his fighting back. He was at the Killer's mercy.

The Killer leaned close. "Don't worry," he said. "You were the only one who came clean." He blinked, as though unsure of his surroundings, then refocused on Jerry. "But I can't let you save the little whore. Those are the rules."

He bore down on Jerry. Jerry's eyes fluttered.

This is it.

Then, a sickening thud.

96

Nothing changed. Nothing, but everything.

The fire still blasted. Heat still flowed over and around everything, drying it and getting it ready to burn. Smoke still roiled in dark clouds that made Jerry's lungs spasm.

The Killer still looked down at him.

But his eyes… his eyes changed. They had been angry, intense, manic. Now: empty.

A thin trickle of blood streamed down the other man's forehead and Jerry felt the charred hands loosen from his neck.

The Killer slumped.

And Jerry saw his daughter, standing above the other man. She held the broken remains of the heavy mahogany box in which Ann had hidden the evidence of her adultery. Now the box was in splinters and the letters curled and flew, born on waves of heat until they fell to fire or simply exploded into flame in midair. Destroyed.

The secrets gone.

Sheri managed to smile at Jerry before she sagged, the last of her strength exhausted.

Jerry pushed out from below the Killer's form and managed to grab her before she fell. He held her tightly. "You came back," he said.

She nodded, even that small movement seeming to cost her. "*You* saved *me* before." She looked down at the sprawled, still form of the Killer, steeled herself, and kicked him hard. "And I don't like being called a whore."

97

Jerry thought for the first few seconds that they wouldn't be able to get back into the attic. And even after Sheri dug deep and managed to find some hidden surplus of strength sufficient to pull herself up and help her exhausted and sadly out-of-shape old man to do the same, he wasn't sure they were much better off.

The attic was a disaster.

The house had visibly started to buckle, canting to the side. Firelight poured in through the attic hatch, but it illuminated little since the attic was full of smoke that had tried to flee the house and instead ended up trapped in this, its highest point.

Just like us.

Jerry tried his best to throw that thought out. How ridiculous would it be to give up now? So close to escape?

What if there is no escape up here?

"Come on," he said, holding Sheri's hand and leading her through the attic. They both crouched automatically, trying without much success to get below the smoke.

And then he saw it. A small patch of light.

He hauled Sheri with him as he hurried over to it, thanking his lucky stars that there was nothing up here, no furniture or family memories to trip over. Just empty space.

A moment later they were at the light. A vent cover. He put his face to it and could feel cool, clean – or at least cool*er* and clean*er* – air wafting through the slatted cover. It was about eighteen inches to a side. Big enough to get through.

He put his fingers through the slats and pulled. Then pushed. Then pulled again.

The vent cover didn't budge. Sheri started to cry, and beyond her Jerry could see the leading edge of the fire licking over the top of the attic hatch.

He pulled harder. Pulled until blood ran down his fingers. His spine popped with the effort he was pulling into it, pulling with his whole body and not just his hands or arms.

The house shifted, seeming to leap to the side a good two feet. Sheri screamed.

Jerry kept pulling.

And with a crash, the vent cover pulled away from the wall. Jerry went down, falling to his back, and every bone and muscle in his body seemed to scream its disapproval. He told them all to shut up, then stood and threw the vent cover aside.

Outside the hole that he had opened up, a red and orange fabric flapped between billows of dark smoke. The termite tent.

And beyond that… freedom.

98

Jerry helped Sheri out of the vent hole, dropping her to a part of the first-story roof that jutted out a few feet below it. He thought she was going to roll over the side and fall right off it, but she managed to hold on. He pushed himself out the hole next, landing semi-gracefully next to her.

They still weren't out of danger. The termite tent was all around them, full of smoke and fire, disorienting and suffocating them. They could die only inches from freedom.

He thought about lowering Sheri off the roof, but couldn't for the life of him remember what was below them. Grass? Concrete? Something else? How ridiculous would it be to die here, dropping down and breaking their backs on a patch of unforgiving architecture or landscaping after all they'd been through?

He could barely see now, the smoke was pressing so close. Sheri was coughing constantly. He was, too, he realized, but hadn't noticed it. Too busy trying to get him and his daughter out of this.

The house shuddered and took another sideways lurch. Wouldn't be long before it came down completely.

Jerry moved slowly to the edge of the roof. Not the edge that hung over nothing, but the edge where it joined the house. He seemed to remember that some of the roofs had… yes! His questing fingers found a thick drainpipe. He didn't know if it would hold them for long – if at all. But if it could give them even a moment or two, they could shimmy down a couple feet and be that much less likely to hurt themselves on the landing.

"Come on," he said to Sheri between fits of coughing. She reached for him and he guided her hand to the pipe. She seemed to understand his intention, dropping over the side of the house without a word.

And then she was gone.

Jerry found himself alone. Alone and suddenly reticent to follow. Lowering a lithe teenage body would be one thing. A middle-age parent's body? The body of a man who led a sedentary life and whose idea of a workout was walking to the television to change channels instead of using the remote?

He pushed himself over the edge. Soot coated the pipe, and at first that was actually helpful, letting him slide more than climb. I can do this, he thought.

Then the pipe became slicker. Too slick. He fell.

He hit something on the way down. Something soft. Sheri. The two of them fell the rest of the way to the ground. He had no idea how far it was, but it felt far Empire-State-Building-far.

The impact was bone-crushing, and Sheri screamed below him. Jerry would have screamed as well, but the impact made every molecule of oxygen rupture out of his lungs. He could do nothing more than lay there, opening and shutting his mouth like a fish waiting calmly to die.

Sheri groaned and he realized she was beneath him. That got him moving. He rolled off her, though it seemed push every single muscle fiber in his body to its final limit.

He couldn't see anything. Completely disoriented. Smoke everywhere. The only break in the black was bright flashes of fire that reached out like hands playing a deadly game of tag.

Jerry shied away from the fire. Reached out, hoping to find Sheri, and felt heavy cloth instead: the termite tent. With the other hand he reached again for Sheri. Touched her. She screamed in pain. He didn't know if he was causing the pain or not, but he couldn't wait. The fire and smoke would kill them soon. Maybe seconds.

He grabbed her. She resisted.

Suddenly brightness was everywhere. The termite tent must have caught fire. It was a burning shroud, flaming pieces falling down from above, fiery pillars leaping at their sides. They couldn't get out here. Besides being on fire, Jerry suspected the fabric of the tent would be too heavy to lift. They had to find some sort of exit.

Jerry pulled Sheri, yanking her along with him as he searched for a hole in the flames, some way to leave.

And found it.

99

Jerry pushed through the termite tent. Engulfed in flame on either side, but a hole the size of a small door had been burned away and he darted through the exit carved out by the fire. He didn't let go of Sheri, either, and dragged her through with him.

Even this close to the fire, the air outside the tent seemed one hundred degrees cooler. He turned his face to the sky, savoring the cool, then felt something hitting him.

He looked at it. It was Sheri, batting at his arm with one hand. Her other hand hung limp and lifeless at the end of an arm that was clearly broken. She was beating out a small fire on his shirt sleeve.

She was beating it out with her bare hand. Not seeming to mind the burns she must be suffering.

The fire snuffed out. Jerry caught her hand in his. Pulled her in for a hug.

She did not resist.

"I love you," he said. And it was true.

"I love you, too," she said.

He looked down. Realized he was standing near the pool, on the same spot that Brian died years ago.

Jerry looked back at Sheri. She was gazing at him with concern.

"It's okay," he said. "I'm okay. We're going to be o –"

And that was when a burning figure reared up behind his daughter.

100

The Killer was on fire. Clothing, hair, *skin*. It was all a single pillar of flame. He came after Sheri, screaming over and over, "You can't live, you can't live, you can't live!"

Sheri screamed. She raised her good hand up to ward off the hellfire-cloaked nightmare that had come for her.

Jerry plowed past her, knocking her aside and then barreling into the Killer. He felt flames licking at him, leaping from the other man's form to his own. Felt the heat settle into his skin and burn. Didn't care. He just had to stop this. Had to stop it *now*.

He felt the Killer's hands, now little more than bone with charred clots of sinew clinging to them, batting at his face, his arms and shoulders.

Jerry gritted his teeth. Bore down harder.

Sheri screamed. He wished he could tell her goodbye. But he couldn't, and that was all right. He had said the more important things.

He drove the Killer forward. Toward the waterfall of flame that had once been a termite tent. To the fiery dome that the Killer had intended to use to hide them from the world.

Jerry gritted his teeth. Plunged them farther. To the edge of the fire. Then farther. *Through* it.

He felt it immediately, the passage from the momentary freedom he had enjoyed back into flame. He remembered Brian, falling to earth, and thought he might have an inkling how he felt in the moment he touched down.

His hands were burning. He realized in a strangely detached moment that he would probably never do another surgery.

That was all right.

His clothing caught fire.

That was all right.

The Killer was struggling, but slowing.

That was best of all.

Jerry threw him into a bright spot in the fire, what he hoped was a part of the house aflame, and was rewarded with the sound of crunching plaster. The Killer shrieked below his hands, and Jerry enjoyed the immense pleasure of seeing the other man's flesh melting off his face.

He hit the madman's body into the house again. Again. And again again again againagainagain....

The fire leapt before him and he fell back instinctively.

The Killer's body slid to the ground. The fire crept over and claimed it.

Jerry knew he himself was burning, too. Knew he was going to die.

That was all right. He was tired. Tired.

I'll just lay down.

Sounds good, Jerry.

He slumped to the ground. But it was too hot, so he pushed himself away from the burning wreckage of the house. It canted to the side, seeming to spill over itself. Jerry watched it dully, then realized something was tugging at him. A hand, reaching through the smoke and fire, pulling him.

Sheri, he thought.

He followed the hand as it pulled him. Through dark clouds, through heat and hell.

It pulled him into clear air. He blinked away smoke and particulate. Tears blurred his vision. And when his sight cleared he saw….

"Hello," said the Killer.

101

Jerry heard something pop, and couldn't be sure if it was the conflagration behind him, or something in his mind. Because the Killer was dead. He had to be dead. Jerry had just killed him.

But here he was. Standing here *completely unmarked* and holding onto Jerry with one arm while Sheri unconscious at the living dead man's feet, blood spurting from her nose and a huge bruise across the side of her face.

"You're dead," Jerry said.

The Killer nodded. But at the same time, he said, "You can't kill me. Not all of me." He nodded at the burning mass that had been Jerry's once-upon-a-time Dream House. "But you had to kill him." The Killer sighed. "He wasn't me anymore. He didn't match anymore."

Jerry remembered the Killer saying that. "I don't match." And suddenly remembered other things:

The lights had turned off in one place in the house while thuds were heard elsewhere....

... there were sounds upstairs only seconds before Sheri was grabbed....

... and several of the videos he had seen had zoomed in or out or changed angles, *even though the Killer was in the scene.*

Jerry felt realization blooming. "There are two of you," he said, speaking more to himself than to anyone else. "Twins."

The Killer frowned. "Father never wanted more than one son. There's only one of me." And then he kicked out suddenly and Jerry went flying forward. His right foot came down on hard ground, but his left touched… nothing. He fell, and realized the Killer –

(*The Killer's brother? Which one did what?*)

– had kicked him into the pool. Jerry came up sputtering, screaming. "Relax!" shouted the Killer, sounding almost jovial. "You were on fire."

Then he picked up Sheri's still form… and moved toward the still-burning pyre of the house, a smile on his face.

102

Jerry screamed and paddled for the edge of the pool, trying to move as fast as he could while at the same time keeping his head high enough that he could see what was happening.

The Killer strode with Sheri to the edge of the fire, gripping her under an arm with no apparent effort. He looked back at Jerry, holding his gaze.

"She *can't* live, Jerry. Those are the rules. We live and die by the rules."

And he reared back to throw her into the fire and there was nothing Jerry could do.

"My life for hers!" he screamed. The words just came out, half garbled by water getting in his mouth as he paddled. He didn't exactly know where they originated, if from anywhere. One moment there was silence, the next moment the words were on his tongue as though by the strangest convolutions of *creation ex nihilo*.

Still, they gave the Killer pause. He stared at the fire but did not move.

There was a loud crackle, a flurry of sparks that rode skyward on a twirling tendril of flame. The house fell in on itself. Still a huge fire, but diminishing in size. Disintegrating as he watched.

Though it was more than enough to burn an unconscious teen alive.

Jerry kept swimming, aware he was saying the words over and over as he paddled. "My life for hers my life for hers my life for hers."

The Killer watched the fire. It seemed to brighten in front of him, a forge of Hell reaching for its master. Then he walked back to Jerry, dragging Sheri with him.

Jerry had reached the edge of the pool. Had his hands on the edge of the deck. He thought for sure the madman would try to shove him back, away from the edge.

But he didn't. The Killer lay a gentle, almost loving hand on Jerry's head. Like a father giving last goodbyes, a patriarch of old endowing his posterity with their blessings from on high.

He looked at Jerry, and the look was calm, bereft of hatred or evil or madness. It was chillingly normal.

Jerry had let the man in his house, over and over. Had let him in, had said, "TV's in there," and then let him alone.

How many times do people do that? he wondered. And how many times are the strangers worthy of that trust? How often are they good people, and how often are they madmen come to prey on our illusions, to eat them up and spit out broken lives in passing?

"Jerry," said the Killer, hand still on his head, "you're going to be all right."

Jerry said the only thing that he could think *to* say. "Why?" So much packed into the word.

Why us? Why this way? Why now?

Why Sheri?

So much meaning, but the word came out less than a whisper. It was a breath, the barest idea of a question, the awestruck, confused utterance of a man before a god.

The Killer looked genuinely confused.

"Don't you understand, Jerry? You were the only one." The Killer waited a moment, as though to see if Jerry would comprehend. "You were the only one who told your secret, who confessed."

"The others. Sheri –"

The Killer shook his head sadly. "The others didn't confess. They were *made* to confess. The truth can only set you free if you embrace it, Jerry. And you were the only one who did that not after you were threatened with death and had your secrets shown to the world, but of your own volition."

Jerry remembered, almost against his will, that the Killer had shown video of Ann, of Drew, of Sheri. Remembered the Killer threatening to kill each of them if they didn't tell their secrets. But he hadn't had a chance with Jerry. Because Jerry was better? No, he didn't think so. Only because he had changed the path before the Killer had a chance to *show* Jerry's video, to threaten Jerry's life.

"I'm no better," Jerry said. "I'm no better than they were."

The Killer laughed. It was a pleasant laugh, the kind of laugh you might hear in a crowded room and be tempted to join in with, just because. "Jerry, I'm not *God*. I'm not here to judge your thoughts. Just to get rid of the secrets." He winked. "You'll be much happier now. Trust me. I know."

"My life for hers," Jerry said again.

The Killer looked like he was considering the matter deeply. Sheri groaned as though to add her thoughts to the conversation. "It would be fair," he said, his eyes faraway on some plane where his mad rules held sway, now and forever. "Fair. But would it be *just*?"

"Please," Jerry said. "She's too young. It's not her *turn* to die."

The Killer went still. And Jerry knew he had said something either terribly right, or dreadfully wrong.

103

Jerry held himself as motionless as possible, the water gently lapping around him, as the Killer's face underwent a panoply of minute changes. Jerry didn't understand fully what he was seeing, but sensed that he was watching something akin to a tornado held in a porcelain vase. They had only seconds. Seconds before the fragile container burst. Seconds before the tempest took them all.

Jerry knew he had to do something. The only problem was that he had no idea *what*. He was burned, bleeding, bruised, beaten. Hanging in water while his enemy stood on firm ground and held all that was precious to him in his hands.

Before he even finished considering his position, the Killer blinked. "No," he said. His voice was firm. His eyes, calm before, took on a strange cast. "It is her turn."

He leaned toward Jerry, hand still on his head, and Jerry thought he was going to shove him under.

But no. He simply screamed, "It *is* her turn!" Then he visibly brought himself under control. "We take turns, Father. We'll always take –"

Jerry didn't hear the rest. Because at that moment he clamped his hands down over the Killer's hand in a double vise grip. He put his feet against the inside of the pool at the same time, bending his knees and then shoving back with every last ounce of strength he had.

There was an enormous splash and the Killer was inside the pool with him.

Jerry didn't know what to do, he hadn't thought beyond this moment.

Hell, Jerry, be honest – you didn't even think of this *moment.*

And that was true. All he was thinking was to get the Killer away from Sheri. But now he was in the water with a monster, and he had no idea what to do. The Killer was pummeling, scratching, pulling Jerry under. Jerry tried to take a breath but he swallowed water instead. He was too tired to fight, too tired to struggle.

Too tired to care.

He felt himself slowing. Felt the muscles in his body slackening. It was almost like he was an observer, someone watching a television show or a movie – and it wasn't even a show he much cared about.

Just like family movie night.

An image appeared in his mind. The family, gathered around the huge television, each of them glancing at the show in between mouthfuls of food and texting and work and all the bits of their worlds that they carried with them, all the walls they kept between one another.

All the lies.

Then he saw something else. Not in his mind, but in reality. He looked up in his diminishing struggles and saw something. It was wavy and irregular, little more than the promise of form. But he recognized it.

Sheri.

She must have awoken. Crawled to the edge of the pool.

A hand was reaching out. Reaching for him. Barely-glimpsed, hardly-seen.

But real.

True.

He reached for her hand. Found it. Held it. Held it tight, held it like it was the only thing left, the only thing that mattered.

Sheri pulled him to her, even as he pulled her to him. Jerry's head broke the surface of the water, and he inhaled a sputtering, coughing, gasping draught of air.

Behind and below him, the Killer pawed and pummeled, but suddenly seemed like *less*. Suddenly seemed like an unreality. A lie that belonged to the fiction of their *before*. And, holding to his daughter, it was abruptly easy for Jerry to pull himself away from the Killer and then to spin as Sheri's good arm encircled him. It was suddenly simple to turn and face down the murdering bastard who had tried to steal what was his, tried to steal what was *real*.

Jerry's legs went around the Killer's shoulders.

He shoved down.

The Killer struggled. Struggled. But Jerry was anchored now. Tethered to the real.

The Killer thrashed and flailed. But he didn't last long.

Lies couldn't.

He slowed. He stilled.

Jerry kept holding on. Just in case. Wisest to keep tabs on the harms of the past, though securely rooted to the realities of the present.

He was still holding on when the first firefighters came. When the police came. Still holding on to the Killer and still held by Sheri, and it wasn't until medics pried her stiff arm away from him that he let the body fall to the bottom of the pool and disappear below the water and the reflections of a funeral pyre that had once been his dreams.

Now he was awake.

EPILOGUE

The man watches. Watches as he works.

He watches from afar, of course. There are police and firefighters and media and even a few neighbors who are curious enough to come out and actually inquire into what has happened. The man doesn't get too close, because has no wish to go to jail.

But he does watch.

He feels strangely *diminished*. Which is natural, he supposes, since two-thirds of him is gone.

Forever? He does not know. He has never died before. Perhaps he will rise up out of the pool, out of the ruins of the house.

But he doubts it. If for no other reason than for the fact that he will no longer match: he cannot be *One* if he is bloated and waterlogged, burnt and charred to bones and tough tendon... and startlingly normal. No, what is three cannot be One. That was one of the things Father always taught him when he came out of Mother and she died because of the strain and Father never let him forget it. Never let him forget that if he had only been *One* she would have lived. Would have survived.

The man pulls his mind away from that. Away from the dark times when he was becoming One.

Back to the house. To what has happened. He knows all, of course. Because he was One until recently. And because of the cameras everywhere and the monitors in the van. So he knows of Jerry's survival, which is well and good.

He knows of Sheri's, as well.

He purses his lips. He is not sure how to think of that. Should he finish the job? She didn't confess, as he himself pointed out to Jerry. So by the rules, she must perish.

But then, those were the rules when he was One. And now he is simply… *one,* he supposes.

He will have to think on this.

He finishes what he is doing. Ripping off the bumper stickers on the front of the van, the one that says "Honk if you Love Jesus" and the other that says "Honk if you Love Satan."

He saw them in a truck stop once, and thought they rather represented his Oneness. Much like a Godhead of religious tracts, though he was not particularly religious. And he had put them on the front of the car as a private joke, as though anyone could ever see him coming.

But now… now he was no longer One, and perhaps people *would* see him coming. Best to be careful. The bumper stickers would go.

He looked at the house, down the street. He could make out a figure – Sheri? – being led limping to an ambulance. He would have to figure out what to do with her.

But not today. Today he died, after all. Forever? He does not know. He has never died before.

But whether forever or not, he is glad that when he *did* die… it was not his turn.

He gets in his black van.

Pulls…

… slowly…

… away.

And is gone.

For now.

AUTHOR'S NOTE

"What's the difference between a writer and a pizza?"

"You can feed a family of four with a pizza!"

[Hilarious laughter]

It's actually a pretty funny joke. Unless you *are* a writer, looking at a month where you know you are going to have trouble paying the bills. I mean, I love my kids, but they insist on *eating every single day.* Sometimes multiple times. Sheesh.

In such a situation, if you're like me and you have next to no marketable skills, you hurry up and write a book. So a few years ago I wrote a short book (40,000 words – more a long fiction piece) called *The Stranger Inside* in the hope that I could make some money for my family.

You know, for that darn eating habit.

But that meant I had to do a rushed job, cranking it out in a few weeks. The basic idea – of a family that wakes up to find out that they have been locked inside their house by a madman intent on teaching them a "valuable life lesson" a la the Disney channel (only with more dead people) – was a good one, but I didn't think I did it justice. It's bothered me since then.

Fast forward a few years. Maybe I have grown in my ability to feed my family. Maybe I'm just more accomplished at self-delusion. Either way, I decided to revisit *The Stranger*

Inside, redo it and (hopefully) make a decent idea into a flat-out good book.

It's been fun. The trip was much darker the second time around. Partly because the story called for it, partly because due to some medical issues I was in a lot of pain during the writing.

But… and this is the thing I want to really drive home, the real reason for this Author's note… no matter how well (or poorly) it turned out, you don't have to worry. *I am not George Lucas.* I have no intention of revisiting everything I have ever done with the idea of "improving" it. This was just a one-off. Just this one time. I swear.

Probably.

\- Michaelbrent Collings

ABOUT THE AUTHOR

Michaelbrent Collings is an award-winning screenwriter and novelist. He has written numerous bestselling horror, thriller, sci-fi, and fantasy novels, including *Darkbound, Apparition, The Haunted, Hooked: A True Faerie Tale,* and the bestselling YA series *The Billy Saga.* Follow him on Facebook or on Twitter @mbcollings.

And if you liked *Strangers,* please leave a review on your favorite book review site… and tell your friends!

Made in the USA
Middletown, DE
21 September 2020